TAKING HART

TAKING HART

by M.A. Noble

M. Hockett
Canton, NY

Taking Hart is a work of fiction;
any resemblance to actual
persons is coincidental.

Copyright © 2012 M.A. Noble

ISBN 978-0-9858345-1-7

• • • • •

Dedicated to the memory of

Mary Tripp Noble
&
Earl Vernon Noble

TABLE of CONTENTS

Note: Check CHARACTERS, p. 253, to see who's who!

1	PATRICK'S POINT	1
2	ON THE ICE	3
3	BEHIND BLUE EYES	31
4	TODAY'S HISTORY LESSON	41
5	P'D OFF	67
6	AUGER'S PUNCH	93
7	STROKE OF FATE	121
8	SNAGGED	139
9	CAPTURED IMAGE	157
10	INCOGNITO	177
11	DOWN TO THE BUCKLE	197
12	A CHANGE OF HART	209
13	FRED'S DISTRACTIONS	229
14	COREY'S COURAGE	241
15	SAIL ON	245
16	FACILITY FOR CORRECTIONS	249

CHARACTERS 253

FACTS BEHIND THE FICTION War of 1812 in the 1000 Islands ... 255

CREDITS 257

A teenager today
has enough to worry about...

So why does Corey care about the
War of 1812?

Somehow, it holds the key to his ancestry, his
mom's whereabouts...and his very life!

A Forgotten Warfront
Piracy, Ambush, and Treachery

The War of 1812 brings images of bursting rockets and spangled banners in the east. But did you know about the *north* coast? The Great Lakes and the St. Lawrence River hosted numerous battles, and the Thousand Islands concealed acts of piracy, ambush, and treachery much like the ones on which this story is based.

MAP of
HARTS LANDING AREA

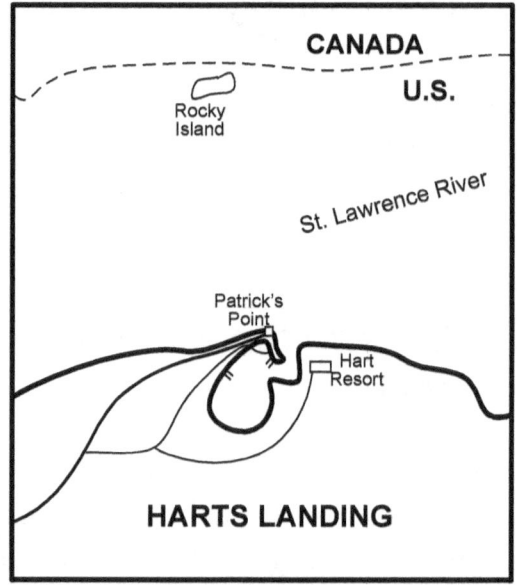

Note: Harts Landing and Rocky Island are fictional locations; any similarities to specific communities or geographical locations are coincidental.

1 PATRICK'S POINT
September 2011, Harts Landing, New York

Peg Stowe leaned over the rail and stared into the St. Lawrence River—the river that had claimed her ancestor nearly two hundred years ago. Her fingers twisted the sapphire at her ear as she imagined the thirty-foot fall. Here at the Point, you could smash into the rocks, and the current would suck you down, maybe wedge your body under a slab of granite. Or drag it downriver towards Montreal.

Peg felt the bump of Topaz above the sapphire. *Corey's birthstone.* How would her son handle the news he was about to hear? In her right hand was the brass buckle that contained an ancient secret, and she gave it a nervous squeeze. She wondered about the chances of surviving the strong current, and then she peered into the object whose secret would soon be revealed. *Irresistible.*

In the next moment, Peg felt herself falling through the night. Some part of her mind registered the blackness of river, the shimmer of moon, and the ripple of hairs on her arms as she plummeted.

A question rattled her skull: How had things come to this? The answer churned within her as she disappeared into the St. Lawrence: *It was the brass buckle.*

Explosions went off in her head. Current sucked and dragged her, tossed her like a rag doll. Memories throbbed like nerves: her father's abuse, her crystal meth addiction; then Corey growing and Charlie's love...and the truth she had learned today.

Her head spun, and she knew her lungs would fill before she ever reached the surface. She had just enough presence to

1

say a prayer: Let Corey find his way. Help Charlie understand. *Let my love flow through them.*

2 ON THE ICE
Six Months Later

Corey Worder gasped as ice ran from his neck right down his back. He yanked his jacket back and forth until the slush plopped on the ground. He wiped at his skin with part of his shirt. Taking this shortcut wasn't such a great idea!

He had felt pretty good on his way to the new job until somebody's shed roof dropped a leftover load of winter. He should be used to it. Harts Landing had been dumping on him since he came last summer. The whole town was all about that privateer Hart, the founder. Fine. Problem was, they looked down on Worders...all because of what happened *two hundred* years ago. Hart's mate, Patrick Worder, was a scoundrel and a deserter.

The town hall chimed the quarter hour.

Better run. Corey couldn't afford to lose another job. Howler was a big dog, and he ate a lot of Chunkies.

In the arena, winter was still rattling its breath on jacketed fans and skating hulks. Corey toweled off his backside. Then he grabbed a broom to push out the tracked-in mud and blew off a patch of hair that fell over his left eye. It fell right back. He cleaned the bathrooms, picked up trash, and manned the concession stand. Then the head janitor sent Corey for the grooming tool, muttering something about the "dam Zamboni" being "broke again."

Corey would have to go out on the ice like a dork, with a giant squeegee on a stick. He could hear the comments already. Like, *Which one is the stick?* Followed by snorts. He'd heard of guys who didn't "sprout" until after sixteen... Did he have to be one of them?

Corey found the squeegee in the closet and clomped it through the locker room. Nonsense words echoed in his head, and he tapped the tool in rhythm to *Zam Damboni...Bony Zam I Am*. His tapping accelerated as he approached the door. He sucked a big breath and entered the bench area, where his thoughts were drowned out by a roar.

Players from both teams had ganged up near the center line, desperate for control of the puck. An "Ice King," one of the opposition, tore out of the cluster and zigzagged to the goal, where the local Patriot goalkeeper skittered back and forth. The Ice King slapped the puck between the keeper's legs and tied the score right at the period buzzer. The visiting fans went wild.

The hometown Patriots skated off the ice and clunked past Corey, looking angry and disappointed. Corey looked away. He didn't notice the gate swing. It flattened him against the boards as one of the guys barked, "Watch yer *back*, Worder!" which erased all the scowls, even brought some whoops.

BackWorder—because Corey was klutzy. Or was it because he dismembered words and slaughtered the language? He hadn't meant to insult the Hart family when he announced their history program at school. Using the PA system made him nervous! That's the only reason he'd swapped the beginning sounds of "Four Harts." Which resulted in a name he would *never*— The teacher's plan to bring him "out of his shell" backfired. He'd never go near a microphone again.

BackWorder. Corey was sick of it, and something dark gnawed at his gut. He wanted to punch the hockey guy. But he felt even shorter than his five-foot-five next to these giants on skates. He rubbed a shoulder and tried to look cool as he pushed himself out onto the rink.

The goal cage had been bumped out of position. With his jackknife, Corey scraped ice out of each hole and fitted the pegs of the cage back in. Then he pushed the squeegee and eyed the crystals that gathered along the rubber strip in front of him as he smoothed the ice so guys like Auger Hart could show off. The local fans wanted to see Auger break some state record for goals...like he needed another trophy.

Corey moved near the opposition stands, where he noticed three pennies in the rink. Coins could make a player skid, so he scooped up the pennies and put them in his pocket. Then he heard someone call out, "Way to scrape it, Kid! Now you're wealthy." Corey gave a half smile, not sure whether the comment was friendly.

He went to the boards, opened a hinged section, and stomped out to the lobby. He bent to fix a flap of duct tape around his heel. His stepfather, Charlie, was a fishing guide, but only off and on, and Corey's dog was "history" if Corey couldn't take care of him. Corey couldn't buy dog food *and* shoes.

He checked to see if anyone was looking. Then he pulled off his left glove—the one with no holes—and uncurled his fingers from a blue stone. Real star sapphire. Next to a small topaz—*that's me*—plus aquamarine, Charlie's birthstone. Corey's stepdad had gotten rid of all Mom's clothes and stuff, but Corey didn't tell Charlie he'd found this earring. Charlie had changed since Mom disappeared. He always seemed angry. And if he couldn't pay all the bills, he'd say, "She can't use it, might as well sell it."

But the gleaming blue earring was all Corey had left of his mother. *She must've dropped it in that old trunk, just before...*

Corey squeezed the sapphire then stuffed it, along with his hand, back in the glove. Then he went into the arena, which was rumbling with laughter. The Patriot mascot was doing some skit. On Corey's ice. Now he'd have to clean it again.

Privateer Warren Hart, the town hero, or at least the school mascot, had entered the rink. He wore a giant "brass" buckle where two straps crossed his chest. At his side, waving a hockey-stick like a sword, was first mate, "Patrick Worder."

The deserter.

Corey's skin prickled. They couldn't do that old battle scene. The school board banned any public display anything "disparaging a member of the student body." He jiggled the coins in his pocket. That Hart mascot was the new girl, Samantha something. She hadn't been in town long, but she'd worked the game last time. *She's too new to be part of something cruel.* Corey started to relax.

But a horn played notes of suspense as a "Royal Marine" challenged the Patriots with a hockey stick. Worder threw down his stick and backed away, and the horn trumpeted Corey's own mood with its *Wah, wah, wah.* Captain Hart got blasted with a shot to the chest, and the crowd moaned. Then they cheered to victory notes as Hart revived and held up the buckle that had shielded him. Next, the local fans started harassing the first mate "Patrick" as he ran off the ice, by shouting, "Worder deserter, Worder deserter!"

A bunch of teenagers nearby were laughing when one pointed at Corey. "Hey isn't that a real Worder?" he whispered just loud enough for Corey to hear.

"Yeah, and get this," another snickered, "his initials are COW. He's a COWorder!"

Corey's neck, recently iced, now burned red hot. Why couldn't Charlie adopt him? Stowe was a perfectly good name. Anything but Coriander Olan Worder. Mom had said that people used "Worder" as a scapegoat, and didn't mean it personally. Well, it was personal to Corey.

His stepdad had said Corey shouldn't change his name because, "You can't solve problems by running away from them." This, from a man who downs a twelve-pack a day. If Corey had any guts he'd tell Charlie where to shove his beer cans.

It was time to go out on the rink, but Corey's feet were glued to the floor. *It's either go out or lose the job.* He had to picture Howler licking an empty bowl before he finally took a breath and jerked one leg forward and then the other. When he made it out to the ice, he scraped and pushed without feeling anything but numb.

Corey blew black strands off his eye as he concentrated on the ice. He knew his brows looked like one straight band over a pirate's "eye patch." If he were a pirate he would sail away from this place where even little kids chanted, "I'm no deserter, I'm a Hart not a Worder." So what if Patrick Worder was Corey's forefather. Corey pictured the branches on his family tree. More like five-or-six father. Anyway, why should it matter? It wouldn't—in any normal town. But people here came from hard-core patriots. Their ancestors had been forced to serve the British before escaping to this hidden Landing where many were killed defending it. That was a big deal around here.

Corey moved away from the giggling kids, towards the opponents' end. He squeezed his left glove and felt Mom's sapphire dig into his palm.

"Why should you care what they think?" she would say, with her deep blue eyes piercing his. And her hand would brush her hair in that slow salute of hers...like *that* one.

Corey halted on the ice. He stared at a woman at the end of the benches. Had she just done Mom's weird hand move? But this woman had short hair—nothing to brush away. *Freakish.*

Corey stood still as he watched the stranger, his hand jiggling the coins in his pocket. When the horn blasted, he finally stumbled off into the stands.

Corey ignored the ice. For him, the action was in the reddish-brown hair dancing around blue eyes in his mind. Bobbing spectators framed an image that put Corey in a trance. The earth spun backwards, and he was a five-year-old sitting on Mom's lap; she sang about a Rolling River, and her hand danced a curve around her cheek as she swept her hair back. A comfort washed over Corey, a feeling he had forgotten. He thawed, allowing himself to relax.

A roar from the stands broke the spell, and the earth spun back. Corey turned to see what was going on. The Ice Kings had taken control and passed the puck towards the goal, where a Hart defender snatched it—then lost it among thrashing arms. Corey turned back to the strange woman in time to see her full-faced gaze on his. Then she twisted away—with a flash of blue from her right ear.

No way! Corey's thoughts were a jumble. *Dork, your mind is messing with you, she's not your mother.* But that sapphire earring... Could it be coincidence? Did she find it? Did she see Mom just before...?

Corey launched himself in the direction of the woman, opening his mouth to yell, "Wait!" But before his shout escaped his lips, she disappeared. He would follow her! He couldn't. Corey was trapped by the hooting crowd that pressed forward. He turned; no way out. On the ice in front of him, a sturdy Patriot had raced out from the mass of bodies. Auger Hart's gray eyes were focused on the puck he now controlled as he skirted the boards towards several dark spots...*pennies?*

The woman vanished from Corey's mind, and his body went cold as the ice. He jerked his hand to his pocket. Nothing. The coins had fallen out of his holey pants. But what were the chances Auger would...

"Ohh...nooooo!" The sounds came from the hometown seats. Fans were standing, looking down on the ice in front of Corey where Auger Hart sprawled. The clock was stopped. The referee picked up a coin, and he seemed to be looking right at Corey.

Corey could feel blood pulsing around his eyes. The rest of his blood seemed to drain right through the floor beneath him. Somehow he squeezed back through the crowd; he threw down the squeegee, ran out the door, and tore down the hill. But he couldn't outdistance the echo of his boss's words: "Don't bother coming back!"

Corey put the ghostly woman out of his mind as he stumbled down to the village. He had other things to worry about now. Two questions beat in time with his flapping sneaker:

What will Charlie say?
What if I lose Howler?

A PATRIOT'S SCORN

Auger Hart could *not* believe it. He had won the puck and outpaced the enemy. He had found an opening; in his mind he saw his stick springing the puck into the net, heard the cheers that would fill the arena. Then disaster.

Instead of cheers, the arena was filled with the hissing of air sucked into hundreds of lungs. His leg had slid sideways, and he had splatted onto the ice. His head hurt. The red face with the eye-patch hair and guilty look drew him like a beacon. That kid with the squeegee—Auger had seen him with the pennies earlier. The stupid BackWorder kid was supposed to take care of the ice, not mess it up.

Auger had limped to the face-off in a daze. The referee threw down the puck, and Auger had whacked at it, but in his mind he was still posed with his stick in anticipation of the shot that never was. The other half was poisoned with thoughts of revenge. Now he was lumbering behind the team as the Ice Kings took control.

"Auger! Wake up, man!" a teammate called.

Just then, the other team scored, and a collective moan descended from the home stands. The Patriots were behind, four to three!

Auger had to put his emotions aside. He was a Hart and that was a lot to live up to; if it hadn't been for Warren Hart, these Patriot descendants wouldn't even be here playing hockey. Auger had better push the limits.

His reflexes quickened as the words of his father slashed his awareness like blades: A Patriot has a mandate, has authority to lead. Auger would own that puck and put it where it belonged: on tomorrow's front page with his own smiling face—and where the most important man in town would see it over coffee. His Dad would finally notice!

Ice scraped, sticks clashed. Auger was back in form. But the Ice Kings still had the edge of adrenaline from their goal, and the black biscuit skittered back and forth between rivals.

Ten seconds. Auger stole the puck and headed for the goal. If he tied the game again, the team could still win—and he would personally set a state record for goals.

Fans jumped to their feet. Their noise pumped him. His eyes sharpened. Every movement was crisp as he passed, received, feinted. He saw an opening; he jetted through before it closed like a wormhole behind him.

"FIVE...FOUR...THREE..."

Auger was in the zone.

"TWO...ONE..."

He sprung the puck forward in a perfect shot to the net, where it would escape the goalie's grab. Auger saw himself riding shoulders, his victory grin brightening the next edition of the "Hart Happenings."

Then the buzzer sounded...before the puck entered the goal.

The Ice Kings roared their approval. The Patriots threw their sticks down in disgust.

Auger undressed slowly. He lumbered towards the showers. He analyzed his moves under the hot water. He had done everything right, until that little slacker had changed everything. Auger had noticed him standing there daydreaming; that's when he must've dropped those pennies. Then Auger remembered the kid's abominable remark during school announcements. The Worder kid had it in for the Harts. *He'll pay for this.*

Auger toweled off then pulled on his street clothes; he hoisted his duffle bag over his shoulder and walked out—didn't feel like hanging with the guys. He threw himself into the sky-blue BMW, turned the ignition, didn't bother with the belt, and spun the wheels as he screeched out of the lot. Dad still wouldn't get him his own car. "Cash flow" problems or something. But at least he had Gran's, which wasn't totally lame. He raced up to the Point, windows open. He was sorry his grandmother couldn't drive, but he was glad to have her wheels. He swerved to the scenic lookout across from Hart Memorial Park.

He ran past the cannon his ancestor Dirk had used to beat the British. He dashed up the steps to the deck of the museum, past the benches and the swiveling, coin-operated viewer to the edge by the plaque proclaiming that a British chest of gold "may still lie buried among the islands." He leaned over the rail and stared at the waves, black struggling with blue. He liked the water but preferred it in a controlled state: only by freezing and shaving the bumps could it be tamed into a form he would call his element.

Across the shipping channel from Harts Landing, a rock island projected from the river, and from this Rocky Island rose the ruins of an old castle. Some crazy guy with more money than brains remade a part of Windsor Castle and its Round Tower. It had been abandoned for decades; no one wanted to spend the millions it would take to renovate it. That's what Dad had said when he checked into buying it, which Auger was not supposed to mention to anyone. Besides, there was already a tour-able castle upstream—Boldt Castle, plus that other one downstream—Singer Castle. How many castles did the river need?

Auger shifted focus to just beyond the lapping waters at the Landing, where he knew the river bottom dropped off to form a deep channel. During shipping season, the channel accommodated friendly vessels from all over the world, carrying merchandise and raw materials into and out of the Great Lakes. But in the Landing's early days, two-hundred years ago, the vessels that plied these waters were often unfriendly. Auger envisioned his ancestor Warren Hart, Warren's son Dirk, and the rest of the *Patriot* crew gunning the British *Spitflame*, only a few hundred yards away, as they saved the town from the British. The story lived on because of one of the few survivors: Warren's son, Dirk. Dirk's account of the battle appeared all over town on plaques and in pamphlets...like the ones right beside Auger. He grabbed a paper from the plastic case and scanned the words of the legend he knew almost by heart.

THE BATTLE OF HARTS LANDING According to Dirk Hart

June 20, 1813 Secret Landing, New York

We approached our hidden village in the *Patriot* after hiding upriver for several days; the weary crew looked forward to their welcoming wives and hot meals. But the lookout had just sighted the British *Spitflame* behind the island of rock, and it was urgent that we move on. The opening to the Landing is nearly invisible, but a sharp eye could spy it from a northern approach, and we all knew that the British *must not* discover our settlement. They were desperate to recover their stolen gold—the richest payroll ever to sail the St. Lawrence. And they would retaliate severely against not only the *Patriot* crew, but our families.

The wind died as we needed it most. The sweeps were brought out to muscle the vessel past the landing. Then I spied first mate, Patrick Worder, taking a course of action that caused me to rub my eyes and take another look. The crew had noticed changes in Patrick of late, though Father seemed blind to them. Worder was eating more than his share of the rations and had grown lazy and secretive. And now I would add *treacherous*: he pushed off in a rowboat and made for the Landing.

Astonished, I cried, "Father, Patrick's abandoning ship!"

The Captain stared at Pat and opened his mouth just as the sentry called, "Enemy ho!" which turned all our heads. Sure enough, the British vessel had appeared from behind the island of rock and was bearing down upon us. Patrick, too, heard the shout. He shot a dark look as my father called sternly, "Remember your duty, Pat!" But the mate turned and fled.

A deadly battle followed, in which Warren Hart took a shot to the chest. But, as if by miracle, his heavy brass buckle absorbed the shot, and he arose, unscathed. He fought to repel the attack as crewman Jackson and I took the remaining rowboat and scrambled ashore to man the 24-pounder hidden on the cliff.

Captain Hart was a hero for saving the Landing. Though I, his son, had the honor of firing the shot that sank the *Spitflame*, the glory fell flat. For, sadly, my dear father succumbed to the final shot from the *Spitflame*; it consigned the Patriot and her brave crew to the depths of the river.

CHEERS TO AUGER

A chirping sound drew Auger's attention: a text message from Rita, his stepmom, reminding him to do an errand for his grandmother.

He stuffed the history pamphlet back in the case and thought of the things that were *not* printed there: Dirk finding Patrick Worder on the cliff with the baby, and the struggle that followed. Auger looked down where the powerful current ripped past the cliff, where Worder had fallen in the river. *Too bad Dirk saved the Worder baby.* If he hadn't, that *Corey* Worder would never have been born. The kid was a pirate: he'd robbed Auger of his trophy...and Auger's chance to impress his father.

Auger ran down a few steps, jumped over the rail by the wheelchair ramp, and dashed to the car. He peeled out of the lot.

When Auger was little, his father was his coach, and he taught him to play hockey; he took him hunting, took him skeet shooting, took him to work. His dad would show him with pride around the hotel, the restaurants, and the tour boats. He would point to the name on his door and say, "That will read 'Mr. August Hart'!" Then after Auger's mother left to "find herself" in the Peace Corps, he and his dad had been even closer. Sure he'd get busy with work now and then, but it had always ended, and Dad would spend time with Auger again...until last fall.

Dad had been working like a maniac when he started ignoring Auger. Now Dad hardly smiled, and he only noticed Auger to warn him to "Keep focused." And he would take his own advice and turn back to his business plans or whatever else was more important than Auger. *I should've left for Africa with Mom.* But Auger didn't really want to live without running water—or frozen water. Besides, he was a Hart like his dad.

When had Dad "checked out"? Wasn't it after his assistant had thrown herself in the river? It was that Worder kid's mother! *Dad shouldn't have hired a Worder in the first place.* A Worder would leave you in the lurch. It was a Worder who took his dad's attention away, and it was a

Worder who stole his chance to get it back. Auger's eyes stung.

On his way home, Auger noticed the box in the passenger seat. He had almost forgotten to leave off Grandma's care package for the geezer in the back room at the Priva-Cheers Saloon. Gran was such a do-gooder. *I'll make it quick.*

Auger finally parked in his own driveway and dragged his feet to the servants' entrance. He had dreaded going in, but what was the difference? Probably no one was even home. He shut the door behind him and headed for the dining room. He'd just grab an apple.

But the dining room was not its silent self. Its cherry buffets and wainscoting tossed voices back and forth, some leaking around the solid paneled door, slightly ajar.

"...should have been there—"

"I told you, I couldn't miss this meeting—"

"On a Saturday? What's so important?"

"Anyway, it would have been awkward..."

Auger felt like running up to his room, but an inner voice urged him: *Push past your limitations.* He opened the door. The talking stopped.

Unusual. Rita, Dad, and Grandma all sitting in the same room. Dad was normally at work, and Rita, Auger's stepmother, was busy at her Glass & Brass art gallery or kickboxing class—she was in good shape for thirty-something. And Gran, well, she spent a lot of time at the care facility.

Rita met his eyes, and a squeak escaped her glossy red lips. "Auger!"

A softer voice said, "Is that my favorite grandson?" Gran wheeled her chair around slowly, and her voice grew stronger. "Come give me a kiss!"

"I'm your only grandson, Gran," Auger forced a smile as he kissed the cheek of the woman who had named him, and sank into the chair she patted.

Dad nodded in Auger's direction and sipped coffee as he read his reports. Auger scratched his slippery palms.

"Oh Auger, have some hors d'oeuvre," Rita said in her best French accent. "They're divine." She held out a tray of little pieces of toast with toppings, like the ones she served at her Glass & Brass gallery. Some kind of...fish?

He hesitated as he reached for one. Gran was always warning him against eating fish from the St. Lawrence. Too many toxins—PCB's or something. At least she cared about him.

"It's Maine lobster!" Rita said, pushing the tray at him. He took one. Not bad.

His grandmother reached for a box by her chair. "Auger, I got you something for your celebration."

"But he didn't—"

"My grandson deserves it." His grandmother's voice took an edge as she glanced towards Rita, but the gentle smile remained. She pulled something out of the box and held it up, her eyes gleaming. As Auger glimpsed the blue and silver jersey, his gray eyes widened and the rock in his throat threatened to choke him. The back of the shirt proclaimed, "It Takes Hart."

"Oh, Mother—" Dad shook his head. Was he annoyed with Grandma or with Auger?

"You should have told us..." Rita said, mostly to herself.

Grandma ignored. "Try it on!" Her voice was shaky, but her eyes danced.

"But I lost..." Auger blurted as he let his grandmother jerk the shirt over his head, trapping his arms so he felt like a mummy—incapable of swinging a hockey stick, much less scoring.

He gazed at his chest. The words appeared upside down, but he could read them just fine: "New York's #1."

Grandma clapped her hands and beamed. "You'll always be my number one."

Auger had never felt more like a zero. He was sure his face was the color of Rita's lipstick as he jumped up, ran out, and tore off the shirt.

HART FAMILY TREE

In the hallway was the cabinet of sports weaponry, and Auger imagined using the Worder kid for target practice. Then he found himself staring at the gold-framed family tree on the opposite wall. His mother, Dorothy, still held her place above his. He wished she were here.

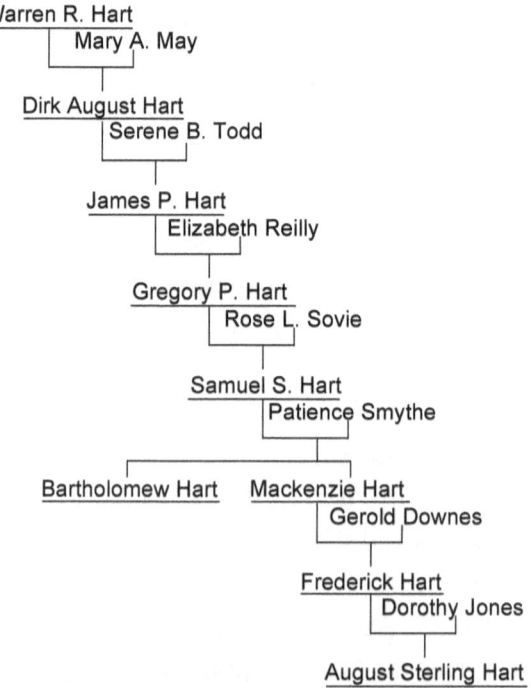

SAM

Corey's feet weighed a hundred pounds each. He had reached the part of town where sidewalks were broken slabs separated by grass shoots. He crushed as many as he could with his heels as he repeated his own version of a rhyme: *Step on a crack, bring your mother back.* Stupid, but he couldn't help it. Sometimes Corey would imagine his ancestor Patrick Worder falling towards the river and then turning into a woman—Corey's mom. After all, taking a dive was a family tradition. And Corey would sometimes imagine Mom, before she slid under the surface, replaced by another Worder: a boy with ragged dark hair and amber eyes.

Dirk Hart shouldn't have saved Patrick's baby. Then Corey wouldn't be here now, wouldn't have to face Charlie.

As Corey got closer to home, lawn ornaments became old cars and junk piles. Corey would have gone somewhere else—like the Glass Inn—but his only human friend, Mr. Murphy, had sold the Inn and moved. Corey did have a buddy at the fort last year, but his dad was deployed to the Middle East and he never made it back. The friend and his mom moved away.

"Corey!"

He jumped—he hadn't heard any footsteps—but he kept walking.

"Aren't you Corey Worder?" the voice insisted. He didn't need any more teasing. He walked faster.

"Wait! Please...I need to apologize."

Something hit him in the back, just hard enough that it stopped him.

He slowed and turned. It was that new girl running to catch up, the mascot responsible for embarrassing him! She'd whacked him with what must've been the season's final snowball. Pitching for winter softball had sharpened her aim.

"Go away, you've done enough," he growled.

"Look, I didn't *know!* Some kids told me about this *drama*—I love the river—and when I found out it was *river* history, I wanted to be part of it. I didn't know anyone was *related* to Worder—didn't even know it was a real guy." She quit jabbering and slowed to catch her breath as she reached his side.

Corey glared at the button on her jacket: RiverGuards. Charlie called them "watchdogs of the waters"—he was always saying how important it was to keep the river healthy.

"Right," he said to the button and kept walking.

"The coach chewed us out," she called after him. "He was busy at the break...I wish he had stopped us." She caught up again, and Corey couldn't help meeting the brown eyes now, level with his own. He'd never seen her this close. She was...hot. But her turned-up nose and freckles made her look harmless. He could almost believe her, but he kept walking. She chattered and tagged along, shoulder to shoulder with Corey. "Randy had to shuttle some people in the *van* and Johnny was *busy*, so he had a guest bring me to the game, and I was *late*...wish I'd been *too* late to do that skit...

"I'm Samantha Clarke." She touched his arm to slow him. "You can call me Sam." She swerved around in front of Corey, blocking him. Her full lips were shiny red, and she tossed a reddish-brown wave. "Do you have a nickname?"

"Uh, just Corey." He moved off the walk to get around the smooth legs covered by a ruffly pink skirt at the top and stuffed into fluffy white boots lower down. *And don't bother wasting your dimples on me.*

"Anyway, I heard you lost your job." She came after him. "I want to make it up. My dads need help..."

"Huh?" He halted. "Did you say *dads?*" Corey squinted sideways.

"Yes." Her smile vanished. "I have two." Her voice took an edge. "Do you have a problem with that?"

"No, I—"

"I thought you might be a little more sensitive than others." Her face was pink, but she shook her head and started again. "Anyway, I live at the old Glass Inn—The Mainsail now. We're fixing it up as a bed and breakfast—"

"So you're the reason," Corey halted. "Mr. Murphy had to go away!"

"It's not like we forced him—" Samantha took a step backward, her face redder. "He was perfectly willing to take what was offered and go south."

"It—it was *you* guys who took my glass sailboat!" He turned away and snarled, "Mr. Murphy left it to *me!*" It was like rubbing salt in a wound. Corey and Mom had already hung it at their house when the new owner insisted that the window was part of the inn. Charlie had ended up taking the glass back to the new owners' real estate guy.

"What?" She acted confused. "Wait! We had a bad start—I wanted to help you!"

Sure you did. Like all girls who looked that good, he knew she would smile at his face then smirk and whisper behind him. He wanted to tell her that he was onto her, he was no fool; instead, he turned and ducked down a side street.

Corey slouched along Thompson, River, and Balsam streets before clearing his mind enough to think about Charlie and how to tell him he'd lost another job. Corey was fired from the bakery because some kid startled him, yelling "Worder desserter! He's got pies, get it—desserts?" Corey had dropped a tray of pastries and slipped on the mess. The kids laughed while Corey wiped custard from his eyes and the boss chewed him out. Later, Corey had lost his job at the museum after he sneaked into the office where Mom was last seen. He'd just wanted to feel her presence. How could she be gone if he still felt her vibes?

He was studying the sidewalk near the Priva-Cheers Saloon, practicing what he would say to Charlie, when a barmaid came out to prop the door. Corey had heard the new owner had repainted, added on, and hired younger help from who-knows-where. Help that was more "energetic." Meaning sexy.

"Like what you see?" the barmaid said with a wink. Corey jerked his head away. She'd caught him staring at her overflowing blouse as she bent over. Samantha popped into his mind and he shook his head, staring at the sidewalk as he moved on, forcing himself to think about Howler. That's when he collided with Humpty Dumpty.

"Tell 'em the truth..." the round old guy was singing.

Corey held onto the man so neither of them would fall over then pushed him back. "Oh, it's you." Corey had seen old Buddy panhandling up at the Point by the museum. Up close, his face looked like one of those contour maps in earth science. Gray hair stuck out here and there, no surprise. But for a guy stumbling around a bar, something was missing. No booze on his breath.

"Tell it like it iz...when itzall you gotta give, tell th' truth..." Buddy sang.

Fine. The truth. Charlie had to know sooner or later.

Corey was rehearsing his latest version of the truth when he got to his own house on Grant Street and his best pal met him at the back gate. Howler peed against the fence then used his hundred-some pounds of Mastiff and fifty-some pounds of who-knew-what to wag more confidence into Corey as they crowded, side-by-side, through the kitchen door.

DROWNING TROUBLES

Charlie Stowe stared at the smart phone in his hand. He had been happy to get it last summer after Peg agreed it was an important business tool for a fishing guide. *Now I'd rather have a dumb phone.*

"I'm real sorry, Charlie, but the wife and kids want to stay at the Hart Resort," the guy on the other end of the connection repeated—the guy Charlie had taken fishing every spring for ten years. "And now that the Harts have added fishing to their package... I won't be needing you."

Wouldn't be needing the guy who knew the river like his own hand? The guy who'd landed a record 59-inch muskie... "Sure, I see, yeah that makes sense I guess..." Charlie's voice grew to a shout, "for a scumbag!" He threw the phone on the table, grabbed an aluminum can, and slurped through the foam of a Genesee Cream Ale.

Couldn't he get a break? That was the third client. Didn't matter that Charlie knew every weed bed, every drop-off, every shoal in these 1800-plus islands *and* had years of hard-won experience through sun and rain. He caught his reflection in the kitchen cabinet and jerked a nod at the leathery face.

Damned Fred Hart and his resort. Knew nothing about fishing but could afford fancy equipment and advertising. Now Hart had something fishy going on over at the island, Charlie just knew it. Charlie had been ice fishing by Rocky Island when he'd heard that airboat buzzing in and dying off behind the island. Hart probably planned to make that old castle into some kind of fishing resort. The guy put on a good act, pretending to care about all the locals, but Fred Hart himself was probably behind all the land grabs. Fred Heartless was more like it.

Charlie sank his wiry five-eleven frame into the sofa. He'd been living on auto-pilot for months trying to make ends meet...and to forget.

Maybe he should've gotten one of those web sites for his guide business, like Peg said, but he didn't want anything to do with the computer—not any more. He spotted the portrait of his late wife hanging, crooked, on the wall. He thought Peg had loved him. Until...

She had "Found a love." He took a swig. "Willing to leave home." He took another. "Join Mr. Hart." He tried to drown each word. But they kept coming up, no matter how many times he swallowed.

Those late nights—special project, hah. He should have known; no one gets that wound up about work. No, Peg had an unstable background, and it had come back to sabotage their relationship.

It was his own fault. He'd persuaded her to her to move here, to be a family. But he'd underestimated the "Worder curse." Supposedly she'd beat it years ago—after running away, doing drugs, and getting pregnant. She had straightened herself out, or so everyone thought. Then last fall she'd deserted *him*.

Charlie finished his beer and snapped open another. He turned on the old boom box. Pretty soon, Jagger was wailing that he couldn't "get no satisfaction." He wailed through several more beers.

At what point had she decided a fisherman was not enough? Charlie's curse was in those big blue eyes that melted all resistance, in the soft voice that... Hell, it was easier to just keep swallowing the beer.

Footsteps interrupted his downhill slide into a stupor.

Now I have a kid to feed.

Charlie mustered a glare towards Corey as he raised his beer can and took the last gulp. He couldn't look at the kid's face; all he'd see was Peg's eyes—not the color, but the pretended innocence. And the kid's yellow-brown eyes pierced him with questions he couldn't answer.

"Good thing ya got a job," he said to his can. "An' yer damn dog peed inside again." This was followed by a snort as Charlie's head nodded to his chest and the can bounced on the gray rug before rolling to a threadbare patch near Corey.

BAD ROOTS

"You—you're drunk!" Corey took a step backwards. But there was no use saying anything to Charlie now. Corey spun around and ran down the hall as the clock struck three-thirty.

He woke up two hours later with his cheek pasted to leather, sprawled over the trunk in Mom's old office. He peeled his face off the trunk and caught sight of his wallet, still open beside him. He lifted the note from it and re-read Mom's last words.

Is it sick to have it in my wallet? Somehow it made her closer...even if she did sign it like a stranger. Not *Mom*, not *Peg*, which everyone called her, but *Margaret*, her legal name. What was that all about?

He stuck it back in the billfold and eyed the chart on the wall. His mother had posted the family tree Corey had done for social studies—before he knew about his rotten roots. He hadn't found any ancestors further back than Patrick himself...just as well.

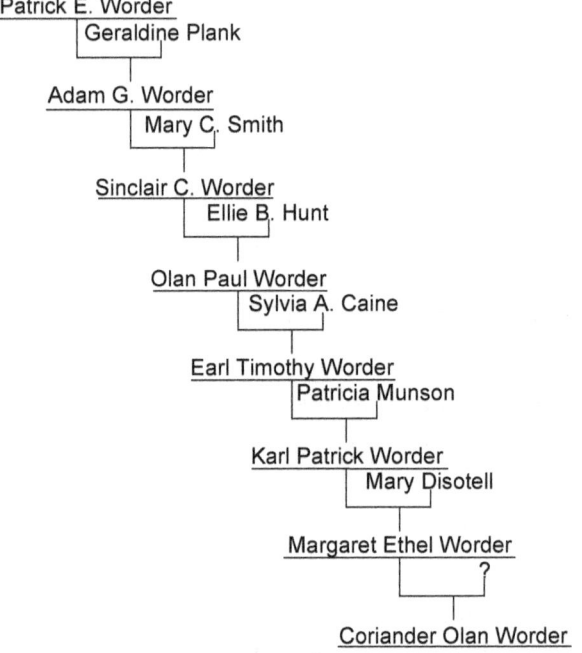

Patrick E. Worder
Geraldine Plank

Adam G. Worder
Mary C. Smith

Sinclair C. Worder
Ellie B. Hunt

Olan Paul Worder
Sylvia A. Caine

Earl Timothy Worder
Patricia Munson

Karl Patrick Worder
Mary Disotell

Margaret Ethel Worder
?

Coriander Olan Worder

Corey's mother had been into crystal meth—she didn't even know who Corey's father was. Then, she'd gotten into healthy weeds and herbs. He still couldn't believe she'd named him after a seed: "Coriander—spice of my life."

Corey stood and yawned, rubbing sleep from his eyes, when he heard Charlie's voice drifting through the dog-shredded doorframe from the kitchen.

"...and that's great! Thanks John, I appreciate your support. And hey, call me any time you need anything."

Corey went to the living room door. He could see Charlie moving in the kitchen and heard him whistling. *That's different.* Corey moved into the kitchen and lowered himself to a vinyl chair.

"C'mon, eat." Charlie said, moving the pork and beans closer to Corey. "Must be hungry after workin' the game." He clapped Corey's shoulder and gave a wink. Give him a little time to sleep it off, and Charlie was a different person. Since September, Charlie had been swinging back and forth between human and troll. Corey almost wished he was sitting with the troll now. *He'll be even meaner next time he swings.*

"Good news." Charlie slid the salt over to Corey. "New fella that took over the Murphy place is sending me some business." He stuck out his chin and stroked the top of his crew cut as he looked into the aluminum fruit bowl. "Said he heard I was the best!" He moved towards the living room. "Finally, somebody on my side."

"Yeah...great." Corey took his dish to the sink. Maybe that would soften the blow. Maybe Charlie could get enough work so Corey's job didn't matter.

Charlie sat in his yellowed easy chair scanning a borrowed issue of *Northern Scales*, a magazine that listed fishing events and record catches. He started muttering about some place where they'd found chemicals in fish. "Experts say *three* parts per million of arsenic is too much. Government says *ten* ppm is okay. Idiot politicians want to kill people off."

He flipped pages for a while. "Jeeze, if I could afford an ad in here... Look at those guides and their fancy *cuisine* and 'spa accommodations.' They make a luxury vacation out of a simple fishing trip..." He threw the magazine down and looked at Corey, hovering by the kitchen door.

"So tell me about the game, Kid."

Corey's stomach flip-flopped. "Ah...it started great, I did everything right." He edged past his stepfather's chair and sank into the sagging sofa from Good Will. Taking his weight, its middle nearly touched the floor. Corey stared at his finger as it enlarged a hole in the couch cushion. The faded yellow daffodils matched somebody else's curtains.

"I cleaned perfect. Then they did this thing, made fun of Patrick—" The words came in a rush. "But I went on the ice. Even then." He sucked in a breath. "B-but there were pennies..."

Charlie stared at Corey's shirt and said nothing.

"I tried, I really did. But—my pants, the hole—"

Charlie frowned. "I already heard about the game."

Corey's eyes grew. The janitor told him. Or Sam's dad. Or her other dad. How many dads could she have?

Corey's words spilled out. "I don't know what happened—everything was fine." He looked down. "Then there was this woman..." He swept his hand past his face. "She moved like—"

"Corey." Charlie's voice was firm. He sat next to Corey. "You've got to stop seeing your mom everywhere, you've got to move on." He swallowed hard and added, quieter, "She's not coming back."

No anger, no storm. That would have been easier than hearing the crack in Charlie's voice. Corey fought to swallow back his own emotions, but he lost the fight.

"Why did she leave?" he hiccupped. "I thought I could count on her."

"Cripes." Charlie sighed. "Me too."

"How could she think we'd be 'better off'...?" Corey wailed. His chest jerked and the couch bounced under him.

"Kept things inside..." Charlie stared at the wall photo. Corey's eyes followed as he gulped back a spasm. Red highlights framed his mom's gaze from blue eyes.

Then Charlie shook himself and stood. "Well, lucky for you the folks at The Mainsail want your help." The rough edge was back.

Corey's stomach churned.

Charlie's voice hardened.

"This is your last chance, Kid. You start working again tomorrow." He walked to the door. "Or," he stabbed his finger towards the hulking mass at Corey's feet, "that dog goes." He slammed the door on his way out.

Corey was stunned. How could he work for those people who took over Mr. Murphy's place, took Corey's sailboat...and humiliated him on the ice?

His brows curved upward, and he gazed into the eyes in the picture. But he'd get no answers from a deserter like his mother. Sure, he and Mom used to have some kind of freaky mind connection...but now his dreams of what went on behind those blue eyes must only be his imagination.

M.A. NOBLE

3 BEHIND BLUE EYES
The Fall of Peg Stowe...Last September

"The replica is perfect!" Peg met her friend Dell for coffee by the pier. "I'm lucky to know the best metal worker at the fort."

"Glad I could help."

"It's a symbol of the Patriot resistance—and I want to surprise my boss with fresh ideas for the bicentennial."

She looked up at the sign above the pier, identifying Harts Landing for all who entered the bay. It simply listed members of the Hart family line. No imagination.

"My plan is to focus on the buckle as a theme. Put up a huge replica here and at the highway. We'll use slogans like 'Buckle Down for the Night' for the hotel, and 'Buckle Under Wonderland' for the diving tour. What do you think? We'll do souvenir buckles, regular size. I figured it would have more impact if I actually showed my boss a good prototype."

"You've thought a lot about this." Dell sipped his coffee.

"I didn't have time to *borrow* the original." Peg frowned. "With my boss away, and you being deployed soon. Anyway, no one will notice it's missing." She hoped. The original buckle had been in a secure case, but Peg's lock-picking skills had come in handy. She had replaced the buckle with a postcard. "No one will look close enough to notice."

Dell raised his brow. "You little thief."

"B-but, I didn't really steal it..."

"Relax." Dell smiled. "I'm sure your boss will love it."

"The celebration is coming, you know, the bicentennial of the War of 1812." She was grateful to Fred Hart. He had taken a chance on her; he gave her a good salary and health benefits, and he respected her skill. He had relied on her more and more, now that the company was tied up with the new project. "I want to do something special to surprise him. And show my creativity."

"Well, I'm glad I could be useful!" Dell tossed his cup in the trash can. "I'll send you my bill." He chuckled and put his arm around her.

"You're the greatest! And Dell, take care of yourself." Peg patted his face and kissed his cheek.

She grinned as she walked home. Maybe she could be the role model Corey needed. He needed something positive. Starting school here was rough; bad enough the kids used to make fun of his first name, plus his "inventive" use of words. Now he was tormented for his last name. She tried to shield him from the shame she too had felt, but she loved Charlie and moved back here to be with him. Besides, Corey would be sixteen soon; shouldn't he be able to handle the truth?

No one should have to deal with that. There were public markers, museum write-ups, even tour boat guides who juiced up the old stories. But even Fred Hart agreed it was time to downplay the villainy of Patrick Worder.

Peg glimpsed herself in a shop window as her earring caught the sun and flashed blue. Sapphire, her birthstone. She stroked the two small stones completing the teardrop formation: topaz and aquamarine. It was like having her two guys wink back at her.

Charlie, her aquamarine, had been so excited when he left to get the almost-new fishing boat. He and Corey, whose bright amber *topaz* eyes shone with excitement, would motor the *Stowe Aweigh* home from Cape Vincent this evening. She and Charlie could afford the thirty-two-foot fiberglass vessel because of her job skills. Her hands were her portal; she read the world through them, and when they felt a keyboard beneath them they flew. She had been the fastest word processor at the fort. But it was a clever mind that drove the hands. She'd finished her business degree and got the job as assistant to Mr. Hart here at the Landing.

"Roll on...rolling river," Peg sang as she left the pier. Granddad had said the lullaby had been passed down all the way from his great-great-grandmother Geraldine Plank. The mute woman had never uttered a sentence; the only words that passed her lips were in her lullaby to baby Adam, Peg's great-great-great-grandfather.

Peg had lost Granddad too soon, and when she sang his song, she felt happy. As she passed the footpath leading up to the Point, she heard a familiar voice echoing her tune through the woods. Buddy, the old panhandler, was like a parrot. "Hello, Buddy!" she called.

" 'ello Buddy" came back.

Later that afternoon, Peg found something that made her forget about marketing and souvenirs. Something in the old trunk from her father's house. She had never known the trunk existed until her father died last summer, and inside it she found clothing of her ancestor Geraldine Plank. It wasn't until today that Peg had found the hidden book—*Patrick's* journal. Maybe Dad finally gave her something of value!

When Charlie called from the Cape, she had just learned something astounding.

"I've got news of my own!" She told him it had to do with an old journal, but that's all she'd say. "Don't mention it to Corey." She was being mysterious, but she wanted to explain it to Corey when they got home. And she needed to make a readable version of "Patrick's" words.

Peg was typing as fast as she could. The original document was delicate, and even she struggled to read it. Living here was hard for Corey, but this could make all the difference. *Because history as we know it is bull!*

She stopped typing mid-sentence, gasped at the clock, and hit "Print." She put the journal back in its hiding place and grabbed her coat. She checked her purse to make sure the two buckles—original and copy—were still there. Then, she noticed the printer had only one sheet of paper. *Skip it—I'll deal with that later.*

It was time to meet with Fred Hart.

Thanks to Charlie for souping up her green Civic, Peg powered into the lot at the Point in just a few minutes. She could see the museum's second story deck jutting out over the cliff as she nosed into a parking space. She thought of the journal and found herself humming again. She'd been surprised to see the words to the river song in the journal: "The moon is my mother, the sun is my father, the Landing's my home but my Hart's on the water." Only she'd always thought of it as "heart's" instead of "Hart's." Actually, it was the other information in the journal that made her sing.

She checked her hair in the rearview mirror. Only one sapphire winked back! She'd had them both on this morning. Must've dropped the other in the trunk. She had caught her hair on the buttons of the old clothes inside it. Now, she tried to remove the earring she had, but it was stuck. *Forget it, better hurry.* She locked the car as she smoothed her hair to cover the bare ear.

Naturally, the Harts had an interest in promoting local history, and Fred was Chairman of the Board. Tonight, he would arrive from an out-of-town meeting about setting up an

Initial Public Offering to get more cash for business expansion. Then he wanted to meet Peg in private to discuss the foul-ups in the reservation system. He valued his assistant's judgment. Maybe she would soon be more than an assistant!

She walked to the back door of the museum, where a sturdy blond boy attempted to enter with several boxes in his arms.

"Oh—let me get that for you, they look heavy."

"Nah, they're not too bad, but thanks." He flashed a grin that showed the cleft in his chin as he passed her to stack the boxes. On his way out, he picked up her purse, which had slipped from her arm as she'd held the door.

"One good turn deserves another." He handed it back, his intense gray eyes fastening on hers. She could see why the Hart boy was popular with the girls.

Forty-five minutes later, she and Fred Hart neared the end of their business, and she was about to show him the buckle. She wouldn't bring up the journal until she'd had more time to digest the information it revealed. If Fred was serious about revising the history literature, she might have something to replace it with. But what the journal suggested was shocking, and she needed more time before confronting Fred Hart with something that would affect his family too. Besides, Fred's mood was already off because he'd been outvoted on the IPO. The company would remain privately owned, and he worried about funding the expansion.

Now Fred was packing his briefcase.

"Wait, I have something..." In her haste to grab the purse, it dropped to the floor. She scrambled to pick up the contents, and Fred dove to help her. She and her boss were head to head on the floor when Peg found herself staring at beige Gucci shoes. She hadn't noticed the door swing open.

As she stuffed the remaining items in her purse, one of the brass buckles nearly escaped, but Peg snapped the purse shut. The right moment had passed for revealing the prototype buckle. She would show Fred tomorrow.

"So...this is your meeting?" Fred's wife said in a pseudo-joking voice as Mr. Hart stood up, a little too quickly. Peg couldn't remember seeing Rita Hart up close, but she had the feeling she knew the red-haired woman from somewhere. Somewhere far from designer labels and gallery art.

"Oh, honestly Rita, we had to go over some numbers," Fred said to his wife as he helped Peg get up and then dusted himself off. He kissed Rita's cheek.

"Anyway, weren't you going to a show? Oh—where are my manners. Rita, meet Peg." His wife gave him a cool glance. "Er...Peg, this is *Mrs.* Hart." Then he gestured towards the woman behind his wife. "And my mother is also Mrs. Hart."

The older woman said "How do you do?" with twinkling brown eyes and a warm smile. But Rita Hart pasted her smile on and held out a gloved hand that barely touched Peg's before she turned back to her husband.

"The show finished early. We decided to kidnap you for a late dinner."

Fred gathered his things and turned to Peg. "Look over that information tonight, will you Peg, and we'll meet on it tomorrow." The meeting was over. "Oh, and lock up here, please."

No problem. Peg would talk to her boss later. She started looking over the online system of reservations he had accessed for her, along with the emailed cancelations that had somehow been delivered to numerous guests. Fred was impressed with Peg's analytical skills and wanted her to look for some kind of pattern.

Twenty minutes later she still could make no sense of it. She would sleep on it. When she picked up her purse, she couldn't resist pulling out the two buckles. She held the original in her right hand, the copy in her left.

Peg looked from one buckle to the other. How alike they were! Fred would be impressed. She hadn't examined the original buckle closely since taking it from its display case at the resort. She felt its weight in her right hand, the coolness of the brass. So this is the buckle that saved Warren Hart. Peg closed her eyes and ran her fingers over every edge of the thick two-by-three-inch rectangle. She had an affinity for metals—she'd found that out as a child.

Peg's dad had locked her in a closet for days when he was drunk. She had learned to read the lock with her fingers, prying with a pin, until the lock gave way. Later, her lock-picking talent had landed her in juvenile detention because she opened locks to steal money for crystal meth—for which she had also developed an affinity. The meth had helped her forget her father's abuse—and made it easy to find men who cared, at least for a night. She had slept around, but the result was Corey, and she had no regrets about having him.

A *snap* interrupted her thoughts. The brass buckle had sprung apart in her right hand. It had a hidden hinge that released when pressed just so...and between the hinged sections was something yellow and folded. She touched the ancient paper gently, full of wonder, and started to extract it from the buckle.

She barely heard the footsteps that preceded the inward swing of the door.

"You're clever, you've found its secret."

Peg jerked at the sound of the voice.

"Oh—you're back!" Peg took a step forward. Then she noticed something hard in the eyes.

"I see there have been...*developments* since I left." The voice held a no-nonsense edge.

"Well, I—" Peg's fingers trembled as she snapped the buckle closed, the unread paper still inside.

"I'm sure you realize the damage it could do. It would affect more than just you and me."

What did *that* mean?

"You'd better give that—"

The head jerked away at the rustling of bushes; the sound came from below the adjoining deck and drifted through the partially opened sliding door. *Just the wind.*

"—give that to me now," finished the voice as the head snapped back.

Peg held out her right hand, the same hand in which her visitor had just spied the original buckle. But it now held the object that had been in Peg's left hand a fraction of a second earlier.

"I thought you'd see it my way." The voice sounded more relaxed as the bogus buckle was accepted and placed in a coat pocket. "Have a pleasant evening." The visitor spun about and exited.

Peg Stowe almost thought she'd imagined the whole thing—except that she now held only one of the buckles. What had possessed her to exchange them? She exhaled and stared at the buckle in her hand. She had to go now, go somewhere she could examine that paper inside it. No telling when her trick would be discovered.

She flipped the office light switch and slipped out the sliding door to the deck; security lights illuminated her way past the coin-operated viewer, past the plaque marking the location of the 1813 battle. But before she made it to the steps at the other end of the deck, she was drawn to the rail. She looked over and down where Pat Worder had fallen. She was thinking about the odds of surviving such a fall, and it barely registered when the security lights went off. Moonbeams playing on the brass buckle had caught her gaze, reminding her to hurry away, when strong hands clenched her arms and started forcing her over the rail. Her head spun to make sense of the bizarre events. Peg's hands jerked and grabbed at the rail for balance, and the buckle flew to the side, out into the bushes. Boosted over the rail by forceful arms, Peg could do nothing but fall through the autumn night to the rocks and powerful current.

Nose broken, forehead smashed—miraculously, some part of her clung to hope and made Peg hold her breath. Such pain in her lungs. Memories came in waves, twisted and merged; she had just enough consciousness to pray for her son and husband before her memory locked itself within.

M.A. NOBLE

4 TODAY'S HISTORY LESSON

Corey came to and sighed. They had never found Mom's body, and he had secretly hoped she was still alive. But he had to face the truth: like the recovery team said, she must've gotten caught in a tree or cave under the lethal current where no diver would risk his life.

Now Mom had been gone six months, and it didn't matter how long he studied her gaze, he'd never know what she was thinking that day. Charlie was right. Her past had gotten to her.

Corey's eyes fell on Howler, and he reached over to give his best buddy a belly scratch. Howler sat up and put his head in Corey's lap.

Corey asked the droopy brown eyes, "Do you think I would let you go without food? Or give you away?" He scratched Howler behind the ears. *I can't get Mom back, but I'll do everything I can to keep you.*

Corey looked once again at the photo. His voice was shaky as he said, "I don't know how you could've deserted me, Mom." His brows met and his voice grew solid. "But I will *not* abandon Howler!"

He would swallow his pride.

He would call The Mainsail.

Monday morning, Corey dreaded school and the new job—but at least Charlie was in his corner now.

"Don't take crap from nobody about that game. Just learn from your mistakes and go forward." Charlie even showed Corey some boxing moves. "You're as good as anybody, even that Hart kid—you can take him on!" Then he muttered, "I'd like to take Hart myself." Corey was pretty sure Charlie wasn't talking about Auger.

But most of the kids at school didn't pay any attention to Corey. Besides a few whispers—BackWorder, Turder, and even DorkWadder—when he tried to push in the one door that opened towards the hallway—no one bothered him.

It was his last class, American history, where Corey tried to block out Orman the Tormenter. Today, Mr. Orman was running on about that war—the War of 1812.

"It wasn't just in 1812—it lasted until 1815. This area was a hotbed of activity. In many border towns, people were against the war—they had friends on both sides. Some made a living smuggling goods to the other side, a few were pirates. But this town was different—a real anomaly."

Orman looked around to make sure all eyes were on him then kept going. "Secret Landing, now called Harts Landing, was founded by an unusual band of men who'd been impressed by the British—who knows what that means?"

"I'm impressed by that new girl's booty..." the class clown said. The kids around him hooted.

"All right, enough," Mr. Orman said as the kid whispered, "Wouldn't mind staying in that 'bed 'n breakfast.'"

Corey was glad Samantha was in an honors class instead of this one.

"To impress," the teacher emphasized with a stern glance at the clown, "was to force into service. American Patriots were taken off their ships and forced to serve the British. So, Hart's privateers wanted to get even with the British. They stopped British ships, stole supplies, and finally battled it out, which is why we have two sunken ships right outside the bay!" He grinned, ear to ear.

"Now," he pursed his lips and raised an eyebrow. "A privateer is not the same as a pirate. Who can define *privateer*?"

Oh great. This topic couldn't lead anywhere good.

"A privateer fought for an established government." This came from front left, some fourteen-year-old brainiac. She continued like she was reciting from a book. "He arrested and plundered enemy ships by the authority of the government, and he carried a *Letter of Marque* to prove it—in this case, a document signed by President Madison!" She inhaled and smirked like she'd won a race.

"Fabulous," Mr. Orman said. "*Privateer* could refer to either the man or his ship, and he had the right to attack the enemy, take their goods, and keep the treasure.

"The men who formed Harts Landing were privateers—that's why we celebrate Privateers Day."

"You mean *Privates Day*," someone said, referring to the local nickname for Privateers Day.

The teacher ignored him. "Now we know what a privateer is; someone tell us what a *pirate*—"

"He doesn't play for a team." It was a new voice, full of confidence, and all heads turned to admire the hockey god who swaggered in. Auger Hart was seventeen and took advanced history, but he assisted the teacher in this class so he'd look good on his resume. He wanted to get early admission to some "ivy league" school.

"A pirate is out for himself," Auger continued, "and he'll abandon the mission if it's not all about him."

Corey could feel Auger's eyes boring into him, and he knew the "history" Auger was talking about was only two days old. Corey sunk lower, head down so his hair fell over his eye. He was busy trying to blend into the floor and block out the rest of the discussion. But he couldn't help hearing the Tormenter's brilliant idea of having Auger recite the legend of the Battle of Harts Landing.

Auger really got into it, even acted out the parts. Then he started wrapping up. "After Warren perished in the battle, Dirk Hart—"

"Another of your famous ancestors!" Mr. Orman couldn't help himself.

Auger pretended to be embarrassed and continued. "Yes...my great, great, great, great grandfather, Dirk Hart...went to his father's cabin at the Point to find Patrick Worder—that's when he, well, you know...." Auger was hinting around just enough to make them want more.

A new kid was saying: "No, *I* don't know. What did he do?"

Orman threw a glance at Corey. "Oh we don't need to get into the details."

The bell rang. Corey wanted to escape, but he didn't want to pass Auger, who was at the door, filling in the newcomer and other bystanders.

"...Worder was about to throw a baby off the cliff. The mute woman staying at Hart's cabin had just given birth." Auger dropped his voice lower. "Supposedly, Worder was the father—and he was trying to 'dispose' of the evidence that he had taken advantage."

Corey heard the whispers and suddenly wished Patrick was alive now. *I'd kill him myself.*

Everyone finally left, and Corey slunk to the door. He imagined Auger's face on the other side as he gave the door a good shove.

The one person in the hallway was knocked to the floor. She sat holding her nose as splayed books surrounded her.

GIVING UP THE SHIP

"S—Sam?!" Corey choked as the girl hoisted herself to her feet. He blushed and scrambled to pick up books.

"It's okay, I wasn't looking either. "Too absorbed in those half lives."

Corey glanced at her science book as he returned it. *Half lives?* Even the evil wizard from that story they read in English class had a half life. *That's more than I get.*

But Sam was talking about chemistry. "A half-life is how long it takes a substance to decay so only half is left." She poked her finger at a table of elements on the cover of a science book. "Like, the half-life of plutonium-238 is eighty-eight years—a long time, right? But to get rid of half of *uranium*-238 takes over four *billion* years!"

Corey stared at her. "You-rainy...what?" Thoughts of history class were evaporating.

"Uranium—the stuff they use in nuclear power plants and weapons. They smash the atoms to split them for fission, plus they can make plutonium-*239*—"

"They use atomic power for fishin'?" Corey said. "I've heard of using dynamite..."

"No, I mean a chain reaction—"

He forced a grin. "I'm just yankin' *your* chain." That was what Charlie would say. But Corey wasn't entirely sure what Sam was talking about.

She snapped the book. "Well, this stuff is no joke. People produce nuclear wastes and think they can just bury it—but it doesn't go away! And it's not just nuclear stuff." She was practically poking Corey in the chest. "People keep screwing around with nature to make their lives easier—more electricity, fuel, *drugs* to feel good—"

Sam was on a roll...probably because of that assembly about addiction where they'd warned all the kids to say "No" to anything more dangerous than scrambled eggs.

"Do you realize that every pound of crystal meth produced makes *seven* pounds of chemical waste?" Sam was going on. "And it doesn't just go away!" Corey was shocked when she grabbed his hand and jammed his finger over the cover of a pamphlet. It showed cans and bottles with crossbones, and some horrible sludge. "They use acids, solvents, even *freon*, and they heat up stuff that releases poisons. They flush chemicals into the groundwater." Her face was red, and her eyes shot daggers into the picture.

Then she looked up at Corey and sighed, like she finally realized that Corey wasn't creating meth, probably couldn't even pronounce its real name.

"Okay," she said, dropping his hand, "I'll stop before you chew off an arm to get away."

Corey ducked to grab her other books and hand them to her while she stuffed them into her bag. By the time she was finished, her whole expression had changed.

"Okay." She gave him a wide smile. "Ready to go hammer some joists?"

He stared at the strawberry lips that made tasty morsels out of construction words.

"We're adding on...my dads are building an extra wing." She kept talking as Corey followed her out the door and down the steps.

He thought he would have to work with Randy and Johnny only at first, and then he'd be on his own. He also thought the job was for sure. So he was surprised when Randy wanted to know his "qualifications."

"Can you hit a nail? How fast are you? You're kind of scrawny." Dark brows came together over eyes the color of mud. Brows sort of like what Corey always saw in the mirror, but with an arch that meant business.

Johnny rescued him. "Sam says you're okay; that's good enough for me." He patted Corey on the back. Corey had seen Johnny around; he managed the dive shop for some unseen owner. *It's obvious who Sam looks like.* Johnny had freckles and reddish brown hair, though curly. And he was friendly and compact.

"Corey, I understand that window—" Johnny nodded to the glass sailboat over the entrance, "—was special to you."

Oh-oh...we're gonna get into that. Corey tightened his lips and looked at his shoes. He didn't know if he would be able to keep his temper. *Think of Howler...Howler.*

"Look, we had no idea." Johnny put his arm around Corey's shoulder. "In fact, I feel so bad..."

Corey's head rose, and his eyes rested on the middle button of Johnny's pressed lavender shirt.

"I don't care what the contract said. You should have it."

Corey froze and held his breath. Was this a trick?

Johnny spoke again. "I understand Mr. Murphy was a friend of yours. It was too bad he couldn't stay, but his son said he had to move for his health."

Corey finally choked out a "Thanks." Maybe these people weren't so bad.

He learned well. Randy showed him how to mark out and nail boards to the floor frame. Corey found that no matter how good Sam looked in her skirts, she was at home with a tool in her hand and plaster dust on her nose. Before long, Corey was feeling at home too.

He cleaned up his work and then went to the entrance to stare at the glass boat. It was framed perfectly by the carved pillars and sweeping tree branches, and the sun's backlighting made the water sparkle like real waves. Where would Corey put the window at home? They'd had to sell his mother's antique sideboard that used to frame a mirror; there was no other worthy place. Besides, how could he get the light to shine through it like that?

"The boat looks good here," he finally said to Johnny, who'd just returned from some errand. "As long as I can come see it when I want."

Corey was walking tall when he left. He'd been forgiving about the window. He had a job, even got paid, and he was going home to his best friend with a whole bag of goodies.

He almost forgot about the game disaster.

DUMMY

It was a good noose, Auger thought. The Worder kid should get the point.

Auger slipped his hand through the gate into the Worder kid's yard and quietly unlatched it. The other hand dragged a bag of straw that resembled a human form. Making the effigy of the Worder kid had taken time away from studying, but the look of terror on his face would be worth seeing over and over—and Auger could get it all with his video cam.

He glanced around, darted to the maple tree, and swung the rope over the branch, a swish of leaves breaking the silence. He caught the end and yanked it tight.

The attack was sudden.

Auger fell backward and scrambled like a crab to get away. *It's a monster!* Auger barely got to the gate while the mutt wasted half of the dummy. Then Auger was barely able to latch the gate against the hulking mass that hurled itself at him.

Heart pounding, Auger limped to the hill overlooking the yard as the monster howled—sounding angry, then pathetic, like he wanted someone to play with. Auger wiped his bloody palm and hated the kid more, the kid with the stupid dog and the rusty old hinge that had punctured his palm. Now he'd have to get a tetanus shot. He'd wait here as long as it took. The pain would be worth it when the kid came home. Auger pulled out the cam and noticed it was already recording. *Huh...must've activated it when I fell.*

Auger had barely hidden himself when he heard footsteps. *Hah!* He eyed the skinny kid with the stupid patch of hair and lopsided mouth. The kid opened the gate, patted the monster and fed it some biscuits. Now the kid was clomping ignorantly towards the maple tree.

Here it comes. Auger could almost taste the kid's terror as he focused the camera...

The shout broke the peace of the neighborhood.

"*Woa*, Charlie! You got me a punching bag—awesome!" The troll actually *hugged* the bag. The mutt had torn the head, limbs, and label off the dummy.

Auger stared with open mouth. He gave the tree a kick. He played his recording and heard the dog's howl and watched the kid again and again in disbelief as if the result would change. Every time he watched, his hatred grew. He didn't know which he loathed more, the Worder kid or his mutt and its horrid yowls.

Auger wiped blood off his hand as he limped to his car parked on the back street. For a few weeks, he would be busy with the college prep tutor—he was a junior, but he was trying for early admission to Dad's college. After that...he would just see.

COLOR SCHEMING

By the fourth week, Corey had loosened up with Sam, who could easily chat with anyone. She was more of a newcomer than Corey, but she knew more people.

"You have to have an *interest*," she said. "Me, I'm into the environment. And I meet people at RiverGuard, plus I volunteer to get signatures on the fracking petition."

"What?" Corey had never heard Sam use a word like that. It sounded obscene coming out of those raspberry lips.

"It means *hydro fracturing*. They use injection wells—they pump fluid down a well and break up the rock to get natural gas out, but some experts say it's bad for the environment."

"Oh, yeah...I knew that." He was hypnotized by her soft voice and earnest gaze. He was ready to sign anything.

Another interest was tutoring, and she showed Corey how she helped kids, like her brother, to focus and keep his syllables in order. *Lavender*, not val-ender. Corey knew she was trying to help him, but somehow it didn't make him feel stupid.

Lulled by her easy chatter, the beating sun, and the rhythm of hammers, Corey imagined telling Sam things. About growing up. About not knowing who his father was. But he couldn't say it out loud. What he finally did say, hiding his eyes as he focused on sanding, was "Must be nice having two dads."

Apparently it wasn't always nice.

"I came here to live when my mom was transferred to Amsterdam." Sam wiped her forehead and chugged a bottle of water. "I'd never had to deal with the remarks before—

about having gay dads, I mean." Something in her voice drew Corey's eyes to hers, and he detected the hurt. He didn't know someone so...*cool* could feel that way.

He told how he had found out about his ancestor last summer. "On Privateers Day, I entered my name for a drawing. The guy actually laughed and said, 'No really, what's your name?'" With her, he could laugh about it.

Samantha really looked at him. Like his feelings were important. Here Corey was, talking to a beautiful girl, like an equal. His voice was getting deeper, and this morning, he'd seen a whisker next to the pimple under the one of the yellow eyes in the mirror.

Then Sam told him about her younger half-brother, Tommy, who left with her mother. "Kind of goofy and lovable...I miss him. And he has trouble with reading too."

Corey reminded her of her little brother? He deflated again.

But Corey kept his mind on the job and started to feel comfortable with the dads, especially Johnny. And now they trusted him enough to paint a room. He'd helped do the *lavender* room. Now he'd be responsible for the next room.

He knew how to figure the area, how much paint was needed, how to gather the tools and prep the area. He was feeling a confidence he hadn't known since moving here.

He couldn't wait to conquer the Safari Room.

AUGER'S B&B TRIP

Why did that hot girl hang out with the goofball? Auger had seen her walking with the Worder kid. He decided to drop in at that Bed and Breakfast place and show her what she was missing.

Sam answered the door. Her sleeveless blouse stuck to her skin, and she wiped perspiration from her brow. He licked his lips and said, "I just wanted to welcome the new business to town. Thought I'd leave you some literature on local history...and I could take some of your brochures up to the resort."

"You'd do that?" She looked at him sideways. "Aren't we the competition?"

He caught himself before laughing at the absurdity. *Compete with the Harts!* Instead he just grinned.

She went to get some pamphlets.

He was deciding how to tell her she'd won the lottery and was his next date when his eyes fell on stringy arms that dragged a bucket that probably weighed half as much as its carrier.

So that's it. Worder was working for them. *Pathetic.* Lugging an open pail of orange paint? Across a freshly sanded floor...surrounded by a perfect violet-tinted wall.

The kid was a puppet, and Auger held the strings. All he had to do was nudge that board.

Auger ambled down the front steps. He could ask the girl out any time. For now, he reveled in the circus he'd just witnessed: the kid's open mouthed shock as he sailed into the sun room; the paint gushing out of its can into numerous branches of splotchiness; the resulting mess. Auger hadn't bothered to wait for Sam in the commotion. He smirked as he listened to the best part: the owner's explosion—and the kid getting the axe!

One trip-up deserves another.

Then Auger thought of the dog and imagined him doused in orange, shaking it off everywhere. Too bad the kid's slobbering mongrel wasn't with him.

A WITNESS

Corey stared through orange-slimed strands of black hair as he gathered his sprawled limbs, but his hands and feet slid in the goop, and his frame once again took the shape of a crime scene body outline. He was still too shocked to feel the humiliation of Randy's rant.

Randy had come downstairs in time to see burnt orange glopping down his delicate lavender walls and was shouting, in colorful detail, what Corey could do with his paintbrush.

But Corey had been so careful! His earlier confidence shriveled. He dragged himself to his feet and hung his head. Another job lost. Would he ever see Howler again?

"I saw that!" Johnny had just breezed in the side door

"About time." Randy waved his hand at the wall. "Look what the kid did." Corey's face burned, and he was glad it was covered with paint.

"Don't mind him." Johnny squeezed Corey's shoulder. "It wasn't your fault."

"I didn't see that board, but— How was it not my fault?"

"I saw that blond kid, the hockey star—" A car door slam could be heard through the open front window.

"Auger? Where did he go?" Sam appeared with a stack of brochures in her hand. When she noticed Corey, her eyes grew wide and the papers slid to the floor.

"The guy tripped Corey on purpose!" Johnny stalked to the front door. "I was just coming up the side steps when he shoved that board." He looked out the front screen.

Randy's stare shifted from Corey to Johnny before he too bolted to door. "Let me at him!"

Corey filled his lungs, relieved. He was more grateful than ever for Johnny.

THE SECRET OF THE TRUNK

All through April and early May, Corey and his stepfather were doing okay. Charlie did short-order cooking and some construction jobs when he wasn't dropping his business cards at the docks and shops. They canceled cable, they bought whatever was on special at Price Slasher, and they fished.

One Saturday in early May, Corey met Charlie at the dock, where he was struggling with his fishing equipment.

"You're late...dragging your feet, mooning over that trunk, no doubt."

"No I wasn't! I took Howler for a checkup."

"Great, well don't expect me to pay a vet's fees."

"Don't worry." Corey had hoped his dog's peeing problem would go away, but it didn't; he'd finally had to offer the animal doctor some yard work in trade for examining Howler. Corey just had to pay for antibiotics.

He scrambled to gather some fishing rods and was carrying them to the boat when he noticed someone entering the dive shop. He turned his whole body to look. "It's that woman from the game!"

"What the—!" Charlie flailed as the rods knocked him off balance, and he fell into the cold water. He had to swim several yards to the ladder. He hopped, shivering, back onto the dock.

"That's it." His face was red as fire. "You're going to quit thinking about her." He shook water from his head. "Get rid of that old trunk. Maybe that will help clear out *your* head."

Charlie wrapped in a towel, his teeth chattering. "Maybe I can still get a few bucks for it." He went to get his jacket in the truck.

You, get a few bucks? Corey had messed up for sure, knocking Charlie in the water. But that trunk belonged to Corey and his mom! Charlie had no right.

Corey didn't speak to Charlie again before they left. He threw gear in back of the truck, got in the cab, and slammed the door. He folded his arms tightly and dipped his brows close to his eyes. He watched the dive shop as they rolled past, but there was nothing to see.

Corey climbed the ladder that cut through the floor of the attic, where Charlie had moved the trunk last week. He'd thought Corey was spending too much time in mom's old room with it. *Must think I'm too lazy to climb up here.*

Corey switched on a lamp, his arm brushing a plastic chicken. Its head bobbled and clattered as Corey looked around and saw a lop-sided rocker his mom used to sit in. He used to climb up on her lap and listen as she read about buried treasure. The books were dirty and torn now, long abandoned by their covers. Corey remembered the fierce pirates pictured there, and he imagined them slashing themselves free of their books. He could relate. It would be great not to be bound by someone else's story. To cut free and write your own.

The nearby chicken head still bobbled, as if to laugh at Corey.

Corey pulled the trunk to the middle of the room and sat on the floor beside it. He stroked it and inhaled the smell of old leather. This trunk somehow held a key to who he was. He released the trunk's catch and held his breath. As he lifted the lid, it gave a moan and showed its insides, mostly clothing of his ancestor Geraldine Plank.

But there was something newer. A sapphire earring winked up at him. This was where he'd found it months ago and where he was careful to return it after borrowing it. The last time he'd seen it on Mom, it had brushed his cheek as she gave him a goodbye kiss. The last time he'd ever seen her.

Corey picked up the sapphire and put it into the center of his palm. This was one reason the trunk pulled at him. His mother must've opened the trunk...*that day*. He folded his hand tightly around the blue earring, willing it to give back some of Mom. He began to feel her presence. He took a deep breath. He could even smell perfume...

But the essence of lilac was rising from below. He heard a couple of creaks from the ladder before seeing Samantha's head. Corey slipped the earring into his shirt pocket.

"Hey. Your stepdad said you were up here." She swung her foot around the risers.

This house never had visitors, even downstairs. What was this shining girl doing around moldy relics? Her brown eyes sparkled with green and gold, her skin glowed in an afternoon sun that spotlighted her through the tiny window, and she made everything here dull by comparison.

Her lips, red from an ice pop, were forming his name...again.

"Uh—ahh..." He pointed at the grime on the floor as she lowered herself next to him, frilly shorts and all.

"Don't worry, they're washable. Anyway, Johnny wanted me to see if you could help us later." She glanced at the trunk. "What's that? Bet there's a good story behind it."

"Er..." Corey shifted his head. "Belonged to my uh, *grand-cestor*, Geraldine. Pat Worder's... woman." Not wife,

not lover. She had made Corey possible because of his evil
man-cestor.

"Oh." Sam eyes were wide. He kicked himself mentally
for bringing it up.

"Charlie thinks this trunk is some kind of symbol and I
should get rid of it."

"Kind of like an exorcism, huh? Do you think it will
work?"

Corey squinted at the trunk, trying to remember what that
word meant. Then he remembered that old movie of his
mom's about an exorcist. "I doubt it." He wished *he'd* be the
one that would disappear.

They both stared at the dusty case. Then Sam squeezed
the lid with a thumb and forefinger. "They sure made them
thick."

Corey pulled the trunk between his legs and held it in
place with his heels. "I'd better make sure nothing is stuck in
the lining." He was finding excuses. The trunk was a
connection to his mother. How many times had Mom run her
own hands over the trunk? Had she left her fingerprints here,
on the top, or here, on the latch?

He slid his hand slowly from under the silky lining, his
fingers pressed against the edge of the lid, not ready to let go.
But maybe Charlie was right. Maybe his attachment to the
trunk was keeping him...crazy. If he let it go, would he stop
seeing his mother in strangers? Would he find that he'd been
imagining *all* his problems? Maybe he'd been—what was the
word?—*paranoid.* Maybe he only imagined people looking at
him, whispering about him. He started to let go of the trunk.

Then he stopped. It was tiny, but he felt a bump that gave
way. With a soft "pop," the inner lid showed a gap. Stunned,
Corey slipped his fingers inside the space and took out a

lump...of old, yellowed papers. He and Sam stared at the faded ink of the cover, which was smudged, blurred, and torn.

"The trunk may have been Geraldine's..." Sam eyed what remained of a name. "But that is *Patrick's* journal!"

FACE THE TRUTH

Corey dropped the bundle as if it had turned into a rattlesnake. Sure, he'd been all about the trunk when it reminded him of Mom and some kindly great-grandmother. But in this journal lived his black-hearted ancestor! As much as the trunk had attracted him before, this object repelled him. Sam would never understand.

He put on a bored look. "Who wants to read that old stuff?" He straightened the clothes in the trunk. "Probably tells how much pork they ate."

"What? C'mon." Sam frowned. "Don't you want to know about the battles? The places they sailed, the treasure they hid—right here on the river. Hey, maybe we can find out what *really* happened. Didn't you say the legend is baloney? This is your chance—"

"I *know* what happened." Corey's icy voice surprised even him. "It's just gonna tell the same thing." The truth was, he was terrified to find out. Until now, he could at least pretend it was a lie. He had to change the subject.

"What's that perfume you're wearing?" He sniffed her hair. "It's like...flowers, right?"

She snorted. "It's lilac. And I know you're just stalling, Corey Worder."

"No—I mean you, uh, do..." He looked away. "Smell nice."

Samantha's silky hair skimmed Corey's shoulder as she reached across to pick up the journal. He looked past his own goose bumps to scan her arm from the tensed bicep to the hand supporting the journal. He caught himself looking at her blouse opening and jerked away to stare at his knees. Samantha was gently turning the cover page.

"Come on, let's see what he says!"

Corey wasn't ready to hear it. He glanced at her face. "Do you know your eyes are like..." What did you call those shiny oil slick colors? "They're eery-dissent!"

"What!"

"You know, like..." He was sweating. What were those things Charlie used for bait? Oh yeah. "Like fishing flies."

"Gee, thanks." She looked at him like he was nuts. "Now, come on—"

"No, really. I mean, they're...all shiny, with colors." He stared straight ahead.

But Samantha was set on reading that journal and was not going to back down. "What are you so afraid of, Corey? You won't even give your own ancestor a chance. What if he isn't such a bad guy?"

Her highlights faded as the sun rose beyond the window's reach. Had he made her into some kind of goddess to distract himself from the truth?

Corey took a big breath. He would have to man up and listen to the not-so-grand-cestor.

WORDS OF A WORDER

It must suck to have a loser for a relative. But Samantha was sure this Patrick couldn't be as bad as people made him out to be. And she thought of another reason Corey wanted to ditch the journal: it was too hard for him to read. She knew he got distracted with letters, and she'd felt sorry about his disaster over the loudspeaker at school.

So Sam would read this journal to Corey. And if it was dull, that would be good; he would see that Patrick Worder was a regular guy. She could help build Corey's confidence.

Sam started reading.

Kingston, Upper Canada, July 1812

We have settled into our quarters near Fort Frederick, where Father has been posted as an officer of the Royal Navy. I know Mother, who remains in England, would be horrified that we are so close to the war front. She thought Upper Canada meant Northern Canada, away from the border! Instead, we are in the focal point of the war effort, on Lake Ontario near the head of the St. Lawrence River.

Though Father still thinks me a child, I am quick and agile, and I have been carefully observing the crews... I have taken up training in secret!

"Patrick must have been young—his parents wouldn't approve of his training?" Sam skimmed over the entries. "Oh—here's where he meets Warren Hart."

Today I visited Father at the fort and was most aggrieved to see a man take a severe whipping with the cat-o-nine tails. The maximum twelve lashes with the cat are enough to cripple a weaker man—but by my count, the man suffered at least double that number! I must see the man in private and express my outrage...and my support.

Sam found a later entry on the same topic.

I have learned the name of the whipped man, a Mr. Hart, and have found several occasions to speak with him. I think I have gained his confidence. He had been impressed from an

American vessel on the high seas and made to serve Britain, but our Royal Navy lost the records of some of the men and sent him to this post so near to his own country! He is not inclined to educate them as to their mistake.

"So Patrick was the son of a British officer at Kingston in Upper Canada," Sam said. "And Warren Hart was really an American, taken to serve in the British navy against his will. Sounds like they struck up a secret friendship."

Corey grunted. "Yeah, well I guess Patrick changed his mind later—about being a friend."

Sam skimmed and read more of Patrick's words.

How disappointed I have become with our mother country, seeing firsthand how our own officers abuse their men. Mr. Hart has revealed his intention to steal away, secure a gunboat, and hide in the islands; he will apply for a Letter of Marque, which will give him the right to attack and detain our British ships. I am learning a great deal from Mr. Hart.

"Warren confided about escaping to fight against Britain? He sure put a lot of trust in Patrick, knowing his father was a British officer! Hey, listen to this entry from August, 1812. Patrick says he still loves his Father—

...and the last thing I want is to hurt him. I am confused and torn. But I have found a love so strong, I am willing to leave home...

"What?" Maybe this guy was gay, like Sam's dads.
"Wait, there's more."

What is this love? The love of freedom and the right to fight for its principles. I have decided to join Mr. Hart. We will meet at his boat at nightfall when he leaves for America. Father believes I am returning to England!

"And here's something later."

I made a show of waving from the bow of the KingsWay, on which I was supposed to leave for England to return to Mother. Then I sneaked off the vessel to join Warren. It has taken ingenuity...

Sam read some more to herself. "Hey, it sounds like Warren Hart was some kind of genius. He stole a boat right from under the Brits' noses, and he built a keel that could be raised for moving in shallow water. They made levers and counterweights to make it easier for just a few men to sail."

"Yeah," Corey said, "it's a real thrill to hear how great the Harts are."

Sam ignored him and summarized some more entries she'd read to herself. "Here, he says they have joined with others who had been impressed by the British. Anyway, they banded together and settled at a hidden bay, Secret Landing— that must be Harts Landing!"

Corey scowled.

"Here it says many of the men were growing their hair and beards—and they altered their British hats and coats. In the winter, they were busy keeping warm and finding food." She was silent for a minute. "And here, in late February, they headed for Fort Presentation—that's downriver in Ogdensburg—where they wanted to help a Captain Forsyth repel the troops from across the river in Prescott. They were too late.

"Ooh, here's something about a secret in June 1813."

The crew get along well, we work as one man. That is, every man but one. To be fair, he's young and a bit out of his element. When we took him off the Queen's Bounty last month and he swore he was an American forced to serve the British, Warren welcomed him into our crew. But I get one of my uncanny feelings around him, and I think he knows *my* secret as well.

"Hmmm...a secret?" she wondered out loud.

"That he was a backstabbing deserter, most likely."

She scanned previous entries. "Oh, here's something I missed from August 1812, after they left Kingston."

Warren has made me his first mate and presented me with an engraved cutlass!

"That's the sword in the museum," Corey interrupted. "Mom let them display it."

"Nice. I'll have to check it out." She read more.

Warren is an apt leader; he reads the world around him with extraordinary skill, using his eyes, his ears, his hands, yet he keeps no log. Having little need for or patience with the written word, he assigns that duty to me, his first mate.

"See, you don't need to be great at reading to be successful." Sam flipped forward again. "Here's something about that supply boat—in May 1813."

Today we found a British supply carrier, the *Queen's Bounty*, that had separated from its convoy and struck a shoal by the island of rock, leaving it unprotected. She was carrying gold for payment of military contracts—a chest of astonishing value. We have relieved her of that burden and have hidden the chest in the island cave. We also got a new crew member off the British ship.

"That chest must be the treasure that was never found. I didn't know Rocky Island had a cave." She found a later entry about the new crew member.

> I must admit, I have my suspicions. I denied it at first; after all, Warren treats him like a son, and he sticks to Warren like an oar to a lock. When I advise caution, Warren scolds me and says, "Dirk was an orphan, like me. He needs a man to guide him." The boy has since presented himself as Dirk Hart.

Sam walked over to Corey, who was now staring out the small attic window. "I didn't know Dirk was *adopted* by Warren Hart." But Corey hadn't been paying attention. He seemed to be lost in a song floating up from the street:

"Rollin', rollin' river..."

Sam glanced through the window to the street below. An old man waddled up the middle of the street. She turned back to the journal, flipped some pages, and read to herself about Warren Hart's brass buckle. "So that buckle was specially made—no wonder it protected him. And it holds a secret—"

Her head jerked up at the sound of a screech, which was followed by a crash. Corey and Sam flew down the stairs.

NEAR MISS

A blue Accord had narrowly missed Buddy and chose to embrace a neighbor's maple tree. Corey checked to see that the driver was okay then headed for Buddy, who was still huffing along, singing that song.

The cops must have been nearby, because they were already pulling up. Corey had to get to Buddy before they did. He had never heard anyone sing that song except Mom—it was an old tune passed down through the family. When Corey tried to find out where Buddy heard it, the man kept repeating, "Where's Rollin' River lady?"

By the time the police finished with them and told Buddy to stay out of the street, Corey didn't have time to question Buddy again: he and Sam were late for work. Corey trotted behind Sam's bike all the way to the B&B, where they were split up and didn't have a chance to discuss the journal again before Sam left to pass out RiverGuard pamphlets somewhere.

As Corey was leaving, Johnny walked him down the side steps. "I have a new guy, wants to fish day after tomorrow." He patted Corey's shoulder. "I told him to call the best guide, your stepdad."

That gave Corey the courage to ask. "Uh—I...er, wondered." Then he blurted, "Did you ever see a woman around the dive shop?"

Johnny looked blank and then laughed. "Well, sure. We don't discriminate. I've seen lots of women there!"

Corey looked down. "I mean, well, this one had, like, short dark hair and brown eyes. About my size?" He held his hand level with the top of his head.

Johnny's smile faded and he glanced towards Randy, who struggled with a pile of junk from the shed. "No. I've never seen a woman like that."

Then he grinned broadly and grabbed the old bike Randy was wheeling.

"This must have been Mr. Murphy's. I think it could be whacked into shape." Together, they aligned it and put in fresh inner tubes and it became transportation. It wasn't a car, but it was better than walking.

Charlie was glad to hear about the fishing client. And Corey's new wheels.

"You can use your bike to do some errands for me. But keep your blinders on. No looking for ghosts!"

5 P'D OFF

Auger felt the breeze lift his hair and the sun warm his face as he stood on the *Hart of the Isles*. It glided past islands of various sizes and shapes, some crowned with lavish estates, some built over a century ago. The boat was only half full, but it was still early in the tour boat season. Auger sheltered his microphone from the wind.

"The early twentieth century was a heyday for this area; it was a 'playground' for the wealthy and famous. They even gambled their money away for fun on that small island—see it? Right next to the village of Alexandria Bay—Casino Island." That casino had burned down long ago.

Auger looked forward. Above the trees outlining a heart-shaped island rose the red turrets and spires of a Rhineland castle. This castle, unlike the one across from the Landing, had been renovated, and opened its doors to tourists. The passengers gawked, caught up in the mystique of the fairytale structure that cast a spell throughout the islands and drew vessels from Canada and the United States.

Auger spoke with confidence. "Before you is a testament to the world's saddest love story." He enjoyed the looks of awe the sappy story evoked, and he liked to think they were inspired by his touch of drama. "The castle was begun in 1900 by George Boldt as a gift to his beloved wife. Mr. Boldt spared no expense, importing exquisite Italian marble and tile…"

The *Hart of the Isles* rippled the waters approaching the castle as Auger spoke.

"When Boldt's wife died in 1904, he stopped all work. No one ever resided in the castle, and it was ravaged by vandals and the passing of time. However, it has undergone massive restoration. And yes, we will be stopping for a visit." He grinned at the girl, about his age, who had asked a lot of silly questions. *Dumb but cute*. She wore a blue sweater...*nice*.

Then he thought of the dummy he'd stuffed with straw and his failure to get revenge—*twice*. Worse, Auger had gotten flak from Dad—how did *he* find out?—about tripping the Worder kid at the B&B. Not only had Dad made Auger buy paint, but he made him, August Sterling Hart, repaint the wall, like a servant. *Dad must hate me*.

Auger was still thinking about the Worder kid after they left the castle and headed back down the river. No matter how hard Auger tried to get even, it backfired. Somehow Corey Worder had kept his job—and he was still spending time with that new girl. The kid must be Samantha's charity case. Then he thought of his own agonizing minutes spent at the nursing home so he'd look good to college reviewers. Samantha probably couldn't wait to get away from the Worder kid.

Some of the tourists got Auger's attention as they pointed to the wildlife they spotted in the trees beyond the shore of a medium-sized island.

"The deer enjoy their summer homes too." Auger gave a chuckle. "But they swim to shore before winter comes." He himself preferred land to water, but he'd rather swim than be trapped on an island.

"Speaking of which, Deer Island is just ahead; you may have heard of its mysterious meeting house. It's owned by the 'Skull & Bones,' a secret society at Yale University. The *Bonesmen* have included several former U.S. presidents and other powerful men." Auger's lips curled into a smile as he imagined himself a future Bonesman. Then his smile disappeared. *But for now, I can't beat that lame Worder idiot.* He became absorbed in thoughts of revenge and almost missed a cue.

"If you look quickly under the water...there, do you see it?" The tourists searched with heads down, eager to spot something. "That's the international border between the U.S. and Canada, folks. We just crossed it!" Good natured groans filled the boat.

Suckers. Auger was glad to focus on the tour.

"The deepest area is two-hundred-fifty feet. Temperatures can reach well below zero Fahrenheit in winter, but in whirlpools and currents, the fast moving water never freezes." Tourists were already fascinated by the river, and Auger had learned to heighten its mystique by pacing his spiel. Delay for suspense...then give them the kick! And they were putty in his hands.

It wasn't the water that attracted Auger; it was the position of authority that drew him to the microphone. He stroked the raised lettering on his embroidered jacket, especially the *Mr.* part. Gran could be a little lame at times, but he wore her latest gift with pride.

They rounded Grenadier Island and headed towards Rocky Island, home of the Round Tower castle ruins, which he had pointed out this morning. "Rumor has it that an unnamed corporation has bought Rocky Island," he had said, "and is renovating the castle as a resort." It could no longer be denied that something was going on there. Boats had been offloading materials, and the sounds of blasting and construction equipment could be heard from the Landing even last winter. But Auger had not been authorized to give specifics. Not that he knew any more.

He focused on history. "Right here next to Rocky Island is where Warren Hart's crew ambushed the *Queen's Bounty*, a British supply boat carrying a huge chest of gold. They hid it on the island to use later in the Patriot cause. But that treasure mysteriously *vanished* from its hiding place." Auger enjoyed keeping the tourists in suspense. For now, he would say no more.

As they headed towards the Landing, Auger launched into a description of how Warren Hart had repelled the British and saved the people of the town before perishing in the river.

"And the privateer vessel *Patriot* and the British *Spitflame* still lie in their final resting places, directly beneath us. They now attract divers from all over."

Then Auger told how Patrick Worder abandoned the crew and exposed the town to the enemy. Fueled by his recent frustrations, Auger embellished the story.

"Just beyond the landing rises 'Patrick's Point,' where the scoundrel ran, and where Warren's son, Dirk, approached him, thinking there might be an explanation. But what Dirk found on the cliff was horrifying." Auger looked around to ensure that each eye was riveted on him. "Patrick was about to throw a baby into the river." He was satisfied to hear several gasps before continuing.

"Warren had been good enough to let not only Patrick stay on the property, but also a mute homeless woman. When Patrick found she had given birth, he went into a rage. You see, Patrick had abused the woman and wanted to get rid of the evidence then run off with the treasure!" Auger took in the large round eyes of the tourists.

"But when Dirk struggled with him, Patrick was the one who fell to the river."

"Got what he deserved!" someone yelled. Others nodded.

Auger had more. "Before disappearing, Dirk mentioned the treasure." Auger could hear the intake of breaths and see the eager looks. "As he fell off the cliff, Patrick shouted: '*I've hidden the gold...where you'll never find it!*'"

As the boat returned to the Landing, people were buzzing about the villainy of Patrick Worder. The driver had eased off the throttle, and he reversed engines as they approached the dock. Auger made sure everyone had time to appreciate the large sign over the bay marking Harts Landing. Then he told them to stay seated until they came to a full stop.

Auger jumped off and carefully hung his jacket on a post before rushing to tie the boat lines. He smiled at the thought of all these people from who-knows-where spreading the story of *Worder the Deserter* to the far corners of the planet. Then he looked up and scowled as he worked the ropes; the Worder kid was walking down the other pier with that crooked grin, clueless.

When Auger turned back to get his jacket, his lips went white.

The Monster.

Was *peeing*.

On his jacket—on the special lettering!

"*AAWRGH*!" Auger blurted and sputtered before he could spit actual words. "That animal is a *public nuisance*!"

The Worder kid just looked dumb with his mouth open.

"That jacket is valuable property!" Auger hyperventilated. "How dare you let him—and right on the Hart *name*!" Then he growled at the kid now running to his dog, "Speaking of which, why don't I see any tags on *him*?"

Still fuming, Auger added, "He belongs at the dog pound." The rant came out of his fury. But something stopped it cold. It was a look in the kid's eye as he put his body in front of the dog. A look of protective fear.

That's what it took to get to the kid. The stupid mutt.

HARTLESS

Over the next few days, Corey tried to forget about Auger as he dreamed through his classes and looked forward to the long Memorial Day weekend. One day Sam, who'd been busy with some honors class, caught him just before he left work.

"I had to check some family history for sociology class, so I decided to look up Harts and Worders too, especially after seeing that journal. We can talk after I do more research."

Some people actually liked to study families. He shrugged. "Whatever."

Corey was glad he didn't have school tomorrow. A couple of unused "snow days" had been added to the long weekend. But he didn't sleep well; he tossed and turned all night with bad dreams. It was late summer and he'd gone to the bank to withdraw his cash. But the teller told him someone had beaten him to it. The teller's name plate was lettered, "Dirk Fooler." Then the face morphed into a familiar one, framed with blond hair, and the name plate became a label on a chest under the boy's face. On the label was the word *Heart.* Corey couldn't keep Howler from ripping it off with his teeth, which also tore open the boy's chest. But then Corey was stunned to see there was nothing inside!

The bed shook him awake at 7:04 AM. *Did the earth really move?* But it was another question that rocked him:

Was Auger really a Hart? He was always bragging about his Hart blood. Could he be a phony?

Corey had missed something—something Sam had read in the journal. Why hadn't he paid attention? He had to read it himself.

He ran up the stairs and flung open the attic door. His eyes swept the room.

There was no trunk. No journal.

THE TRUNK & THE DRUNK

"Where's that trunk? I have to see it!" Corey blurted. He had taken the stairs three at a time and burst into the kitchen. "It tells what *really* happened about Pat Worder."

Charlie had just come in the door, slap-wiping his hands together. "I just got rid of it."

"What?!" Corey glared at him then glanced at the clock. The garbage truck was due. He ran outside.

The truck hadn't reached his house. But there was no trunk on the sidewalk. Corey opened the dumpster and looked inside.

"Whatcha doin', looking for breakfast?" Ruby, the trash collector, jumped off the truck.

Corey was in no mood for jokes. "Where is that trunk?" he shouted, looking up and down the street.

"That black thing? All I know is a white van stopped, and when they left it was gone."

Corey ran back inside to find Charlie.

"I have to find it! Patrick tells about Dirk, and..."

"No!" Charlie held up a calloused hand. "I won't hear any more about it. I told you to haul it down, and what did you do? You had to go diving deeper. I should have put it out before. Anyway, we have plumbing to do." Charlie practically knocked the wind out of Corey, slapping a wrench against his stomach. "Just do your work. That old book won't put food in the bowl." Then he turned away and mumbled, "She had to go messing around with it too..."

"What! Mom knew about the journal?" Corey let the wrench slide to the floor.

The answering voice cracked with anger. "Didn't do *her* any good."

Corey took a sharp breath. He jabbed his finger at his stepfather, but only spit came out of his mouth. The dark thing inside him was clawing its way out. Corey closed his mouth and clenched his jaw against it.

"Now I *have* to find that journal!" he said through clamped teeth. He reached for the door, but his stepfather blocked it with his arm.

"Don't you *even*–!"

Corey felt like he'd been punched. The trunk was his only anchor to Mom, and now it held his only hope. The information might even change his life.

"You—you can't tell *me* what to do!" The beast was out. "You're not my father!" Corey shoved Charlie out of the way. "You're a pathetic loser, just a...a *drunk!*"

He ran outside, jumped on his bike, and tore out of the driveway.

Corey wasn't sure where he was going—he just pedaled. His head buzzed in anger and shame. *How dare Charlie!* He had no right. But had Corey really just called him *that?* He pedaled hard. He found himself at the village docks and collapsed off the bike. He sat on the ground. There was the dive shop. He thought of the strange woman with the blue earring, but now he only saw a kid and an old man go in and out. He picked himself up off the ground and wiped his pants. He pulled his bike up and wondered where to go to find a white van.

Stupid. He'd never find it like this. Maybe Sam could help. He'd go to the B&B.

He swung a leg over the bike and pumped a couple of times before he was almost knocked off.

"Hey!" he yelled at the driver. A woman had just sped out of the Glass & Brass parking lot with a cell phone to her ear. She never even saw him as she drove away...in a white van.

THE DRIVER

They were running her ragged. Rita Hart jerked her foot back, releasing the accelerator after the monstrous vehicle had lurched. She'd borrowed the van and still wasn't used to the gas pedal.

"I just got back from the museum, now I have to pick up my mother-in-law, and you want me back here *when?*" She paused and looked up from the phone as she turned right. In the side mirror she noticed some kid zigzagging on his bicycle as if he were drunk. She shook her head. *They start so young.* She sighed. "Fine, Jack, I'll be there by two."

Fred could certainly have had someone else bring his mother and her precious chair home—but no, he said she wanted *family* to come for her. God knows Fred himself couldn't be bothered; his head was buried in his business affairs. Rita had borrowed the van not only to pick up Mother Hart, but to do another delivery, something of "historical" importance, before leaving town. Thank god she found someone to help with the old monstrosity—Rita didn't want to touch that thing full of cobwebs.

WOMAN OF ACTION

Corey regained his balance and pedaled. He soon found himself bounding up the whitewashed steps of the B&B. He pushed into the "Private" door at the opposite end of the lobby and heard several voices at once.

"The books still don't balance—"

"We'll be okay..."

"—and that woman in the back room, she can't stay for free!"

"I'll take care of it."

"Will you guys take a chill pill?"

"Sam!" Corey gasped, out of breath, swinging the kitchen door open.

Randy's heavy brows shot up. "Did you lose your knocking hand?" He moved a stack of plates to the sink while Johnny sat at the table and Sam jumped up.

"Ignore him." She grabbed her bag and yelled, "Later!"

"I hate being in the middle of arguments." She ran down the steps. "They've been at it since seven this morning. Did you feel that earthquake? Anyway, you saved me from their nonsense."

Corey passed his heap of bicycle and just walked. Sam trotted alongside, and they soon reached the end of the street. Corey had no destination. He shook his head and hissed air like a leaky tire as he sank onto a tree stump.

"The journal's gone." He looked up as if she could tell him where it was.

"What?" She searched his face as she lowered herself to the stump. She was so close he couldn't help noticing each curly brown lash and the constellation of freckles framing eyes that locked on his. Then he felt the warmth of her leg and jerked his knee away.

She didn't notice. "But I thought you didn't care about the journal...?"

Corey stiffened. "I changed my mind." The words came out harsher than he'd meant.

"*Sorry.*"

Corey dug his fingernails into the woody stump and blurted, "I don't think Dirk was a real Hart!"

"At least not by birth." Sam was shaking her head. "But you knew that, I read it to you."

Corey squeezed his brows. "I guess I missed that part."

She rolled her eyes. "So where could it have gone?"

Corey's chin fell to his chest. "Charlie put it out, now it's gone. But I got a feeling that book's important."

"Are you sure you put it back before we ran downstairs to the accident?"

"Me? You're the one who had it last! I thought you put it back..."

"No, I handed it to you when we got up."

Corey frowned and said, "You prob'ly dropped it back in the trunk."

"*I* dropped it? Come on, don't blame *me*..."

"Okay, okay." He probably did put it back in its hiding place. It wouldn't be the first time he'd done something without thinking.

"But if I didn't hide it, whoever opens the trunk'll find it."

"Unless 'we' dropped it by the window—"

"No, I would've seen it this morning."

"Any chance someone took the journal out before the trunk left the house?"

"No, Charlie sure wouldn't keep it, and no one else could get past Howler. Anyway, the garbage woman says a white van came by..." His words rushed, "and I saw a white van this morning—almost ran me down!"

Sam stared at him. She stood up and pulled out her phone. She walked the other way, punching buttons.

She came back and said, "We have to go to the museum."

"What?"

"We have an old Dodge van for B&B business. I heard Johnny tell someone on the phone they could use the van and pick up a 'parcel' for the museum. Johnny arranged it for Charlie—the museum will pay him five hundred dollars for the trunk. And, Johnny says whatever was in the trunk is probably still there."

Corey was impressed. Sam was smart and decisive. Like Mom used to be. "A woman of action," as Charlie would say. Corey felt something like hope. But how could they look in the trunk?

"Has to be when nobody is looking. The museum's closed now."

"You worked there, right?" Sam asked. "Do you still have a key?"

RAMBLINGS

Rita cursed the long weekend traffic as she tried to pass a camper driving north on route 37. She had a lot on her mind. *Gotta make this quick... Hope he locked the museum... Will Auger make it on time to accept the other package?*

This trip was one too many. "Can't you do it?" she'd asked Fred. Of course not. He had more important things to do, as usual. And he thought Rita's time was "free."

"But I have to be in three pla— Oh, never mind," she'd given in. She'd suck it up. When she had married Fred, Rita loved his confidence, and he'd made her feel important. They had met at a graduate school reunion, and when he'd invited her, she couldn't resist returning to the place where she'd played as Mama worked in the hotel. But Fred had no idea about that.

It was satisfying, living the life of the people her Latina mother had worked her butt off to cook and clean for. Rita felt she had finally "made it"—for both her mother and herself.

But Rita worked hard, too. Hart money had financed the Glass & Brass, but it was *her* hard work and talent that built it. And her looks were no accident; she cultivated that perfectly balanced spicy but classy look with exercise and grooming.

She finally nosed into the parking space and click-clacked through the day room at the east wing of the care facility to find her mother-in-law. This place gave her the creeps. She tried to ignore the bodies draped here and there. She jumped when a thin hand dared to fondle her arm. She picked it off and moved on.

Finally, she found the door and entered. The older Mrs. Hart sat back in her favorite chair, surrounded by piles of well-worn books. Books that had yet to be boxed. The woman raised her head, haloed by wisps of gray, and she stared at her daughter-in-law. Finally she said, "Are my boys here?"

"Mother Hart," Rita began slowly, her voice notched up a few decibels. "Auger has tutoring, and Frederick has been managing the resort. He's just too busy, you understand. The resort, boat line, new project, *finances...*"

"Of course." The older woman spoke with sudden energy. "Hart *jobs* give opportunity—and *pride*, to so many."

Rita rolled her eyes. "Let's get someone to pack up and load this stuff."

As they settled into the van, Rita glanced at the passenger belt. "Don't forget the buckle."

"Buckle?" Her mother-in-law drew the seatbelt across her body and eyed the clasp before inserting the tab—as if she'd never seen one. Then the older woman smiled and closed her eyes.

Good. Maybe she'll sleep the whole way.

No such luck. The woman started babbling. She was murmuring about "that other buckle" and "Dirk Hart's wisdom" in providing for the family "through all the generations." *Blah, blah, blah.*

Then: "My grandson, he's a good boy. My Augie, he'll carry the Harts into the *future.*" Then she sat straighter and came up with, "That buckle, the one at the resort, where on earth do you suppose it went?"

Rita's foot jerked and the van lurched ahead. *Probably under the river, with that Worder woman.*

"My grandfather used to let me play with that buckle. Granddad died too soon. Then my poor brother, Bartholomew, went to Vietnam, never returned." Fred's mother rubbed her eyes and picked up the Watertown Times from between the seats. Maybe she was done rambling.

Rita saw her reading the headline and remembered seeing the article about a drug bust near the reservation after an illegal methamphetamine lab got blown up. The authorities had found substances used to make crystal meth—solvents, acids, sinus medication packaging, red phosphorus from match sticks...

"Tsk, tsk, why do people get involved in such business?" Mother Hart said, obviously referring to the woman, about Rita's age, who'd been arrested. "Embarrassing their families, getting people killed." She reached over and patted Rita's arm. "I'm glad my Freddie found a good girl."

The car almost veered off the road. The one thing Fred's mother was consistent about was family honor. It would be a disaster if she ever found out about Rita.

Growing up in foster homes had been difficult. Rita's father died when she was born, and her mother died in the accident Rita had been accused of causing, the accident that had also claimed Fred's father. Ridiculous! She had loved her mother dearly—it was only after losing Mama that Rita had become an addict and a thief. But she had overcome! She had vowed to better herself, to be respected. And now she would keep her past from the Harts, even if she had to break the law again to do so. The only person who could have known her from the juvenile lock-up was Peg Worder...Peg *Stowe*. She hadn't been seen or heard from since last fall.

Somehow, another person knew Rita's past. A guy named Jack had entered the picture, claiming Rita's past would be revealed if she didn't cooperate. Supposedly, Jack's "boss" was pulling the strings.

Rita parked the van and helped Fred's mother settle into her suite at the estate. When the woman finally ran out of chores for her, Rita looked at her watch and gasped.

FACE OF A MERMAID

Jack Thomas sipped coffee at the back door of the dive shop. His eyes darted back and forth.

The Hart woman was late. Was she trying to get out of her end of the deal? Well she'd better continue to "donate" her skills if she wanted her past to remain secret.

Her gallery was back-to-back with Jack's shop, and he could see that the delivery truck of "glass art supplies" had arrived. The police were out in force for the weekend, and a village cop was telling the driver to "Move along." The idiot driver was holding one of *those* packages right under the cop's nose.

"This is the last box," the guy said, "and I'll get the van right out of there for ya'!" Then the cop walked away, and Jack breathed freely.

The woman's stepson took delivery at the back door. *The Hart kid.* Did he know what was in the shipment? Would he open it? *Rita better get herself over here!*

In another two minutes, the van screeched into the owner's spot. Finally. He'd give her and the kid a few minutes to do inventory.

Jack slowly finished his coffee, giving himself a mental pat on the back. He was proud of his ability to make connections and use them in his operation. He had impressed the boss, who would use Jack's business to help finance a bigger scheme. *And my cut will make me rich!*

His idea of hiding cocaine in scuba tanks was brilliant, but he'd needed someone to do the metal work to alter the tanks. The art lady had skills, good for more than glass and metal sculpture. Maybe she learned them in the kiddie slammer. She could solder, weld, cut pipe... Plus, she had things to hide from her uppity husband, like the fact that she'd been arrested for his father's "accident" then stole money for drugs. She'd claimed innocence, but so what? She was blackmailable. Rita had turned completely white when she heard Jack recite a few tidbits from her past. She'd caved, and he'd put her to use converting tanks to hold the white powder.

These days, onshore dealing was risky. And the old "rum runners" trick was unreliable. During Prohibition, boaters would drag kegs of illegal alcohol, with rock salt attached, across the border. If they were chased, the smugglers cut the line and let the booze sink. Later, they would return for the keg, which floated up after the salt dissolved.

Nowadays, the waters were patrolled constantly. *On the surface.*

His boss had access to Rocky Island, right across from the Landing. And the international border was only a few hundred yards off the other side. Water was shallow enough for a contact to retrieve a tank concealed among rocks. *But deep enough to escape notice from the surface.*

Jack remembered the night back in the fall when he and Dave, his former partner, had taken the first tank for a "test drive" near the Point—to see if the seal worked under pressure. It was that September night when he had scooped a mermaid out of the river.

He had been squinting into darkness as the moonlight glinted off ripples. Where was Dave? He'd had a simple enough task: dive deep among the rocks and leave the tank, check it for leaks, and surface. They'd return the next day to see if it was still watertight. But Dave had been taking a very long time down there. Jack was already annoyed with Dave— the man talked too much, and he ate too many fried foods for a serious diver. Now the annoyance was increasing.

A splash interrupted Jack's thoughts. Finally! He heard a gasp.

"Where ya been?" Jack grabbed for Dave in the darkness. He grunted and heaved the body into the boat. "Jeeze, what's wrong with y—"

The drone of a motorboat cut the air.

"Great, it's the Border Patrol." He left the body he thought was Dave sprawled on the floor of the boat.

"Stay still and be quiet. Let's hope they won't follow us."

Lights off, he glided down the river, pulled into Runners Creek, and sat in darkness to be sure he wasn't followed. He turned on the scanner to check the airwaves.

Disconnected words sputtered: "Body...possible drowning... heart attack...male, five seven...two hundred pounds..."

"Okay," he said, "I guess the patrol must've come across some dead guy..." He added, "Hey, you did real good, this time, Dave, staying down and shutting up."

No answer.

"It's okay, you can talk now." He turned the light on Dave—but *that* wasn't Dave! Hell, that didn't even look like a him! Where was Dave?

Then it hit him who the dead guy was on the scanner. Poor Dave. *Must've got caught in the current then floated up where the Patrol spotted him.* It was too late to do anything for him now. Jack looked downriver. He sure wasn't going to volunteer information to the authorities.

He turned back to the body in his boat. Where had this woman come from? How did she get so beat up? And how had she survived underwater? Had she found the tank Dave dropped? Dave had lost his life for the tank, but maybe it saved this woman. So she owed her life to Jack.

"Who are you?"

The bloodied face stared back. "Mm—me...?"

Jack felt bad about Dave, but he had to think about business. He was going to need someone who wouldn't talk.

That had been months ago. Since then, the "partner" had worked out great. In fact, the boss had given Jack a bonus! The boss knew a surgeon who owed a favor, so the woman got a new face, besides a new name. "Marie" believed she was Jack's sister, wanted for serious crimes, and would be imprisoned for life if recognized. *She* wouldn't go blabbing.

Jack couldn't help grinning. He had two talented women working for him for next to nothing, and he'd been clever enough to keep them from meeting.

His head snapped up at the roar of a motor, and he watched the blond kid peel out of the lot. It meant Rita would be ready to work. Jack went in the back door to his shop. *I'll meet her in the basement.*

RELICS

Corey and Sam had cut through the woods to the museum, careful to stay out of sight. The museum had been built at the site of the old cabin where Dirk Hart had confronted Patrick Worder and saved baby Adam, Corey's ancestor.

Just before they came out of the woods, Corey held up his hand to stop Sam. They stayed out of sight while a Ford Focus slowed near the museum door, where the hours were posted, and then circled the lot and sped back towards the highway.

They crept to the building, watching for signs of life. Corey put his key to the hole.

"Figures. They changed it."

"Try the window."

It was loose. They raised it and squeezed through. Corey squinted in the darkness, wishing for a flashlight, when the wall suddenly lit up, making him jump.

He took a breath and smiled. Sam was always prepared.

"It's a flashlight app." Sam swept the beacon from her cell phone around the room.

His smile disappeared when he saw the inner door. It was locked. "I forgot about that—it was always open before." Without much hope, he poked and probed the lock with Sam's RiverGuard pin. He was ready to give up when he heard a click, and the lock released.

Sam looked at him with surprise.

"Couldn't have been a very good lock." He blew hair off his eye.

They split up to search the display rooms. After twenty minutes, Corey had found nothing; he came back to the front room where Sam was ogling a wax dummy of Warren Hart dressed in period clothing that looked familiar.

"That's like the outfit Fred Hart wears in the Privateers Parade. There must be two of them."

Sam moved along. She drew her breath. "Can this be...the actual *Letter of Marque* signed by James Madison? And look at this." She pointed to a case holding a short, curved sword. It was Patrick Worder's cutlass.

"'On loan from Margaret Stowe.' That was your mom, right?"

Corey barely nodded.

Sam's eyes were inches from the metal and wood handle. "It even has Patrick's name engraved on it, like the journal said." She reached around behind the case and traced the tiny letters. "Huh. That's weird."

The sight of the cutlass brought back the scene from the hockey rink, and Corey felt the lead weight he'd buried inside that day. The museum walls were closing in, and he wanted to heave.

"Look." Sam's fingers were on the sword. "The words *First Mate* are separated. Plus it feels rough in between—"

"Gotta get...out." Core's breathing was shallow and fast as he stared at the cutlass.

He felt Sam take his elbow and lead him out to a seat near the window they had entered. She sat with him and put her hand on his, giving him a "poor baby" smile. He pulled away. *Must think I'm a real loser.* He had to straighten up.

"You should've eaten some breakfast." She took something from her bag.

"Yeah, yeah...I'm just hungry." He took the granola bar and chewed on it while she wandered the room.

"Hey, that old shawl looks familiar." She stood by a table in a dark corner. "It—it's the stuff from the trunk! The pieces are all laid out with labels."

His curiosity won out, and Corey joined her as they checked the room further. The wood box they thought was a bench turned out to be a cabinet, and the trunk was inside. They eased it out then Corey laced his fingers together and stretched them backwards.

"Shh! Do you hear that?"

"Don't worry, it's my knuckles cracking." Corey was definitely feeling better as he slid his fingers under the lining of the trunk.

"Can you find the release?" Sam whispered.

Corey felt along the backing until he found the tiny raised spot. He pushed and it gave way. The back of the lid opened forward, just as before. He couldn't wait to have the journal in his hands! Now maybe he would find some answers that would solve his problems. He took a sharp breath and stuck his hand inside. His eyes widened.

"It's not there!"

They both slid to the floor under the window.

He'd gotten his hopes up just to be ripped with disappointment, as usual. He glanced at Sam and saw frustration on her face, too. At least he had someone to share it with, a—did he dare think it?—a *friend*. He was good at keeping his feelings to himself. But Sam could be trusted—hadn't she shown that?

"Mom knew about the journal. I wonder if it had—you know, something to do with her ending up..." He couldn't say *dead*.

Sam's voice was soft. "Well if it does, we'll find it."

Before he knew it, Corey was spilling his "ghost" tales about seeing someone that reminded him of Mom. He admitted his mind was playing tricks. "I even asked Johnny—probably thought I was a fool."

"Hey, you're still mourning your mom. It's normal."

Nobody ever called him normal. He smiled at her. He would not give up on the journal. There had to be somewhere else they could look. He stood up. "Let's go ask Johnny who else could have seen the trunk!"

Sam called a warning but it was too late. Corey had hoisted himself halfway through the window before a man's voice stopped him.

"You're trespassing!"

WHO SAW THE TRUNK

Corey jerked his head up and banged it on the window frame.

The guy was crossing the walkway under the window. "Did you find the big box? Is that what you're after? Well, you sh'n't take anything without askin'!"

Corey rubbed his head as Sam whimpered behind him, "Dad will kill me if I'm caught..."

Corey ignored her. "You scared the crap out of me," he told the man before turning to Sam. "C'mon, it's just Buddy. I forgot he hangs out up here."

"I saw it first, through the window," Buddy continued. "I'm gonna ask for it. I could use it for my *effects*." His head bobbled like the plastic chicken in Corey's attic, and he opened his cloth sack. It held clothing, a flashlight, and a paper bag that showed through to the black of some very ripe bananas. Corey jerked his head away.

"What's that smell?" Sam slid to the ground behind him and wrinkled her nose as she pulled the window closed.

Corey turned back to Buddy. "I need to know more. What did you see?"

But Buddy had spotted an old wrist watch at the edge of the driveway and made a beeline for it. "*Time*. Better find th' owner and give it back." He put the watch in his pocket then looked down the river. "Laker heading in..."

Corey looked up and down the river, but there was no ship in sight. Then he saw Buddy look towards the bay as he said, "Old sign shaking—coming loose." Buddy was looking in the direction of the Harts Landing sign over the pier. *He must be remembering the quake.* He probably saw the top of the sign this morning from his hiding place.

Corey tried again. "No, Buddy, I mean, who opened the trunk?"

"Oh. That blond kid, the *hakky* player."

"I knew it!" Corey held his breath. "Did he find anything besides clothes?"

Buddy looked confused. "Dunno. Di'n see him af'er he open'd it up 'n took off." Corey watched as Buddy disappeared into the bushes at the far side of the museum. Corey envied the old man. He didn't have to go to school, went where he wanted. He'd sit up here where he could watch the boats all day without being seen. And Buddy didn't care what people thought.

So what was Corey supposed to do now? He had a sinking feeling. "If the journal was in that trunk when it came here, Auger has it now. And I'll never see it again."

"Oh, no." Sam was looking at her wrist. "We're going to be late to the B & B."

The journal would have to wait.

"Buddy, we were never here, got it?" Corey yelled to the bushes, and a "Never 'ere" came back. They had to run all the way to the B&B.

They worked hard and long. Though they asked Johnny about the trunk, all he knew was that he'd loaned the van to that Hart woman, who had something to do with the museum acquisitions.

It was late, but Corey was still angry at his stepfather. "No way I'm going back home." Johnny insisted on calling Charlie to let him know.

"You can sleep in here." Sam showed him the door to a small unfinished room at the back of the inn. "Just be quiet in the morning—the guest in the next room comes in late." She held out a rolled-up sleeping bag.

Corey stared past her.

"Hello?" Sam dropped her arms.

He looked up. "How am I ever going to find out what really happened?"

"Well, go to bed, maybe you'll dream of something..." She forced the bedding at him. "Maybe we should check out that brass buckle." She turned away but added over her shoulder, "It's supposed to have something."

"What, you mean the Hart buckle?"

She stopped. "The journal said it had some kind of secret."

"It did? How could it?"

"How do I know? Maybe it has an inscription."

"But it would have been discovered by now..."

"Anyway, we could take a look at it tomorrow."

"Huh? How?"

"You don't know? When I came with my dads last summer to check out the Landing, we stayed at the resort. The buckle's right there on display."

M.A. NOBLE

6 AUGER'S PUNCH

Corey felt cool air when he and Sam went into the Hart Luxury Resort Hotel, but sweat trickled down his neck as he glanced from the chandelier to the fresh flowers. It took nerve to walk right into the enemy's den, especially when he was so tired. He'd had bad dreams: he kept hearing someone humming as he tossed and turned, and then he was on his mother's lap as she rocked him to sleep with her Rolling River song. Then the song stopped, and he looked up to see a stranger. But the voice came through again, and that face broke away to reveal his mother's underneath.

Corey had finally dragged himself out of bed to ride with Sam to the resort. Now he pulled his cap down over his head and followed her to the registration desk.

"What d'ya mean, we have no reservations?" The customer's voice grew louder. "We've had them for six months!" The harried clerk apologized and tapped on a keyboard.

Maybe we can walk right by without being noticed.

Nope.

"Can I help you?" A woman emerged from behind a heavy oak door to their left. Her concerned gaze traveled down Corey's dirty cutoffs. Then her eyes turned warm as they worked their way up Samantha's clean sun dress and shiny hair.

"Yes, please." Sam used her best kiss-up voice. "Where would I find an application for summer help?"

The woman smiled. "It's a little late, Dear, but you can get one from Marvin at the reservation desk." She gestured towards a man who had just appeared. Her smile faded as she glanced at Corey and hurried back to her office to pick up a ringing phone.

Sam chatted up Marvin and asked for help with the application. Meanwhile, Corey slowly backed down the hall and out of sight to find The Fireside Room.

It didn't take long. The room was lined with honors and plaques for everything from "Resort of the Year" to Auger's "Little League MVP." Corey seemed to be shrinking, surrounded by gleaming reminders of Auger's superiority. He backed away from hockey trophies that seemed force him out the door like a puck. He was breathing fast; his head pounded and swirled. Then *puck* became *buck*, which became *buckle*, and Corey stopped in his tracks. He had a purpose here. He and Sam had a plan. He couldn't wimp out just because of a bunch of tin cups! He drew a breath and walked back.

He looked from one trophy to another on the walls. Ten minutes of careful inspection revealed no buckle. Maybe there was another room. He turned to go check it out, and a glint of sun on glass caught his eye from a recessed part of the side wall, opposite the bay windows. It was a small case holding a brass buckle.

Corey would have to work fast. He didn't know if he could open the case without leaving evidence. For a moment, he forgot to watch the door as he lost himself in the object. Even through the glass, he could see it had a dent. *Does it really hide a secret?*

Corey's head snapped up at the sound of a tick. It was just the clock. From his back pocket, he pulled the latex gloves Sam had given him. Corey reached around the side of the case and found a clasp. He pulled gently. It opened. It was not even locked!

He teased the buckle out of the case. His right hand barely felt the inscribed *W* and *H* through the glove. He turned the buckle to look at the back. He turned it every way he could, trying to find where something could be hidden. Nothing.

Finally, he sagged with frustration. The journal was baloney. Manning a gun boat, being on constant alert—the monotony messed with Patrick's mind. He made things up. Mysterious buckle with a "secret"? Pure fiction. Charlie was right, this whole thing was a waste of time.

Corey never heard the footsteps.

"I knew it!"

He froze.

"Not only a quitter but a *thief.*"

Corey turned and found himself eye-to-nose with Auger Hart. Then he felt his face swelling like a ripe tomato as he looked into the icy stare of the hockey player.

"I...I—"

Auger swaggered to the back wall. "You know, I'd have a plaque—right here." His gaze pierced the frame he made with his hands. "But you stole that from me with your little ice caper. Just like your good old granddad. Desert the team and steal what belongs to the *Harts.*" His voice was cold as the ice he ruled.

Corey had felt terrible about the game, but no way would he apologize.

"You're too late to steal the Hart buckle." Auger crossed his arms over his chest. "This one's a fake. The real one was stolen by another Worder—your mother!"

Corey staggered backward. "Mm—Mom didn't *steal!*"

"She was a Worder wasn't she? Another loser."

Corey's eyes widened.

"Not only a thief..." Auger's eyes turned black and hard.

"She was a...a slut!"

Corey's jaw dropped, but no sound came out. His eyebrows met in a war conference, and his shocked anger began to harden into a ball at the end of his right arm.

"Coming on to a married guy, thought she'd tap into the wealth... I bet she launched herself when she couldn't con my dad!"

Corey's knuckles curled so tightly, his fingernails dug into his palms right through the gloves.

"You—you're lying," he choked.

"Of course, Dad would never say anything. '*Poor little Corey Worder's been through enough.*'"

The dark thing inside Corey had enjoyed yesterday's taste of freedom; now it was gaining power. The weight at the end of Corey's arm started to swing like a wrecking ball.

The taunting, the bullying, judgments...all were like giant pills Corey had been forced to swallow every day. And Auger Hart's medicine was the nastiest.

Auger started to step away as he tossed the final blow: "At least my dad has some class, even if it is wasted on a *Worder.*"

All the strength in Corey's body gathered in his right arm; Corey felt disconnected as he watched the wrecking ball move like a pendulum. It swung out and met the other boy's nose with a *crunch;* the chin jerked up and back, the body following, thudding and skidding on the plush gold carpet.

Corey looked at his fist numbly. Then he howled at the searing pain in his hand as he ripped off the glove, tossed it on the floor, and ran out of the building.

HOWLING HUNGRY

Corey stumbled down the resort steps, his hand throbbing at his side. His brows turned in opposite directions; he was scared by what he'd done but enraged by what he had heard. *My mother would never!* Auger was lying.

Stealing? Only when she was young and the addiction made her do it. And if she really took the buckle, it was for a good reason. But coming on to another man? Never! Corey's mind reached for explanations. Auger was a liar. Mom loved both Corey and Charlie. She would never look at anyone else.

Corey ran half a mile in fury before a gnawing memory made him halt. It was almost a year ago, when his mother had disappeared for a few days.

"When is Mom coming back?" he'd asked. "I don't know," Charlie had said. "She's working some things out." Mom had returned, but she and Charlie had been quiet.

Had...had she left Charlie for someone else and then changed her mind? Had she come back because of Corey? Was it *possible* Auger was right? The one person he had thought was loyal, loving, and devoted—was she *that* kind of deserter too?

No. Corey would not believe that. Auger was just out for revenge.

But what about that buckle being fake? Maybe not. Corey wasn't great at reading words, but he could read objects—and that buckle was blank. Had Mom found a secret in the real buckle? Did she replace it with a fake?

He wished he knew more. Corey's brain was scrambled, but he had no friend he could call—he couldn't tell Sam he'd punched Auger. And he couldn't call his old friend even if he could find his number. He had no phone, and he wasn't about to ask Charlie for *anything*. Corey had to go to someone he could count on—someone loyal without question. Someone wagging his tail as he waited for Corey right now.

"Howler!" Corey had not fed his dog since yesterday. He would be ready to eat the mail carrier.

BUDDIES ON CALL

Auger spit blood and felt his nose. Had that imbecile broken his face? The strong, straight nose over the charming smile that got him past first base with any girl he wanted? He was astonished that the twerp had it in him to punch anybody. Auger had never even considered a physical fight. It would have been like...hitting a girl.

He wasn't sorry for what he'd said. After all, Auger had heard his stepmother grumbling about that woman getting "cozy" with dad...so what if he'd embellished a little?

Nose hurts. Need ice.

The Worder kid deserved payback. It was time to pull out the stops. One of his buddies was working in the kitchen. Another drove for animal control. They would jump when he gave the word.

Auger jerked out his phone and punched it.

HART SICK

Corey had run from the opposite side of town to pick up his bike at the B&B and was out of breath by the time he saw his house.

"Howler! Hang on, I'm coming!" Corey had taken a shortcut through the alley behind Larry's Luncheon and was just in time to grab some meat that had been scraped into the trash. He felt guilty and wanted an extra treat for Howler. He was a block away when he saw the stray animal van pull up to his house.

"Hey!" He pedaled faster. Could that be Howler nosing into the back of the van for...a juicy steak?

"Hey! Howler, wait, I'm coming!"

He could hear laughter as the back of the van slammed shut and the van screeched off towards the village.

Corey dropped his foot to the street and stared after the van. Howler had been inside the yard. Could he have been hungry enough to go with a stranger?

Corey pumped the bike again, tearing after the van. Was this Auger's doing? Where was Charlie? Who was in the van?

He raced down to Main Street in time to see the van by the water. Two guys were manhandling a large cage...onto one of the Hart Tour boats!

"Ahhhwoooooooo!" floated from the boat. Corey saw a blond head at the controls—a head with white gauze over his nose.

Auger was moving the boat out towards the river.

Corey reached the dock and ran back and forth under the sign listing names of the "honorable" Harts. He yelled curses, waved his arms...then just his fist. The boat continued out of the bay. Corey ran for Charlie's boat—*no key, plus the tank is empty*—then scrambled up the bluff to the Point, yanking shrubs as he climbed, ignoring the pain in his right hand.

Corey jumped over the guardrail by the sign, "DANGER: UNSTABLE CLIFF."

Could he see Howler from here? He scanned the river channel for the boat. There it was, just floating. He could hear the pathetic howls, over and over, coming across the water like they were on the tour boat's speaker system.

"Ahhwwwoooooooooooo! Ahrrooooooo!" The sound trailed off as the three boys muscled the cage to the edge of the boat and looked out over the water. The cage was covered with something black so Corey couldn't see inside, but he heard muffled howls.

"Here's your mutt, Corey Worder!" The voice definitely came over the speaker system. "He's not so vicious now!"

A heavy *splash* resounded when Auger shoved the cage overboard, and the howling ceased when the cage disappeared beneath the waves, leaving only a floating black blanket.

SHAKEN

Corey let out his own howl, and it echoed over the Landing. He stumbled back and forth, holding his hair and eyeing the rocks below. The mighty St. Lawrence rolled on, as if the world had not just turned upside down.

Howler was the only friend on earth he could count on.

And Corey had failed him.

I'll jump in the river...I'll save him! But Corey knew that if he survived the rocks and the current, it would be too late to save Howler.

All at once, he felt the earth shake itself. *Like Howler when he's wet.* Even Corey's thoughts were shaken, and they jumped in his head like the balls in a lottery hopper.

He fell to his knees. His hands pulled at his sticky face as the cliff trembled and sifted him closer to the edge. *Why not add another Worder to the St. Lawrence?* If he died in the river, at least he would be *with* Howler—and Mom too.

Corey rocked back and forth. His mind worked to numb itself, and he had no idea how much time had passed when he was jerked by another tremor.

The ground bucked, and Corey grabbed at clumps of weeds with one hand and dug into the soil with the other. The earth rumbled, and the churning river pulled at him like a magnet. Resisting hurt too much. Besides, water was his element...*why fight it?* Charlie would be happier without him.

He hesitated...then released his grip.

"YOU ARE GETTING SLEEPY"

Marie exhaled as she settled into the easy chair, letting its warmth penetrate her legs and back. The room was dark and cozy, the voice soothing.

"Take a deep breath and close your eyes." The voice came from the shadows. "Let your mind become free..."

Much as she had tried, she couldn't block out the dreams that left her crying out. And whenever she looked in the mirror, she still couldn't find herself. The only thing that made her feel connected was that blue earring she'd found on Jack's boat. The small yellow and blue-green stones were like the eyes of mysterious friends watching over her, and they soothed her.

Jack had explained how she'd collided with a speed boat during a getaway. That's how she'd lost her memory. He'd filled her in about her life BC—"Before the Collision." How she had masterminded the business operations and was wanted for a list of crimes. And that she'd be locked up for life if she were recognized. Jack was so sweet, apologizing over and over, "I should never have let you drive" and "I could have lost my dear sister." He had found Marie a therapist, and she had been coming for weeks. But she felt no closer to remembering herself. Maybe this time...

Marie trusted Dr. Poole and never questioned her methods, which included bringing Marie through the trauma of the accident and recent past before the regression to "BC."

Marie's breath settled into a rhythm, and her mind began to scan the memories that revealed themselves only in this chair: Falling to the river, excruciating pain, lungs screaming for oxygen, then—miraculously!—sucking glorious air from a scuba tank. A tank stuck in the rocks deep underwater. Marie had filled her lungs again and again before fighting her way to the surface and feeling Jack's arms pull her to safety.

"Now tell me how you found that book you brought me," the therapist prodded gently. "The one you thought was tied to your identity."

Marie described it as she relived it. "I am passing a house with a big dog—familiar somehow—I park down the street and get out. Some deranged man follows me, loosening his belt! I walk faster. A driver in a blue Accord is looking at house numbers—she's going to hit the man! The car swerves, it hits a tree..."

Marie described entering the side door of the house while people ran out the front. Then: "Something pulls at me, the place is oddly familiar. I go upstairs, where I find old pages under a window."

"You did well to bring them here." The voice was reassuring. "This book appears to be highly symbolic for you. It must be kept safe.

"Now I'd like you to go further." The therapist used a litany of suggestions to allow Marie to access deeper memories.

Marie took a long breath. *Let go of fear.* She tightened and released her muscles as instructed by Dr. Poole. *Let go of judgment.*

She envisioned wispy fingers probing her mind. Hazy images formed, like those of her dreams: a man with a fish body; a boy staring with one eye; her own fingers picking locks. Then she saw herself holding a strange object.

"I feel smooth metal, a heavy rounded rectangle..."

The therapist's hand stopped writing. It was trembling.

So was the crystal chandelier.

Then the whole building shook as the earth quaked beneath them.

A BAD FALL

With splitting fingernails and bleeding hands, Corey slid towards the point of no return...where the river's magnetism and the earth's gravity would escort him to the Beyond. Already, he could hear the sound signaling his departure. He'd expected a bell...or maybe a harp, but not a *screech.*

The cliff's edge was getting closer; another second and Corey would be halfway off. Would he really see Mom? He heard a voice in the distance. "Cooorey..."

It came closer.

"Corey! Come quick!" It had more of an edge than he'd expected. In fact, it was more like...*Sam's.* The realization jarred him.

What the...! He latched onto a piece of rock. He couldn't hold it for long.

"It's Charlie—he's been hurt!"

Charlie? Corey grabbed and pulled at the last sprig of weeds—which came out by the roots. But their resistance slowed him, and with his other hand on the rock, he stopped sliding.

Strong, self-sufficient Charlie—*hurt?* His stepdad would be all alone. Corey *thunked* his forehead to the cliff. He tested his right leg. His thigh was still supported, but he had to pull his knee up, sideways to reach solid earth. He pushed his knee against the ground while pulling at rock and dirt. With throbbing pain in his hand, Corey pulled and shifted his body towards the guard rail.

By the time he limped to the parking lot, Sam was running out the museum door, calling "Corey!" again.

"Where *were* you? You left me and I had no *idea*—You look like you've been in a war. Never mind. Charlie's..." Her voice softened. "He's unconscious. He fell off a chair during the quake—and he hit his head. Johnny found him. Somebody saw you come up here."

By now they were both in the van. Corey's head was a jumble. Had he really just almost fallen to oblivion? More like *death-ion.* What would Sam think about him punching Auger? Or about him almost dropping himself off the cliff? He wasn't about to tell her.

Now his stepdad was hurt. Was Charlie even alive? Yesterday, Corey had said something awful. Was there time— could he be forgiven? Corey blocked everything else out of his mind as they pulled onto Route 12. Five minutes later they were in the waiting room at Landing General.

Corey walked back and forth, jiggling money in his pockets—change from one of Charlie's errands. "Please, I'll do anything he wants from now on," he whispered. "Just let him be okay." He tried to distract himself by watching the TV on the wall. The local news was saying some old buildings could fall because of the quake—a four-point-five on the Rickety scale or something.

Then the low, confident voice of Fred Hart came on.

"You may have heard rumors that an anonymous developer has been buying area businesses and real estate, displacing residential renters. The Harts have always been there for the local people; we share an important history together, and the Hart Corporation will not be tempted by any offer. We Harts will do everything possible to fend off these riverfront pirates!"

"Good thing Charlie didn't see that. He says Hart's probably the one behind the land-grabbing himself."

Sam was grinning at him. Probably just glad to hear him finally say something. Corey told her what else Charlie had said: "'Well, what would *you* do if you wanted to exploit the town? Swallow up the land, put up hotels, bars, entertainment—wipe out the residential sections. That's what Fred Hart is doing. Sure he'll bring business—for Harts! He'll drive out all the independents, us fishing guides...'" Corey thought Charlie had gone off the deep end.

A woman in light blue scrubs came out.

"Looks like your dad will be okay, but he may have suffered a concussion—we'll want to keep him overnight. You can see him soon."

Corey let out a sigh; he didn't even correct the nurse by saying *stepdad,* and he collapsed into the nearest chair with his eyes closed. He was exhausted, and in five minutes, he was hearing his mother's lullabies. The songs turned into howls.

Corey awoke and jumped up, gasping at the image of Howler's questioning eyes, eyes that asked why Corey had not protected him. Corey couldn't deny the reality of today's events. He darted toward the exit. He needed air! As he passed the gift shop, his eye caught sight of a stuffed dog, and he shuddered. He lurched towards the door. He should have watched where he was going.

The exit was too soft for a door.

At first, Corey thought he had run into Charlie. The man who entered was the same size and shape, but *duh,* Charlie was in a hospital bed. Corey mumbled *Sorry,* but it wasn't until he got outside that he realized he'd almost taken down another Hart!

MR. HART'S SURPRISE

Corey saw Mr. Hart do a double take and come back outside. Was he going to have Corey arrested? Corey didn't care. He should have killed Auger! Then Howler would still be...

"Aren't you Corey Worder?" Mr. Hart extended a forearm, and offered a glimpse of straight white teeth.

Corey froze as he stared at the man dressed in golfing clothes. Probably schmoozing the out-of-towners he claims to be fighting. *Instead of controlling his son.*

"I heard your stepfather was here in the hospital." Hart finally dropped his arm. "I'm sorry he got hurt."

Corey stared at his shoes, his lips tight. He wanted Mr. Hart to be mean; he wanted to hate him.

"But I also wanted to tell you..." Mr. Hart put his hand on Corey's shoulder. "I'm sorry about what Auger did out on the river." He turned towards a row of parked vehicles, saying "I made him go back out and dive for that cage." The man seemed to be talking to himself. "He can't leave stuff like that in the river." He drew something from his pocket. "Oh yes, I have the recording."

Corey couldn't help blurting out.

"You're worried about the cage?! What about Howler, doesn't he matter?" Corey followed Mr. Hart, flailing his arms, unable to stop himself. "And why would I want a stupid *recording?*" Corey's face was on fire, and he felt like throwing up right here by this...van. An animal van.

"Your dog?" Mr. Hart was opening the back of the van. "Of course he matters."

Corey stared dumbly at the hulking mass just before it bounded out the van doors and knocked him to the ground.

Mr. Hart held up an electronic device. "Auger copied it off his phone to play over the speaker." Corey could hear the same howls that had rolled over the water. Mr. Hart punched it off quickly, his face full of concern. "Auger was out on the boat being childish, but rest assured, your dog was safe onshore." He shook his head as he watched boy and dog on the hospital lawn.

Corey himself howled and rolled, his legs tangled with his dog, happy tears washing away the grief that had nearly drowned him.

NOT THE CLOSET!

Corey was walking on air as he headed towards Charlie's hospital room. He'd left Sam waiting with Howler in her van, though he hadn't been clear about why Howler was there. Fortunately, she didn't ask questions.

Now he was entering Charlie's room, where strange moaning sounds came from the bed.

"...foun' luv huh... thawt you'd leave 'ome. *Heart* din' work out for ya..." Then snoring.

Charlie was on pain killers, he wasn't making any sense. Charlie's grunts and Corey's sudden stomach growls persuaded Corey to find a vending machine.

When he came back, Corey squeezed a bulky chair between the wall and the bed. He sat down as he finished his candy bar. Charlie was more alert now. Corey was glad he didn't mention what happened between them yesterday.

"That was some shaker—hadn't felt one of those since I was a boy, then we get two in a row," Charlie's voice wavered. "People forget there's a fault through the river. Good thing Johnny came by or I might still be lying there on the bedroom floor."

Corey didn't mention where *he* could be lying right now if Sam hadn't come to the Point when she did.

Corey wondered why his stepfather had been standing on a chair in the bedroom, but then a more important question occurred to him. He got up and paced. He didn't want to upset Charlie, but...after all, he *was* on pain killers. And Corey just had to know.

"Charlie, when Mom went away last summer, where did she go?"

His stepfather drew a long breath and closed his eyes.

It was the wrong thing to bring up. "N-never mind—"

"She went to see her father. The old drunk."

What? The same thing Corey had called Charlie.

"Her...father?" Corey shifted from one foot to the other.

"Your mother had a rough time growing up. Father was an abusive S.O.B. She heard he was dying, thought they could patch things up."

"Did...did they?"

"No. Pathetic man couldn't even remember his own daughter."

Corey sat down, feeling a stab of resentment. "How—how come I never knew?"

"She never wanted anything to do with him. Wanted to protect you."

Corey stared at Charlie. *That* explained the absence—and the sadness. Corey felt lighter. Mom had *not* left Charlie and him!

Charlie picked up his water cup. "Pills make me thirsty."

Corey thought of something else. "What were you doing standing on a chair in the bedroom, anyway?" An innocent question.

Charlie sputtered and spilled the water.

"I had to just—Never mind what I was doing in the closet!"

Closet? Corey watched Charlie's face redden as the two nurses outside stopped talking and looked his way. Charlie lowered his voice. "I mean, nothing you need to worry about, just rearranging things." He took another sip. He licked his lips as his brows drew together.

"Listen, we got problems. Hospital bill, no insurance..."

Corey hadn't thought of that.

"And, I won't be able to do it all, not for a while. I'll have to depend on you, Kid."

Corey would have to work harder. Even then, the bills would drown them.

The nurse appeared in the doorway. "Time for a pain killer, Mr. Stowe."

"What's *that* gonna set me back?" Charlie asked, but he took it.

Corey got up. "Guess I better go look for some money. Maybe I'll find a chest of gold."

"Speaking of chests," Charlie called, "bring me socks and underwear. They're in the drawer." Then he added, "No need to look anywhere else!"

Corey didn't pay much attention—he was already halfway down the stairwell.

A REVEALING ROBE

Corey insisted on riding in the back of the van with Howler while Sam drove.

"You're more excited to see your dog than you were about seeing Charlie! As if you hadn't seen Howler in ages." She braked to a stop by the pier and became quiet. She pointed to the heap of metal. "What on *earth* did you do to that bike?"

Corey ignored her and let Howler out the sliding door as she continued. "I don't know what's gotten into you today. First you leave the resort without telling me. Then I find you've gone up to the Point after *dumping* the bike Johnny fixed for you. That's a nice thanks."

"I had a bad day, okay?" Corey surprised himself. He didn't usually stand up to a girl's criticism. It felt good to rebel.

"Well." Her voice softened. "Whatever."

He picked up the bike and wheeled it onto the street. "See, it's fine!" He waved as he pedaled, Howler trailing behind him.

Corey dug through coats, pants, and shirts in the bedroom closet. He had found the socks and underwear. He was relieved Charlie was okay, and he was sorry for what he'd almost done at the Point. If Charlie had not fallen and Sam had not come to get him, Cory would be dead now...just because an idiot dumped a cage in the river.

Corey was glad to be alive, for a change. He had Howler back, and Charlie would be all right too. Corey knew he had been selfish, and Charlie had had a lot on his mind. He wanted to make it up to Charlie. At least make him comfortable.

Where's his robe? There—the belt was hanging from the closet shelf. It was attached to a terry cloth bundle, and Corey pulled at it.

"Whoa!" Something heavy started to fall on his head. He pushed it back so it rested on the shelf. He looked around. There was a closed folding chair leaning against the wall. Corey dragged it to the shelf, opened it, and climbed up to see what had almost knocked him down. But he stood too far back, and the chair started to collapse. He fell sideways and barely got his left foot onto the floor to catch his weight while his right was stuck in the chair. *That's* what happened to Charlie! He had lost his balance, and his feet got caught; then he had hit his head against the door frame.

Corey got back up and balanced carefully to probe the bundle on the shelf. Wrapped up in the robe was...Mom's laptop. So this was what Charlie was looking at! Probably meant to get rid of it. Could they sell it? They could use the money. Corey could help Charlie by getting it ready.

He would delete the files first. He took the computer to the desk in Mom's old office. He opened it, ignoring the folded paper that fell out, and booted up. Most files were right on the desktop, just recipes. Then Corey noticed the email application.

Crap. He needed a password. He idly punched letters as he wondered what to try. He hit *Enter* and was amazed to find that his own name worked.

He scanned the inbox and saw a whole lot of junk mail.

He went to open the *Sent* folder, and clicked on the last email he saw.

It's a message to Fred Hart.

He couldn't read it.

Corey *had* to read it. He tapped his foot. He jingled the change in his pocket.

He couldn't *possibly* read it.

He shut his eyes then opened one. His foot stopped tapping. His head leaned forward, and his hand swept hair from his eye.

He read:

> I look forward to meeting with you at the Point; there is so much to talk about! I hope you are ready to make a change, one that could affect your whole family as well as mine. It will be big news to Corey. He will find out the truth when he returns from the Cape.

A prickling heat crept up Corey's neck. He turned from the screen, his mind reeling, his stomach churning. His eyes locked on the folded paper on the floor. With a trembling hand, he picked it up. Anything to take his mind off the screen. Every other line on the paper was faded out. The printer ink must have been running low.

> I am confused and torn. But I have found a love so strong, I am willing to leave home...

Then:

> I have decided to join Mr. Hart. We will meet at his boat at nightfall...

Corey's stomach lurched. Had his mom left this note for Charlie? Then it was true! She *had* been planning to leave Charlie for Fred Hart. Had Fred changed his mind—was that why she'd called herself worthless in her suicide note, and said she didn't deserve anyone's love?

He turned his head and the world spun. He'd been so sure Auger was lying. Corey clutched his stomach as images of his mother and Mr. Hart rippled from his mind to his belly.

He was on the verge of spewing into the wastebasket when some other words popped into his head:

> What is this love? The love of freedom and the right to fight for its principles.

Corey blanked, and his brows became one. He tried to recall where he'd heard those words.

In the attic. Sam had read them.

His mom had typed and printed...a *quote from the journal!* This was the reason Charlie hated Mr. Hart—why he'd been drinking. He'd thought that the printout was a letter to him, *Charlie*—and that the email was a love letter to Mr. Hart. That's what he'd been babbling about in the hospital.

Had Charlie seen this page before Mom disappeared? When Corey and Charlie had returned from the Cape, Mom was not home. Corey had fallen asleep, but Charlie had gone to look for her and returned with that note. Had he *done* something...

"Crazy." Corey shook off what had crossed his mind.

He looked back at the email and squinted. At the bottom was more that had ended up in tiny font:

> Again, I am grateful that you suggested updating the legend, but I need time to digest what I have found and talk it over with Corey before we make plans.

Why didn't Mom want to tell Fred Hart more? Did she find something good about Patrick Worder in the journal? Maybe she found something terrible. She probably got her hopes up when Patrick seemed okay—then she found out he really was no good.

Corey spotted the name of the folder he had opened. He'd missed the *Sent* folder and clicked on *Draft.* This email had never been sent to Fred Hart.

Corey's mind raced. Was there any proof that Mom intended to leave Charlie?

No. And there was no evidence Mom ever wanted to be with Fred Hart. Corey knew that Mom was no cheat! He couldn't wait to tell Charlie.

Now Corey could focus on helping him—he'd do whatever Charlie needed, and keep Howler fed too. It was time to forget about that journal. It was bad news.

CHARLIE'S REFUSAL

"Fred Hart wanted to pay your bill? And you refused?" Corey had dumped the underwear and robe on Charlie's bed, forgetting to offer the wildflowers clenched in his other hand. He was excited to tell him about Mom's email. But Charlie was in a rant.

"I wouldn't take a dime from Fred Hart, not if I was dying!"

Corey was sure Charlie would change his mind when he heard the news. "It's okay now. I found something in that computer in the closet—"

" *What?* I told you not to go in there."

"But Charlie, I saw the email..."

"I don't want to hear it. That machine is to be destroyed!"

It was almost a scream, and people in the hall were looking inside.

"I will not discuss it," Charlie hissed, spattering his gown.

"What's going on in here?" The nurse had popped her head in the door. "I think you'd better leave now."

"No!" Corey pleaded as the nurse came in and closed her hand around his arm. "I have something he needs to hear..." He pulled away and put his face in front of Charlie's. "I read the whole thing. It was *not* a love letter to...anyone." He was careful not to supply a name for other ears to hear.

Charlie's head twisted to the side, eyes glaring at the wall.

"That's enough," the nurse scolded. "Can't you see he's upset—he needs rest." She sank her fingers into Corey's shoulder and yanked him towards the door with the other. He had to squelch the urge to fight her as he was jerked along, his hand releasing blossoms that scattered on the floor.

A small voice, muffled by the pillow, made Corey plant his feet at the door.

"Then what was it?"

Corey straightened. He turned back, his spirit surging. "It was just a quote, Charlie—" He pulled free of the nurse, who was called away on an emergency.

"She was copying the journal." It took a lot of explaining before Charlie's scowl broke up.

"Why would she make such a big deal of changing the legend—nobody should *care*..."

Corey tightened his lips—Charlie still didn't get it.

"Remember, Kid, a bad relative does not make *you* a bad guy." Charlie sighed. "But I guess she knew better than me, how it affects a kid like you." He became quiet.

As Corey left, he heard Charlie's murmur. "Maybe she *wasn't* seeing him."

The hospital bill was taken care of the next day.

HART TO HART

Fred was working from his home office. He had convinced Charlie Stowe that his medical expense was covered under a clause in Peg's insurance. But the man had questioned it, and Fred had had to think fast.

It had been months since Fred had lost his assistant. Peg was good, but he hadn't appreciated her enough. Finding a replacement was impossible—just when he'd find a good one, they'd quit. Fred ended up doing it all himself and had become overworked. Plus, he worried about the island plan. Could the corporation afford to remodel the Rocky Island castle as the special resort Fred envisioned? The operation would absorb a lot of cash before it could start paying back. But it wasn't Fred's job to worry. He'd been assured things were under control; Fred's job was to take care of the rest of the business.

Being a Hart, Fred was an *Eli*, a Yale graduate. He was talented and worked hard, but it wasn't enough. He needed an edge. The island was not going to have just another hotel. Gambling had previously been restricted to native control; tourists went to the gaming tables at the Mohawk reservation downriver. But new legislation would mean big money for the Harts. They had friends in high places, and Fred had been assured not only of the casino bill's passage—but that his site would be one of the chosen locations.

When things settled a bit, he would take a breather. He had neglected his wife, but he would make it up to Rita. He would dedicate the casino to "The woman who stands by me." And she would ride in the bicentennial parade as Queen of Harts Landing. Even Mother herself, after some confusion, was thrilled to be "dethroned." Mackenzie Hart had occupied the seat of honor every year since Fred's first wife left, but now she insisted the honor belonged to Rita.

Mother had lost her adored grandfather to cancer, her brother to Vietnam, and her husband to an accident. And she herself had helped build the Hart enterprises. She deserved to sit back and watch the parade that honored her family.

Unfortunately, Mother had heard rumors of "hostile forces" buying up local properties. It would destroy her to see outsiders exploiting Harts Landing. "Impossible," Fred had assured her.

Fred was working seven days a week, but there had been so many interruptions. Maybe Fred had been harsh on Auger, but the boy needed to keep control. Not make a spectacle with the dog thing. His son had looked miserable when Fred commanded him to be a man. And the boy had refused when Fred told him to take the dog back to the poor Worder kid. After all, they couldn't afford to damage the Hart image now.

A soft knock came at the door.

For Pete's sake, *now what?*

The door cracked open, and Fred's mother peered inside. Fred instinctively covered the papers on the desk.

"I hate to be a bother," she whispered, "but she left. With that man from the shop." She blinked. "My bridge game?"

"Oh, *great...*"

Mother's bones were healing well, but she couldn't drive yet and her chauffeur was off today.

"Er, I mean, it's *great* that I'm still here." Where was Auger? "I'll take you, Mother."

Another interruption.

"Wait." Fred had started the Cadillac before it dawned on him. "There aren't any men who work at the Glass & Brass. Or did you mean the man from that shop behind Rita's?"

"Oh..." Mother looked confused. "Well, I'm sure I'm wrong, she'd have nothing to do with *that* man!" She chuckled. "Must have been a woman—I can't tell the difference these days."

Fred turned the Caddy onto the main road. Mother had heard that the dive shop owner was a shady character. She was mistaken, wouldn't be the first time.

When Fred got back to his office, he found Auger waiting, his arms full. Fred hadn't talked to him since the dog incident. Auger followed him inside and deposited an armload of junk on Fred's desk.

"What the blazes!" Fred dove to protect his documents from metal, plastic, and paper items. His hand stopped on a Kindergarten award for Best Manners. Then he recognized the Best Player trophy from Peewee hockey. Dozens of other awards competed for attention.

"What's this about? I have no time for games."

Auger's face had been like stone, but it began to crumble. His hand shook as he pointed at his father.

"I only wanted you to be proud of me." His voice was a growl. "I did everything you said. Paid attention. Kept focus..." Auger punctuated with a clenched fist. "Tried to impress you with trophies!"

Fred looked at his watch. He was already behind schedule, and this display was annoying and childish.

"You don't even notice." Auger swung his arm back. "You care more about that Worder kid!" He swiped his arm across the desk, sending trophies crashing to the floor.

Fred threw his hands up. "Now look what you've done." He bent to pick up the junk as Auger backed to the wall and slid to the floor. "Look, it's the Hart image we need to protect by..." He noticed the wave in Auger's hair. "I mean we must..." Was that a cleft in his chin? The jaw line was that of a man. Fred stared. How long had it been since he'd really *seen* his son?

He crept to the wall. He sat on the floor next to his son and let air out in a long sigh. "I know I haven't spent much time." He looked into his son's tortured face. "I thought you knew how important you are...you're my *son*."

Auger stared at his knees.

Fred scratched his chin, still unshaven, and rubbed his eyes.

"I've been tough." He grasped his son's shoulder. "You know I rely on you." He dropped his arm. "But I guess I only pay attention when something goes wrong."

Auger looked up.

Fred stood and extended his hand to pull his son to his feet. He hesitated a moment. "I think I should let you in on some company plans." Fred steered Auger to the sofa. He walked back to the door and latched it before settling down next to his son.

M.A. NOBLE

7 STROKE OF FATE

Charlie had been home for three weeks. June weather was great, and Corey didn't have to pretend to study anymore. Even better, he didn't have to listen to kids and teachers go on about "Privates Week." He would rather work his tail off on the fishing boat or at the B&B, or just roll around on the grass with Howler, than be around the Privates celebration. He had let go of the idea of finding the journal. The thing probably got chucked. Anyway, so what if Auger wasn't a blood descendent of Warren Hart? What difference would it make?

Corey was walking away from Bay Cellular, punching numbers in his new phone. The bicentennial had brought more activity to the islands, which meant more fishing business. Charlie wanted to be able to reach Corey easily, so he added a phone to his plan for a few bucks a month.

Corey punched Sam's number into his contacts list; she was his only contact besides Charlie. He was thinking of adding Johnny but didn't have the number. He'd ask Sam when he saw her. Then he looked up and did see her—she was sitting at an outdoor table at the Juice Tap, slurping pink stuff through a straw and studying the papers spread out on the table. Thank god *he* didn't have to study anything. Sam cleared a spot as Corey dropped into the opposite seat.

"I was using my dads' genealogy software—"

"Studying rocks?"

"No, that's *geology*." She tried to hide a smile.

"Oh yeah...I knew that."

"Anyway, I was looking up family histories. I tried to trace the Worders—"

"Why would you do *that*?" Corey rolled his eyes. He'd thought he had finally escaped history class. He went back to scrolling through his phone's features.

"The thing is, there *aren't* any Worders!"

Corey scowled. "Good, maybe I don't exist. Anyway, I won't have time to chase ghosts with Charlie needing me."

"I see." Her voice was cool. "So I guess you wouldn't be interested in my news about Patrick."

Corey's fingers paused over the phone. He looked up, waiting for more, but Sam was gathering her things. "But you just said there *weren't* any Worders..."

She continued stuffing her bag.

"Okay, okay." Corey put his phone away. "What did you find?"

Sam stopped packing and looked up. "Corey, I've been thinking about this since I saw Patrick's cutlass at the museum." She leaned over the table and glanced side to side like some kind of secret agent. "I think someone tampered with the engraving!"

Corey smiled. She was messing with him—he wouldn't get a lecture after all. He started to laugh.

She cut him off with a look. "I'm dead serious." She pulled out the papers. "I came across an old document listing a body found in 1813. In the water. Downriver from here."

"But no one ever found Patrick's body."

"I know. This body was female. Her identity was confirmed as Emeline P. Redrow, daughter of a Royal Naval officer at Kingston."

"So...some woman from Kingston drowned, so what?"

"She'd been missing since the year before, in 1812. She was supposed to have sailed back to England."

"So what's that got to do..."

"Don't you remember in the journal, how 'Patrick' was pretending to sail home to England but went off with Warren Hart instead?"

Corey sort of remembered.

Sam wrote something on a piece of paper then she shoved it in front of him. It was a name: *Redrow.*

"Red-uh..."

"Red-row," she pronounced. She grabbed the paper and penciled something before shoving it back. "Now read what it spells *backwards.*"

His eyes widened, and he drew his brows together. "That's my name." Corey's mouth went dry, but this woman's name and the fact that she was in the river that year... "It—it's just circumstandable."

"Circumstantial. But no, it isn't." Sam took the paper and drew a picture of Pat's cutlass.

Corey's eyes were glued to the picture as he picked up her cup to drain the leftover ice. Sam started writing the letters that had been engraved on the real cutlass; she turned the picture so he could see. Then she added one vertical line—a simple stroke.

The cup slid out of his hand and splattered on the sidewalk.

"I gotta see that sword," he sputtered.

TO SEE CLEARLY

Sam rushed into the B&B, leaving Corey outside, and ran up the blue carpeted staircase to grab a magnifying glass to take to the museum. As she turned right to enter the upstairs reading room, she yelled *Hi* to Randy, who was running a planer over the oak floor in the suite down the hall. But the thing was deafening; he didn't even look up.

She moved piles of magazines on the reading table; she'd seen the magnifier up here when she'd read that article, the one about that Texas earthquake supposedly caused by injection mining. *Oh—there.* The magnifier was under a River Life magazine.

Sam looked up. It had become very quiet. *Thank goodness Randy's turned off that ungodly thing.* She peeked out of the reading room, past the scrolled woodwork, and noticed the door down the hall was now partly closed. But she heard voices—she hadn't realized the guys were both home. And arguing again.

"...you're either fartin' around on the computer or gone, while I'm wearing myself out..."

"We can't ignore public relations—"

"Schmoozing you mean. Hell, Johnny, I don't even know where you *are* half the time—"

"I'm working double—my other job? That's what we agreed."

"The books are a pain in the—"

"It will be worth it." That was Johnny. "We've just got to be patient."

Same old theme: Randy, pessimistic and brooding and Johnny, optimistic and happy-go-lucky. *Opposites.* Sam and Corey were opposites too, but Corey was more like a brother. Maybe an odd one, but endearing. Plus, he had a lot more potential than he saw himself; he just needed confidence.

The two men had now come out of the other room and paused at the top of the back stairs. Sam glimpsed Johnny's red waves and Randy's dark head, a few inches higher, and she stepped backward. Randy and Johnny had a whirlwind relationship, and sometimes it became a cyclone! Sam didn't want to get caught in the crosswinds.

Randy huffed down the creaky back stairs, but at least he could joke: "Yeah, well, *maybe* it'll work out—if you've got some rich relatives!" Did he mean the relationship or the business would work out?

Randy had already disappeared when she heard Johnny murmur, "Only if the Harts qualify." Then Johnny himself padded down the back stairs. Sam squinted at the back of his head, trying to read his thoughts, but she couldn't see what that remark could possibly mean.

Sam tiptoed down the front stairs, hoping the magnifier would be more useful at the museum.

THE CUTLASS

Corey was out of breath when he and Sam ran up the wooden steps of the museum's main entrance, but he tried to be casual as he walked inside. Corey veered off towards the displays while Sam dropped a donation at the front desk.

He looked around to see if anyone was watching before drawing the cutlass out of its case. He held the sword at an angle so he could read the inscription inside the handle. There was a space between the words *First* and *Mate*. But he was more interested in the name that appeared above those words; he traced the letters with his fingers as he read the name. Then, from his pocket, he pulled out the magnifier Sam had given him.

All the letters of the name *Patrick* had the same look, same texture, like they'd been formed at the same time by the same hand. All, that is, except for part of the last letter, the *k*.

"Jeeze," Corey whispered to Sam, who had now joined him. "You're right, the straight-line *is* different!"

"Somebody added a stroke later to make it look like a *k*," Sam said. "The other part is a loop—so the original letter was an *e*."

They stared at each other.

"*Patrice* Worder?" Corey said

"Emeline *Patrice Redrow!*" Sam corrected.

"So let me get this straight..." Corey sank to a cushioned bench as Sam replaced the cutlass. "Patrick Worder, my great-something 'grandfather'—the guy who deserted the ship—was a woman?"

"That's my guess." Sam sat next to Corey. "The woman later found in the river was expected in London, where her mother was waiting for her."

"Now I remember, you read something in the journal about him—I mean her—sneaking off a ship to go off with Warren Hart."

"And I thought you heard nothing I read that day." Sam gave a foxy smile that delivered an unexpected jolt to Corey's groin. "She pretended to leave the area, even waved to her father, before she sneaked off the ship. She must have used 'Redrow' so she couldn't be traced."

"So, were they like...lovers?" Corey avoided Sam's eyes.

"Not necessarily. Remember, she said her love was for *freedom.* That's why she joined Hart."

Love of freedom. He could relate to that.

"Well, there's one good thing," Corey said, looking back at Sam. "If Pat Worder was really Patrice Redrow, then Pat Worder was not anybody's great-*grandfather!*"

MASTER PLANNING

A Persian carpet graced the maple floor supporting a mahogany desk. A bronze lamp illuminated the occupant of the desk's matching high-backed chair, which swiveled as thoughts flowed like a river...in the mind of the Boss.

Nearly two hundred years ago that *other* "Worder" woman—*Patrice*—had gotten in the way. Then last fall, *Margaret Worder Stowe* had been a threat because she had learned too much. Her death note had been easy to fake, but the woman had been clever enough to substitute a copy of Warren Hart's buckle, and the real buckle had not been found anywhere near the museum. Miraculously, Peg Stowe herself had turned up alive, thanks to Jack, but she couldn't remember anything. *Double-edged sword.* At least now the woman was controllable as "Marie." She had been given not only a new name, but a new face and a new history and, because of her, the journal had surfaced. Soon, the buckle should be found,

The Boss had eyes and ears all over town. Some of those eyes had been tracking old Buddy. Who'd have thought he would make his way back to the Landing after forty years? Aging and the ravages of post-traumatic stress disorder had made him nearly unrecognizable. Now he was getting "treatment" and a free room downtown. But Buddy liked to spend his time among the trees and bushes. The vegetation at the Point gave him cover while allowing a clear view up and down the river. And the man's habit of picking up discarded objects had not gone unnoticed.

Strong fingers punched a phone.

"Change of plan. Have *Marie* make the next delivery to Buddy's room." Marie was familiar with the lost object, and she was best suited to retrieve it. "It would not be prudent for *me* to show up in that part of town."

The carved mahogany chair tilted backward as business points were ticked off:

- Silent partners had been found
- Control of the island had been established
- Local properties were being acquired
- Cash was being generated for the new project
- "Renovations" would cloak the treasure digging
- A lab was being prepared

Maybe it wasn't obvious to the casual observer, but the Boss was a brilliant multi-tasker and believed in "diversifying" efforts. There was more than one way to get power, and several ways had come together—a sign that the time would soon arrive for taking total control. With a team of discreet associates, all fronts could be managed.

The casino project would be completed eventually. Fellow *Bonesmen* would ensure the green light; then island after island would fall under control. The Vegas-style mega-theme park would attract hordes of gambling tourists to the St. Lawrence, with the Rocky Island Casino the centerpiece of the *ThousanDiceLands*.

But something more important had trumped the castle's immediate renovation. Blasting had revealed more than a cave!

The latest project, cloaked by the castle, required extra capital, and though Jack's operation was "small potatoes," it did provide starter money. The thought of the junior associate brought a chuckle. *Imagine Jack thinking he would call the shots.* Actually, his idea for the cocaine tanks was...creative. Plus, it had sparked the idea for the larger production scheme: *meth*, the "poor man's cocaine." And, if it weren't for Jack's scuba testing, they might never have found "Marie." Jack just needed to believe he had some control while being kept *under* control.

Above all, the most valuable asset in fulfilling the mission was a name. *Hart* stood for honor, patriotism, and power. Any obstruction to its use must be prevented. The fishing guide had asked a lot of questions, and the boy was getting curious again. Best to get them out of the way.

An email went out to JackofHarts@takeadive.com: "Time to do some *planting.*"

A LURING SONG

Corey had fastened down the package he'd picked up for Charlie and wheeled his bike away from the bait shop. He thought about the cutlass as he waited on the corner of Stillman Drive for a truck to pass. He was convinced that a woman named Patrice Redrow had posed as a man and called herself "Patrick Worder." He wanted explanations, but he didn't know where to look for them. Today he had to help Charlie, and Sam had left for some river meeting about invasive species in the river.

The morning's gray mist had turned to drizzle, and he pulled his cap over his forehead. Then he kept hearing Mom's river song in his head: *Rolling...rolling river.* He missed her! She was the only one who ever sang that song.

Except Buddy.

Corey realized the tune wasn't just in his head. Buddy himself was singing it as he wobbled down Bay, the side street.

Buddy was like a parrot; he had probably heard Corey's mom singing that song. What else had he heard? Or seen? Maybe he saw Corey's mom when she disappeared!

Buddy was wrapped in something like a black garbage bag. It covered his short, round body but had a hole for his face. He was holding out a plastic pill box like Corey had seen in the drugstore for old people. Then Buddy put the pill box up to his face. "Where's my Wednesday?" Buddy wailed as he plodded down Bay Street, like a plastic covered Humpty Dumpty, asking each person he saw, crossing the street several times. But even those who didn't turn away couldn't help him. Buddy started singing again.

"Rollin' river..." He kept his eye on the box, as if a pill might appear.

Corey left his bike and ran into the street. "Buddy!"

Buddy jumped. He seemed to be flustered to have someone approach *him*. He kept going.

"Wait." Corey caught up and grabbed Buddy's round, slippery shoulder. "I just want to know something."

Buddy pulled away as his eyes widened in recognition. "You...from the Point." He scowled. "Tried to take the trunk!"

"No...it was mine—never mind. I want to know where you heard that song." Corey swiped at the drops spattering his face.

Buddy stared blankly, touching his head.

"You know, like, 'Rolling, Rolling River'...."

"Rollin' River..." The old man picked up the rhythm, singing along, "...the St. Lawrence River rolls on."

"Okay, Buddy, good." Corey grabbed Buddy's other shoulder. "But I need to know where you heard it."

Buddy turned his head towards the sound of car engines in the distance. He started singing again. "Rollin'...."

Corey shook Buddy. "No, Buddy concentrate! *Where* have you heard that song?"

Buddy jerked away and stared into Corey's eyes. Then he pointed at Corey as he clutched at the slick black bag covering his stomach. "That woman...I've got to give her..." His eyes darted around, and his breath quickened.

The sound of racing engines got louder.

Buddy grabbed his head with both hands. "Stop the pounding!"

SOBERING VISION

Charlie was pushing the Civic, but even though he'd tweaked the engine, it was no match for a Mustang. If he could just get closer...

He was back to normal after his concussion, actually better than his old self. He felt fifty pounds lighter now that he knew Peg had not meant to leave him for Fred Hart. But why *had* she left? The whole thing was playing games with his mind. He'd thought *Corey* was flaky, but now he decided he was nuts himself.

Because he'd caught a glimpse. A glimpse of a woman. The look, the posture, the set of the head. And the vibration that passed right through to his gut. He couldn't explain it in any way that made sense, but he knew it was something.

Charlie's hands gripped the wheel and he heard the tires give a screech as he took another corner, tailing the woman in the Mustang.

Did Peg have a relative he didn't know about? Did her father have another child her age? It was a crazy thought, but it was saner than the one that burned deeply in his chest. The one he didn't dare admit.

Whoever that woman was driving the black Mustang, he had to follow her. He tried to keep up without being seen, but when he swung around Stillman Drive, she had disappeared.

Now he was left with a feeling he didn't know how to cope with. He'd always been sure of himself, and if he wasn't, he'd drown the unwelcome feeling in beer. Now alcohol was the last thing he wanted.

He wanted a look at that woman.

REARVIEW

Marie squeezed the steering wheel. She was already late making the delivery to the back of the Priva-Cheers when she noticed a green Civic following her. She had turned down several random streets, and it kept coming.

Could it be an unmarked police car? She could *not* take a chance on being identified! She might have lost her memory, but she knew in her bones what jail would be like. And if Jack was right, they'd put her away for life.

She gunned the motor and yanked the wheel. The Mustang barreled down the side road as Marie turned her head to see if the Civic was following. She was more interested in what was behind her than what was in front of her.

SEALED

"Tell me, Buddy!" Corey was sure Buddy had heard that song from his mother. Plus, he'd said he had to give "that woman" something.

"Who was she—and what do you have to give her?" He ignored the sound of the approaching engine.

Buddy's hands slipped from the sides of his head as he pointed a stubby finger at Corey's face. "Like you—" he stammered as a car screeched around the corner.

"Incoming!" Buddy pushed Corey away and ducked, never seeing the speeding black mass that ran him over. Corey caught a look at the driver's eyes as she rolled through.

Then everything was in slow motion: Corey kneeling by Buddy, tearing away Buddy's "raincoat," seeing the red stain spread through his shirt, fumbling to loosen Buddy's belt—frustrated as part of it came off in his hand—while Buddy's chest jerked for air. Then, Corey holding his own T-shirt against Buddy's side and hollering "Stay with me, Buddy!" as his own shirt became soaked with rain and blood.

Next thing Corey knew, the round man was being loaded onto a stretcher. Corey stuck with him and slid into the back of the ambulance in time to hear Buddy's weak voice.

"That lady, Rollin' River..."

"What? Yes, the Rolling River lady, did you see her? What happened?" No response. "Hang on, Buddy! Hang on...the Rolling River woman was Mom! What did you want to give her? Did you find something?" Corey squeezed Buddy's moist hand with his own.

Buddy opened his eyes once more, touched his stomach, and whispered, "That lady, she left..."

Corey hardly dared breathe. "What did she leave?" Was Buddy the one who found Mom's earring? Had he seen that *other* woman, too? Maybe she ran over him on purpose!

But Buddy's mouth was closed now, and his eyes too.

"You need to step away," the medic was saying.

"No...my mother—he's my last hope!"

Whatever Buddy knew remained inside him.

WHOSE MUSTANG?

The police were finally done questioning Corey; they closed their notebooks and turned towards the squad car. Corey walked behind them, hoping to hear the plan for finding the driver.

"Wasn't that the same guy who caused the accident on Grant Street?" one said. The other answered, "Guy couldn't stay out of the road, looks like it did him in."

"Buddy did not cause this!" Corey knotted his fists. "Go find that woman. *She's* to blame!"

He didn't wait to hear more; he splashed through a puddle, jerked his bike up, and jumped on it. He spun down the street where the car had disappeared. The Mustang could be anywhere by now, but he had to pump out his anger.

Those eyes! The same ones that had lost him the job at the rink. And got him in trouble with Charlie. And she wore that earring. She had raised his hopes, got him fired. *How dare she remind me of Mom!*

The worst was, she had taken away the man who might have had a clue. Buddy had been trying to tell Corey something, and now he might never find out. He shook with emotion; he wanted to strangle that woman. But he needed a cool head.

Near the downtown business section, Corey calmed enough to slow down, pull over, and punch a number in his new phone—how had he ever lived without it?

"Didn't you see anything that could identify the car?" Sam was being practical, as usual.

"I didn't see the plate numbers." He only remembered the dark brown eyes as the woman had turned her head.

"Like I told the police, the car was black. And it was a Mustang." He had glimpsed the rear as he ran to help Buddy. "The shiny bumper, the pony picture by the—" He lifted his brows. "Ronnie's Rentals!"

Maybe he did stand a chance of catching the woman. He wasn't ready to tell the cops what he remembered—he was still mad at them. But he persuaded Sam to help him.

BRASS AND IRONY

Marie gripped the steering wheel to steady her hands. She'd had a simple enough job to do, but she had not only failed; she had almost hit that boy! She'd felt a bump and, looking back through the gray drizzle, saw the shapeless bundle covered by a trash bag. It must have been the boy's gear. But she couldn't stop. She would not go to jail. She just hoped she hadn't broken anything important. She sped up Water Street.

A bead of sweat trickled down Marie's cheek, and she dabbed it with the cotton of her right glove. He had seen her—that same boy she had seen at the arena. Marie trembled all over. She'd been careless to go inside at the hockey game that day when she'd given Samantha a ride. But she'd had such a strong feeling when she saw the school. Then she saw that boy's face. Why did he affect her so? She had wanted to stop and look him over. But she didn't know who he was. Maybe he would recognize her and turn her in.

Marie hid the car the best she could. She was late, but she found her way to the back of the Priva-Cheers. She pushed some buttons on her phone, just as she'd been told. She heard the pattern of tones, which triggered a response: she immediately went inside, like a robot, to do the job she had been assigned. No one was there, but she left a full pill box;

then she worked over the room, trancelike, responding to unseen instructions. Her fingers probed every inch of the room for....*something.* She would know it when she found it.

"The boss is *not* going to be happy!" Jack was angry. "You'd better not have messed up the chance for that brass thing. You were supposed to *find* it."

"Wh—what do you mean?" Marie felt bad enough that she'd hit something with the car; now Jack was talking in riddles. Nobody had told her to find anything. Not that she remembered.

"Never mind, just stay out of sight!"

A DISCLOSURE

Sam parked Randy's Hyundai at the rental place. She carefully put on her lipstick and combed her hair, using the rearview mirror while Corey fidgeted in the passenger seat. "Sam, this is no time to worry about your looks."

But she knew what she was doing. She had a plan, and as she sat in the rental office a few minutes later, Ronnie himself spilled the information without Sam even asking.

She walked out slowly, feeling tense, and when Corey badgered her, she muttered a name without meeting his eyes.

"Auger's *grandmother!*" Corey yelled as they pulled out of the rental lot. "I didn't even know she could drive! Isn't she like fifty or sixty?"

"I...think she's at least functional." Sam turned away, her face hot. She'd pulled the name out of thin air—or at least off the "Hart History" brochure she'd seen in the lobby. It wasn't like her to lie, but she couldn't tell Corey the name Ronnie had really given her.

Sam had been ready to trick Ronnie into telling her the name, but he told her before she'd uttered a word: "Well, hello there, Samantha Clarke. Tell me now, how is that Mustang working out for Johnny? He thought he'd only need it for the weekend, but I told him, I says 'I'll give ya a deal, seeing as how you guys're sending the tourists my way...' I says, 'take it for the full week.'"

Sam had left her mouth open three full seconds before words came out. "Oh—oh, it's great so far..." Then she'd muttered something about having Ron display rental brochures for the Mainsail.

On the second floor of the B&B, Samantha waited outside the open bathroom door.

"Let's see...yeah, Johnny rented a black Mustang...hand me that wrench." Randy's lengthy form was jammed into an unnatural position under the sink. "I wish he had a little more talent for plumbing and less for chatting people up."

"But why did he—"

"*Why?*" Randy avoided a spraying leak and squinted through clumps of hair. "Samantha, this is a hotel. There are all kinds of demands, as you can see!" He got up, wiped his long face on his gray sweatshirt, and stalked out of "The Rose Room"— *Where Love Blooms.*

Randy was a practical man to a fault, and Samantha wondered at Johnny's patience with him.

She flew down the steps and out the front door, where she ran into Johnny, who wore a scowl and seemed lost in thought.

"Oh!" she gasped as he caught and folded her in his aqua-sleeved arms. He changed shirts almost as often as his expression, which now brightened.

"How's my favorite girl—hey you look kind of upset." He smoothed her hair.

She scowled and jabbed her finger towards the upstairs. "Randy can be a real *pri—*

"A prince, he can be a prince." Johnny patted his own red curls. "You should know him by now, Sam. He may have his moods, but he's smart, he's loyal—and you should be proud."

"I guess." She sighed. "By the way...do you know who was driving the black Mustang early today?"

"The rental?" His dimples vanished and he clenched her arm. "What do you know about it?"

"Ow, you're pinching me!" She jerked her arm away.

"Sorry...it's just—it got stolen!" he blurted. "Someone recognized it after hearing a police description. The thief ran over somebody." He stalked into the house muttering, "The idiot."

8 SNAGGED

It was Thursday morning, and Corey was helping Charlie with a guide job.

"Watch that side, Kid!" Charlie had eased up to the helm.

"I got it, don't worry."

"Fine, I'll shut up and drive, you take care of Sage." They passed the Harts Landing sign and were finally underway.

Corey wanted to look for the hit-and-run woman again, but he couldn't abandon Charlie, even if the client had. Some guy had brought his 11-year-old up north for a fishing trip then ditched him this morning for a woman he'd just met.

"But dad, you said we'd go *together!*" Sage had said.

"Yvonne wants to try her luck with the slot machines at the reservation," his dad had said. "You can fish for both of us, Sage. We'll see Boldt Castle tomorrow." Then he had run off to a rented Highlander, where a pretty brunette waited.

Corey felt sorry for Sage, but at least it took his mind off other things.

"Sucks not to be with your dad, huh," Corey said as Charlie maneuvered the fishing boat towards the river channel.

The boy lifted his head. "How would you know, you prob'ly come out here with him..." he pouted and nodded towards Charlie, "all the time."

"That's my stepdad. I never knew my father."

Sage lost his scowl. "Never?"

"Nope. But I had my mom, growing up. Where's yours?"

"She's home. I see her all the time."

"Lucky."

"I guess." Sage squinted at the shoreline. His pout disappeared as his fingers plucked make-believe strings. "She's teaching me to play guitar." He looked at Corey. "What about yours? Don't you see *her?*"

"Not any longer." Corey gazed across the river. "She drowned last fall."

"Oh." Sage looked down and frowned.

"Forget it." Corey pointed outward. "Looks like a good day to fish." He turned on the radio; it was fixed on a news station.

> "...revision of state gambling rules could mean casinos in the area..."

He knew a lot of people went downriver to the Mohawk reservation—the "rez"— to gamble, but the new law could bring casinos right here to the islands. Lots of people didn't like the idea, said it would ruin the *aura* of the islands. Corey smiled at the idea of a slot machine pouring coins into his hand. *Dream on.* He turned the dial to the rock-and-roll station his mom had always listened to.

> "...due to the recent tremors recorded at the Eisenhower Locks, New York Power Authority cites concerns about the Moses Power Dam at Massena; inspections are also planned for the international bridges at Ogdensburg and Alexandria Bay..."

Corey imagined the bridge falling to the water with all its traffic. For once, he was glad he never got to go over it.

> "...and now it's back to the music."

"About time!" Corey and Sage slathered sunscreen on each other's backs and started singing along with a tune they'd both heard on TV. Instead of *"Dance*-ing With My-*seh*-elf," Corey announced he would be *"Lan*-din' me a *Mus*-kie!" Sage joined in on air guitar and added, "*Danc*e-ing with my *bah*-ass"—when he wasn't going hysterical over Corey's bouncing eyebrows.

The boat slowed and rounded Rocky Island as the song ended, and Charlie yelled something about finding bass near the island. "Time to quit yer foolin' and wet a line!"

Corey looked up at the old castle, with its huge round tower, on the island. "Private Property" signs and other warnings lined the shore, much of it rock cliffs that dropped straight down to the water. Construction noises came from the tower even though you couldn't see anything from the outside. He'd heard people were "discouraged" from hanging around here, but Charlie swore they had a right to fish here. The signs included the words, "For your safety," and something about falling rocks. Charlie said, "Baloney, Hart doesn't want you to see what he's doing—probably taking shortcuts on building code, paying off the inspectors so they'll look the other way."

The only other fishing boat was just to the north, near the Canadian border that ran through the river. Charlie scowled at it. "I've never had much luck over there." He stuck an ear bud in the side of his head; probably wanted to listen to his own radio.

All of a sudden, Corey got a whiff of something nasty. He shot a look at Sage, but the kid pinched his nose and asked, "Did you fart?"

"Me! I thought you did it." They both looked at Charlie, who was bobbing his head to some country tune no doubt. "Charlie, you could at least warn us—that's like rotten eggs!"

Charlie pulled his bud out. "They found a muskie with arsenic down by the dam. Almost *twenty-five* parts per million. Bet there's lots of industrial chemicals down there. Fishin' should be all right up here though." Corey hoped so.

Charlie sniffed a couple of times. "Wonder what that sulfur smell is." He turned to Corey. "Well, don't just sit there, why don't ya help Sage get baited up?"

Soon Corey and Sage each pulled out a small bass. A few minutes later, Corey threw his rod and ran to Sage. "Looks like you've got a monster! Maybe it's a giant muskie." Both boys pulled, but the fish wouldn't budge. That was no fish.

"You've got the bottom." Corey started stripping off his pants, the ones he'd worn yesterday. "I'll unsnag it, you can see pretty good under the water here."

"Yeah, it's clear because of the alien mussels," Charlie hollered. "They oughta tighten the shipping regulations."

Sage looked at Charlie like *he* was an alien. "*What* kind of muscles?"

"Zebra mussels," Corey said. "Used to be you couldn't see anything underwater, but then some foreign species hitched a ride on the ships from overseas; now the mussels eat the stuff that used to cloudy up the water."

"Yeah, divers think it's great." Charlie took a swig of fake beer. He never had alcohol when he worked. "But new species screw up the river."

"You sound like Sam now." Corey put on his goggles.

"Yeah, well she's got a good head on her. You should ask her out."

Right. *Corey* would have to be a new species for that to happen.

Corey had experience scuba diving—he'd learned with his mom—but he wouldn't need a tank for this. He lowered himself into the cool water, goose bumps popping up on his arms, and followed the fish line. It was caught on some weeds. He pulled it free and looked out to the north. Zebra mussels sure did a good job here, and he could see a long way. He noticed the sun's reflection off something underwater near the border. A...scuba tank? Wedged in some rocks? Maybe it fell off a boat.

I could use some air myself. Corey looked up towards the bright surface, but something drew his eye back to the tank. There was a diver! A hand appeared through a haze of bubbles, and it curved in salute before dragging the tank away.

Corey sucked in some water, forgetting where he was. He panicked and kicked hard for the surface, where he sputtered and gasped before his breathing returned to normal. Then he remembered thinking he saw the hit-and-run driver down there. His head throbbed. Was he nuts? Maybe *he* had some kind of poisoning!

STICKING UP

It took a half hour of sunlight and fresh air to wash away Corey's alarm.

He forgot about the diver as he and Sage laughed and sang, and Charlie joined them for lunch. Then Charlie went to the helm for something, and Sage was getting a drink when Corey heard his last name rolling over the water.

"Ahead, we'll see where the infamous Patrick Worder fell to his death, after abandoning the Patriots in 1813..."

Great. The Hart tour boat was fully loaded.

"The Worder family still continues..." Auger turned his head from the microphone, spotted Corey, and leaned over the side. "Oh, there's one *below* us." Corey felt his stomach seize up like it always did before that sinking sensation.

"What're you fishing for, Worder—family members?"

Last month, Corey would have hung his head and slunk away, deserting himself. But this time, something was different. A fire burned in his stomach, a fire like...self-respect.

Corey heard his own voice, deep, almost like a stranger's, but it wasn't his inner beast; it was more controlled. "You're just scared that all you have is a famous name, Hart," Corey roared as the tour boat glided past. "Or is that even your real name?"

Auger dropped his jaw and turned away.

"Wow!" Sage looked at Corey with big, admiring eyes. "That guy was mean. But you didn't back down." Nobody had ever looked at Corey that way. His chest swelled as he helped the younger boy ice down his fish.

Sage had a great time the rest of the afternoon, and some decent bass to show for it. Best of all, Corey had showed him how to stand up for himself.

Sage held out his catch as he ran to his dad. "Bet I had a better time than you!" He stopped as his father reached out.

"They're not yours. You broke your promise!"

"I know." His father slumped. "Yvonne deserted me for some scuba instructor. I won't do that to *you* again."

Corey couldn't help grinning as he wiped himself down with a towel and pulled on the fresh T-shirt he'd brought. He gathered gear and headed down the dock to dump it in the back of Charlie's truck. He was still smiling as he walked to his bike and waved to Charlie, whose radio was blaring as he drove out, and saw Sage play-boxing with his dad by the ice cream stand.

Corey watched his stepdad speed up the street then suddenly screech to a halt and back up. Charlie jumped out of the truck, ran to Sage, and grabbed his iced fish. *What the—* Was Charlie insane?

"You can't eat those!" Charlie hollered. "Bulletin came— they tracked the arsenic here. Bass has *forty* parts per million."

Charlie threw the package in his truck, saying he'd send it to the lab, apologized, and took off. Corey stared as the truck roared up the street. He didn't know too much about arsenic or math, but he knew that if ten parts was too much, *forty* parts was four times too much.

WAKE UP CALL

It had been his first day out on the river, and Corey didn't realize how tired he was until he sank onto the bench next to the bike rack. Through heavy lids, he noticed street workers putting out orange cones. Oh yeah, Privates Day was tomorrow. *Big deal.* There'd be costumed dorks drinking from tankards, and skirmishes between Redcoats and Privateers. Whole town would look two hundred years old. Corey's enemy would be celebrated and Corey's family would be smeared. And Corey was stuck here.

Sleep took him prisoner...

Corey was gripping the bars of a cage way too small for him. If he could just stretch to full size, and break it open... But the bars became arms and legs, and he was caught in their grasp. He struggled, panting and sweating, until he had to give up. When he relaxed, the arms became gentle, and a soothing voice hummed a lullaby. It was a voice from the river, where a hand rose and brushed away darkness to reveal a blue gem. The gem's sheen became a white light that shone in Corey's eyes. The hum droned noisily.

He scratched his face. He squinted through rays of setting sun to see the boat that had interrupted his dream. "Go away," he mumbled. "No, not you!" he said to the dream. But his mother had evaporated and left him alone on the bench.

Corey rubbed his eyes. He stretched and scowled at the diver who was now heading up the dock with a tank. *Thanks for waking me up.* Then his eyes opened wide as they followed the form of a woman slinking into the dive shop.

Corey sprinted across the parking lot, past the line of wave runners, up the front steps past the Privates Day Sales sign, and right into the shop. Seeing no one in the sale aisles, he flew to the rear hallway past the "Employees Only" sign. He halted just inside the office, dazed, when a muscular guy about twenty rushed in, leaving his customer outdoors.

"You don't belong in here." The guy gave a nasty frown.

"Who—I mean, where did she go, the woman?" Corey was still breathing hard.

The guy narrowed his eyes and glanced side to side. "I didn't see any woman." He latched onto Corey's shoulder and ushered him to the front. "Maybe she flew off to Never Never Land. Go find her there." He gave Corey a push out the door.

COMPUTING

Sam stared at the spreadsheet with her mouth open. The income from scuba tank rentals must be off—by a few decimals!

Twenty minutes ago she'd found the key to the B&B office. She wasn't supposed to use the computer in here, but Sam's laptop had died, and she'd been desperate to finish research for her RiverGuard report. Some experts believed hydro-fracking for natural gas could cause seismic activity because it pumped liquids into the ground. The resulting pressure could breach faults in the ground and cause groundwater contamination. But that couldn't happen here, could it? The river geology was all wrong for the presence of natural gas.

Then she'd learned that it wasn't only hydro-fracking that injected chemicals into the ground. There were other drilling operations that pumped chemicals down to force materials *up*. The injected chemicals could even release natural substances that lay underground—and make them lethal.

Like arsenic.

Sam had learned the location of the epicenter of the last two earthquakes, and it was pretty close. But there was nothing fishy going on nearby...was there? An image of an island with a castle tower flashed through her mind. But that was only a renovation project.

She had printed out the information, and then, in her excitement to find further answers, Sam had accidentally double-clicked on the spreadsheets showing property sales and scuba tank income.

"Sam?" Randy's voice came from the parking lot.

Her hand jerked. She closed the program, shut down the computer, and grabbed the printout.

Outside the office, she tucked the key into her palm as Randy turned the corner. His dark eyes shifted from her to the door.

"Don't even think about going in there. Took me all morning to get the paperwork straightened out, and I have to enter my QuickBiz—"

"Oh—I was just...um, knocking to see if you guys were in there."

"Anyway, listen. Me and Johnny are both busy tonight, I've got a business workshop and Johnny has to do inventory downtown. Can you stick around and check the Trevors in? They're coming after dinner."

"Sh-sure—I'll take care of them." In her head, rows and columns of names and figures were flashing and spinning then jerking to periodic stops like the fruit on a slot machine. Nothing matched any idea that made sense.

She followed Randy's stare through the back door and was surprised to see Johnny standing with a police woman by a car in the lot. It was a black Mustang.

"I only know what I saw," Johnny was saying. "I left it parked on the street yesterday, and when I came back out, it was gone. But now it has reappeared."

The police had been dusting the car for prints and questioning people, but no one had seen the hit-and-run driver. And so far, the cops hadn't found any prints.

Johnny shook hands with the officer, who flipped her notebook closed. "Well, all we know is the woman has short dark hair and brown eyes and is probably around five foot five. One good thing, she left the car behind—even if she didn't leave any prints."

Johnny walked towards the door, muttering, "Thank god," as Sam pictured a familiar short-haired, brown-eyed face. Sam opened her mouth to speak but stopped when Johnny gave her a scowl and a slight shake of the head.

WHAT A DIVE SHOP

Corey stumbled down the steps of the dive shop as the sales guy turned back to his customers, but Corey knew the woman had gone in. And no one had left. He had to see where she went.

The sales guy had reached the other side of the shop lawn, and his customers were asking about the dive sites just outside the bay—where the sunken *Patriot* and *Spitflame* lay. Corey looked back up at the door. It dared him to enter. *It's now or never.* Corey grabbed the rail and vaulted back up the six steps, two at a time, keeping his eye on the sales guy.

Bang!

Corey froze, crouching at the front door. He'd knocked over the sales sign, which slid down the stairs. He held his breath as the shop guy started to turn Corey's way—but the customer grabbed him and shoved a pamphlet in his face.

Corey let his breath out and crept through the front entrance, careful not to let the screen door slam. He could feel his sweat gluing his T-shirt to his back as he ran, quiet as possible, to the rear hallway. There, down past the office was another door. He opened it and saw lighted stairs leading down to the basement. *She must be down there.* As he crept down, he felt cooler, and he smelled that stale smell you get in old basements. Near the bottom, he noticed pipes running along the edges of the ceiling. Then he scraped his elbow on the rough stacked-stone foundation. He rubbed it as he stepped onto a cement floor holding boxes of inventory: swimsuits, goggles, wetsuits, skimboards... He worked his way around them, swinging his head back and forth.

But he found nothing unusual until he moved around a stack of unmarked boxes. Then he saw him, face-to-face: a tall, burly man with an eye patch wielding a nasty looking blade. Corey's blood ran cold—until he realized it was only a cardboard cutout of a pirate wearing a pair of the board shorts on sale. Corey let his heart settle down; there was nothing here except storage for inventory, plus some repair and maintenance items at a workbench: hammers, wrenches, nails, pieces of wire...

A few shelves along the back wall held scuba tanks, hoses, and regulators. Corey knew that a *first stage regulator,* attached directly to a tank, was used to lower the pressure of air flowing from the tank. The *second stage regulator* would attach to the first stage by a hose and had a mouthpiece for the diver; it supplied just the right air pressure for breathing. Here was a generator, welding machine, pipe threader; the place was ventilated—*must be for tank maintenance.*

Corey was about to turn around when he noticed a part of the wall that stuck out. It was a small, hinged door, hard to see because it looked like the wall. Corey pulled it carefully to reveal a dark tunnel with a soft glow at the other end. He grabbed a flashlight from the bench by the door and stepped inside, closing the door behind him. *Never know when that jerk might come down here.*

He was halfway down the narrow space, wondering why the place had a secret tunnel when he noticed a panel, slightly ajar; it hid a cabinet with several scuba tanks, and one seemed to be cut in half. Then a rare event occurred: Corey flashed on a history lesson—about the Underground Railroad, one of the few lessons he found interesting. On their way to Canada, slaves who escaped the South stayed with people friendly to their cause. Maybe this was one of the old buildings that had concealed slaves! Maybe they had used the tunnel and hid in the wall cutout that now held a cabinet.

There was no hit-and-run driver hiding here, so Corey kept going. At the end of the tunnel, he stopped at a partially opened door and nudged it open.

Corey's heart raced as he crept through another basement room, this one holding crates of glass, shelves, spools of soft metal, and a big table with pieces of colored glass, before he got to the stairs. *Stairs to what?*

He slowly crept upward, testing each step for creaks before committing his weight. At the top was a closed door. He pressed his ear to it as he held his breath. A muffled voice leaked through the wood panel: "And how would you like to pay for that?" Then, in a few moments, a tinkling sound and a door closing. *Must be the art gallery shop.* Corey pushed gently on the door. No give. He looked under the knob to see an old-style keyhole, one for a skeleton key. The hit-and-run woman must have locked it behind her then went out the gallery door to the street. She could be anywhere in town now!

Corey slumped back down the stairs. He had missed his chance.

THE REAL THING

Corey started to walk back through the basement, past the shelves of art supplies. He was no longer in a hurry, and he didn't look forward to facing the guy in the dive shop. He looked around at the supplies. Channeled lead for making stained glass designs, like on Corey's sailboat window. Spare lampworking equipment, solder, tools. Boxes and boxes of ...what was it? He read the label: *Whiting.* There was an open bag of the stuff on the workbench. He found a how-to book that said whiting was for making putty and cleaning leaded windows. The white powder in the picture looked just like this bag of stuff. He dabbed a finger in it, sniffed it, and touched it to his mouth. It was like chalk. Judging from all the boxes here, they must need to make a lot of putty!

He sauntered back through the tunnel, but he heard the floor creaking upstairs. Maybe if he waited a few minutes, the guy would leave the shop again. Corey checked out the scuba tanks in the cabinet in the secret tunnel. Next to the tank that was cut in two, he noticed some kind of residue on the shelf, like white powder. Was that whiting, too? The tank parts looked like they were threaded so they could be screwed together; the seam would be hidden under the edge of the boot, the rubber protector at the base of the tank. *Why?*

He stuck his finger in the powder and held it to his nose to make sure it was the same whiting stuff.

A loud *creak* made him jump, jamming his finger into his mouth. He froze for a moment but heard no more sound. He relaxed. Must be the floor of the office above.

Now his mouth tingled and his lips were numb. This powder was *not* whiting. He tried to remember what he'd seen on some TV show about a white powder that had this effect. *Cocaine?* Then it hit him. The dive shop owner was *smuggling* the powder!

Uh-oh. Corey had seen a few movies; he knew what drug dealers did to people who got in their way. He'd be in it deep if he was caught in here.

He heard creaks again; this time definitely from the stairs. Was the drug dealer coming? Corey's head buzzed, and he was breathing fast. His eyes darted around. If he folded up, he could just fit under that low cabinet shelf. He pulled the panel in to hide himself just as someone cracked the tunnel door open. His heart pounded...what if they pulled the panel open?

Then a shout fell from upstairs: "I need authorization for this check!"

Corey heard the tunnel door close and then someone dashing up the stairs.

He fell out onto the tunnel floor. Now what? He couldn't go back up to the dive shop, but if he stayed down here, the guy would come back, find Corey and... He glanced around desperately until something by the cabinet caught his notice— the skeleton of a dead rat. A skeleton might be all that was left of *Corey* pretty soon. He was trembling.

Wait. Skeleton? He took a breath, hauled his body off the floor, and slipped out the secret door into the dive shop basement. Corey heard the top stair creak as his eyes shifted back and forth at the workbench. The guy was coming down again! Corey grabbed a piece of wire and ducked back in the tunnel, closing the door quietly as he heard the lower step creak. Breathing fast, Corey retreated through the tunnel as steps approached the door behind him. He hurried through the gallery supply room door and shut it as the guy started through the tunnel. Was he coming for a package of "whiting"? Corey tiptoed up the glass gallery stairs.

His hand shook as he stuck the wire into the skeleton keyhole. The basement door was opening! Corey forced his mind to clear. He had to let instinct take over. He probed the lock several times with the wire; it gave way just as the guy got to the shelves with boxes. If he looked up...he'd see Corey.

There was no time to listen through the door. Corey opened it, stepped inside the shop, and shut the door. The clerk was up by the front window, but she turned back. Corey had to duck and crawl on all fours along the display case that separated them. He made it to the front door, which betrayed him with a tinkle as he dashed out, but he never looked back.

ROUGH DETOUR

He'd made it! Corey ran back around the shops to the bike rack by the docks. He caught his breath as he put the key in the bike lock but thought *Who needs a key?* He'd been awesome at the glass shop.

Wait 'til Johnny heard what his dive shop boss was up to. Johnny would quit working there for sure. For now, Corey still wanted to find that hit-and-run woman. He had no idea who she was or where she came from. Was she in on the smuggling? He touched his lips, and they tingled with the memory of the powder. He'd read a story once about how a kid overdosed. Corey hoped *he* didn't get enough to have a bad reaction.

By the time Sam answered her phone, Corey was focused. "I saw her," he said as he wheeled his bike out of the lot. "And I need to talk to Johnny."

Sam was hard to hear. "Well, I can't talk, I'm in the library. And Johnny's not home." Then she spoke even lower. "But I can tell you this...that Mustang was *stolen*. I—I guess I heard it on the news."

So there was no connection between Mrs. Hart and the driver of the car. Corey was glad. He thought Auger's grandmother was the only Hart who *had* a heart. But he still had to find that driver. She had run over Buddy, she had worn Mom's sapphire—maybe she'd seen Mom.

"Come on, this is important, can't you help me?"

"I have to finish this report then I have to get some guests settled. You can come over later tonight."

Corey sighed and hung up. He swung his leg over the bike and pedaled hard, his head twisting back and forth at each intersection. *You never know where she might turn up.* He looked everywhere except where he was going. He didn't see the dog limping on Pine Street until he was almost on top of it, and he swerved into the ditch without thinking.

"Urg-gugg—" His teeth rattled, the bike jolted, and he felt like he'd been punched in the crotch. He thought he'd felt something come off the bike, but nothing was missing.

Corey hoisted the bike up and wheeled it, hunched in pain. He was about to limp across Winford Street when he saw a police car coming. He waited for it to pass, but instead the cop pulled up next to him.

"Bad news, Son."

FRAMED

Corey was shocked.

Charlie *arrested*–for possession of cocaine? The cops said they had found it on the *Stowe Aweigh*.

And what was just as bad, they had a warrant to search Corey and his bike. Corey nearly doubled over when the cop pressed near his groin, still tender from getting mashed on the bike.

The other cop checked under the bike seat. He even took it apart while the first one guarded Corey.

He fumed. *That woman is a demon.* Did she see Corey following her? Did she plant the white stuff to get rid of him? Why would she plant it on Charlie's boat? Charlie couldn't be involved with illegal drugs...could he? Maybe the beer just didn't do it for him anymore.

Now the other cop was talking on his radio; Corey heard him say something about the "the kid" being a "dead end."

"Of course I don't know anything about it!" Charlie had phoned Corey from the court, where he was being arraigned. "I may have a couple of beers now and then, but I'd never touch that stuff."

Corey was quiet.

"Well this is a disaster. I won't be taking anybody fishing, and neither will you–the boat's impounded." Charlie sighed. "You just gotta do your best. Use the cash in the cupboard for food. Check my calendar, make cancellations." He paused. "I just don't understand how that stuff could've got on the *Stowe Aweigh*. Who would've done it?"

Corey decided to explain about the hit-and-run woman—
after all, she was real, she had caused an accident. He
described her and told Charlie how he had followed her. He
was shocked to hear Charlie admit with a whisper: "I've seen
her myself."

9 CAPTURED IMAGE

Corey pounded up the front stairs of The Mainsail. He thought Sam would be free by now, but he could hear her through the screen, saying, "Follow me, I'll show you up to your room..."

Great. She'd be another fifteen minutes giving the spiel. He'd wait out on the back patio. He picked up his bike and walked it through the hedges and trees. He dumped it behind a bush and burst into the opening at the foot of the lower back deck, where he collided with someone. He backed up and got his balance just as the woman did. He began to apologize as she darted past him.

"Wait! I didn't mean to..."

She glanced back long enough for him to recognize the last person he expected to see.

"*You!*"

Her eyes betrayed panic as she snapped her head forward and kept running.

"You ran over Buddy!" Corey growled, running after her. "Or—were you trying to kill *me*?"

She never slowed as she shouted, "No!" over her shoulder. "I never ran over a *person!*" She headed for the scenic walkway behind the B&B.

"*Liar!*" he bellowed. "Why did you steal that Mustang?" Then he had an idea. He dashed through the brush to shortcut his way to the walk ahead of her. He skidded to a halt and pulled out the phone. Just as she rounded the corner and turned his way, he snapped her picture.

"The cops will be interested in this!" His voice shook with anger as he waved his phone. Then she slowed down. She hesitated. She sank to a slatted bench.

She held her head and moaned, "Please don't turn me in."

"You put Buddy in a coma!" Corey rushed to the bench.

"What? I would *never* leave if I hit someone!" Her brown eyes were wide. "I—I saw you there with...with your gear." Her eyes were questioning, and she appeared unsure.

Her look of innocence stopped him in his tracks. *Don't get drawn in.* "That wasn't my 'gear,' that was Buddy, and you put him in the hospital."

"No." She shook her head slowly. Then she covered her face and broke down in sobs. "How could I...? I deserve to go to jail. But I'd never get out, with my horrible record."

Corey wasn't sure what to do. Her sobs were stifling his rage: he had never figured out how to deal with tears. Now the sobs were dwindling to whimpers.

He shook his finger. "If you're in the habit of running over people, you *should* be put away."

She started sobbing again.

He sighed and bit his lip. "So, um...what else did you do?"

She stared at her lap, and Corey looked back in time to see her hand float to her brow and brush the side of her face.

Mom? He blinked. His mind was playing tricks again. He cursed himself as he tore his eyes away. *This woman is not my mother.*

She repeated his question. "'What else did I do?'" Now he was even hearing Mom's voice, though gravelly. He had to get over this craziness.

"That's the problem." She threw her hands skyward. "I only know what my brother tells me."

"Huh?" Corey turned back.

"I need to do some...investigating."

"That's your job?" Did she work for the government?

"Lost identity..."

"Identity theft?" Maybe she dealt with computer crimes. He sat on the bench as the river held his gaze with its silver tongues lapping up rocky shores.

"No." She was now under control. "I don't believe I'm telling you this." The river had carried her gaze seaward too. "But somehow I trust you." She looked back at his face.

He fought to keep his eyes on the water.

"It's *my* identity I'm looking for," she whispered. "I can't remember who I am."

He glanced at her face.

"That river holds my secrets." She gave it a nod. "But in my dreams," she whispered, "I see *you*."

Corey's skin prickled. His eyes followed the river to the western horizon, where an explosion of colors froze.

"I have no idea where I came from, before I was pulled out of that river..."

Corey stopped breathing.

"...last September."

The sky colors started to run. Corey's head swiveled slowly to meet her eyes, only inches from his own.

"My face had to be reconstructed."

Corey was reeling; a familiar face was emerging from behind the unfamiliar nose. "B-but you have brown eyes."

She turned her head away and dipped it towards the sunset, her hands touching each eye. Her fingers had shiny drops. *Oh please don't cry again.* He looked away. He couldn't take much more of this.

But something made him look back. Those drops on her hands. They were *rounded plastic.*

When she looked back up at Corey, he was pierced to the heart...by eyes of sapphire blue.

I KNOW YOU!

Corey forgot to breathe. He lost himself in those eyes, blue magnets that trumped the river's pull. He had no idea how long he sat there without moving.

When words came, they came strong. They came from something growing deep inside. "*I* know who you are." He touched her face. "Mom."

She stared.

"I am Corey—your *son*? You're *Mom*...Peg Stowe."

He didn't care about the broad forehead and the rounded nose—they meant nothing. His mother lived in those eyes.

Corey felt a tremble that became the shake of a delirious laugh. He sprang off the bench and raced to the tree line above the river. He stopped. Somehow, the scenery had changed. The old river was a liar that showed castles upside down and islands gliding backwards against stationary ships. But now he could see right through to solid earth. He turned back to the woman—the woman who had given him life. He walked to the bench and sat down.

"Mom, it's really you." His voice cracked as he leaned towards her. Then he stiffened, and something entirely different came out: "Why didn't you come and find me?" He jumped to his feet and spread his hands palms up. "How could you just leave me...for six *months*?"

She searched his face as tears welled up in her eyes. He dropped his hands. Now he felt terrible—this was his mom— but someone else too, someone who had no memory of him.

Who knew what she'd been through? He dropped to the seat again. "I—I guess you couldn't help it."

He pulled out his wallet and flipped it open. She looked at the earlier picture of herself with hungry eyes as she touched her cheek and then her forehead. "Jack said I would go to prison if anyone recognized me."

"I don't know who *Jack* is..." Corey jumped up again. "But—you're my mom." He paced back and forth a couple of times, still trying to calm his warring emotions. He jerked to a stop again. She probably couldn't answer his questions, but he had to ask.

"Where have you *been* since September—did you really fall in the river?—but how'd you get out? Why didn't you come find me?" He choked out the last words and sat back down.

He took a breath and asked, quieter, "What *happened* to you?" All she could do was shake her head. How could he make her remember him? He'd take her to the house. Show her to Charlie. Have her get one of those maternity tests! His thoughts were a jumble. He got up and walked again. His nerves were wires, his system electrified, with no outlet.

Then he plugged into an idea.

He sat down next to her and took something from his shirt. He held it out in the palm of his hand. Her eyes lost the dazed look and locked on the object, never wavering from it, as she reached into her own pocket and pulled out its mate. She held it in her hand next to Corey's.

The two blue stones, reunited, shone back.

As his mother looked from the sapphires and their topaz partners, to Corey, her eyes shone to match the gems. She nodded. "My son."

He leaned into her, and she folded him in her arms. For now, anger and euphoria reconciled and poured out of Corey in a mixture of tears and nonsense syllables. The sun almost touched the skyline before Corey gathered himself to face a whole new universe: Mom had come back from the dead! But Corey's new world still contained a lot of questions, and his mom couldn't give him the answers.

FILLING THE BLANKS

"I don't know what to ask first." Peg Stowe settled onto a fallen pine tree trunk. She was trying to stop thinking of herself as Marie. She, *Peg*, and Corey—her *son*—had left the scenic walkway for more privacy. Now they watched from the trees as the sun melted into the horizon.

"Maybe you can tell me what happened just before— before I ended up, you know...in the river?" Even if Peg didn't have her memory, she felt it in her bones that this boy was her own flesh and blood. Even at the arena she'd known he was *someone*. But fear had cloaked her instincts. Jack said she'd go to prison and so she'd turned her feelings towards her son into avoidance. Now, seeing the gemstones together had triggered something, and they had provided a conduit, a channel, for connection.

Her son was educating her.

"Before you married Charlie, you were Margaret Worder. And everyone in town thought our ancestor was a *deserter*." Then he explained that this *Patrick* had turned out to be a *Patrice*. Corey and his friend had done some detective work of their own.

Peg's past life sounded like fiction to her. She'd been locked up first by her father, then by the state? "Maybe *that's* why I'm so afraid of jail."

"But you straightened out. You took care of me, read bedtime stories—" Corey thought of something. "Where are you staying? And what were you doing at The Mainsail?"

Finally, questions she could answer.

"I have a small place upriver, on Wellesley Island—Jack says I've had it for years." She frowned. "But I work late a lot—so I keep a small room at that Bed and Breakfast."

Corey looked blank then suddenly pounded his forehead with his palm. "When I slept over at The Mainsail...*you* were the one singing in the room next to me!"

She did have trouble sleeping and sometimes found herself humming in the night.

He was shaking his head. "You were only—a few feet away from me."

He scratched loose dirt with a stick before blurting, "So you've probably seen Sam." He looked at her sideways. "And she's seen you?"

"Sam...Samantha? I gave her a ride the day I saw you on the ice."

He looked astonished. "She did say a guest brought her that day. So Sam knows you? I wonder if she...no, she would've told me." Peg couldn't tell whether Corey was angry or amused. Samantha must be his friend.

Peg was caught off guard by his next question.

"What do you do for work?"

"I ah...work with my brother. I dive." She looked downriver, to the northeast. "I deliver scuba tanks. Replace them, I mean."

He might as well know it all. She turned to face him. "Look, what I do is illegal." Her protective shell was dissolving, but it felt good. She'd been trying to hide an identity she didn't even remember, but her son was *real*.

"I don't feel good about the work." She swallowed. "We're using the tanks for smuggling."

Her son was touching his lip. "The white powder... I found it in the basement." He told her about following her into the dive shop and what he had seen.

"I should have locked that door to the tunnel. Jack would have a fit." She explained how the tanks had a special compartment for the bags of the powder, but there was enough room for air to fool inspectors.

WANTED

Corey couldn't tell Charlie, not yet. Corey's world had changed, and he needed to get things straight before bringing his stepdad into it. Plus Mom didn't remember him. She needed more time, too.

Corey followed his mother through the bushes back to The Mainsail to get his bike. He couldn't wait to see Sam's face when he told her that "Marie" was his mom! As they got closer, he could hear Sam's voice. They were just about to break out of the woods to the parking lot when his mom gasped. She stood as stiff as the birch tree Corey grabbed to keep from running into her. Through the branches, Corey saw a patrol car. The back of a uniform hid most of Sam. The officer was holding out something.

"Sort of reminds me of Marie," Sam was telling the guy.

Corey looked at his mother. She was trembling like the leaves of the shrubs.

"And this boy?" the cop said, showing another picture.

"Corey?" Sam said then clapped her hand over her mouth. She let her hand go and said, "I just talked to him a couple hours ago. Is...is he in trouble?"

Corey stood beside his mother, holding her tightly around the shoulder. He could see his bike from where he stood. The cop wouldn't be able to see it unless he turned his head about thirty degrees. Corey held his breath.

"He lives on Grant Street," Sam was saying.

What? Why was she ratting him out? *Calm down.* The police already knew where he lived. The officer got back in his car, and Corey breathed. But then Sam got in the B&B van and drove away too.

They couldn't afford to be seen. Corey and his mom couldn't go to his house or her room; the cops probably had an eye on both places.

It would be dark soon, but it would be a warm night.

****

Peg stared at the back of the B&B. Only a few moments ago she had found her son and even envisioned life with a family. But that wasn't in the cards. *Face it, you're trapped.* She couldn't just take up where she'd left off. Even if Jack had lied about her being "wanted," it didn't matter. She was guilty *now*. She not only smuggled cocaine—she had run over a man.

Now the police were hot on her trail.

SIGNATURE MATCH

Corey watched his mother tapping her head as she looked over the cliff. "Something's coming back, but—I just don't know!"

She's too close. "Stay back by the guardrail." Corey realized she was standing near *that* spot, and he couldn't help thinking how he'd almost slid off to his own end.

"I've never been up here before—I mean, that I remember. Anyway, I don't go many places."

It was Corey's idea to bring her to the Point, the last place she'd been *herself.* They had walked up the pathway through the trees, careful to avoid meeting anybody. He thought maybe the scene where she had fallen to the river would make something click. *But it's not working.*

They sat with their backs to the guardrail, facing the river. Hidden by tall weeds, they relaxed and talked as the red streaks near the western horizon dissolved into a dome of star-studded black velvet.

Corey stretched out and laid his head on Mom's lap. He looked up at her sleepily through his dark strands.

"My son." Her gaze was fixed on his. He felt her stroke his hair as his eyes closed, and he heard her whisper, "I know there's a lot I don't remember, but I know you are the boy in my dreams."

When Corey opened his eyes again, the east glowed yellow and the air held a chill. He tried to rub out the creases on his cheek where he'd crushed the grass.

Mom was standing, looking at the back side of the museum.

"I have a feeling about this place. I need to go inside."

"Okay, no one should be around for a couple hours." He stood up and stretched.

They went in the back window, and his mom made her way to the office upstairs. She glanced at the floor then walked out the sliding door to the deck.

"This seems familiar," she said. Then he saw her eyes lock on the railing, and she started shaking. She took gulps of air and made gasping noises.

"Okay, this is a bad idea." Corey grabbed his mother by the arm. Who knew how the scene would affect her? After all, she'd jumped right into the current the last time she was here. He was not going to take a chance on losing her again.

"I'm all right." She pulled away. But Corey stayed very close to her.

She took a long breath. "*Let go of fear.*" Corey shadowed her as she moved closer to the rail. She closed her eyes and breathed heavily.

"Something fell."

"Uh...er—" Corey couldn't say it out loud. *You are the one that fell.*

"Something from my hand." She made a sudden grab for the rail, like she was possessed by a demon. Corey grabbed his mother. *Oh god, she's freaking out...*

Then she opened her eyes, pulled away again, and ran down the steps to the bushes.

"That's where it would have landed. It was a piece of gold-colored metal..."

"*Brass?*" She'd had that old buckle up here?

Corey joined her, and for twenty-five minutes they searched the weeds and bushes. Mom stopped first.

"Let's take a break, I'm thirsty."

She rested in the upstairs office while Corey went to get her a drink. When he returned, a drawer from the file cabinet blocked his way. Mom was sitting on the floor with dozens of papers and pamphlets around her. She had been reading the museum literature about the town legend. But it was something else she waved at him.

"Didn't you say this was my name?" She held a form with a signature at the bottom.

"Hey, that's the loan agreement for Patrick's cutlass—You signed it last summer so the museum could display it."

Mom took a pen and wrote her name. They both looked from one signature to the other.

"Your handwriting's still the same." Corey thought of something. *Maybe it's time for more shock therapy.* He took out his wallet.

"You...signed this, too." His eyes darted from the note to her face. Then he stared at the signature, waiting as Mom read the suicide note. She was silent for a minute.

"I—I just can't believe I wrote such a thing." She looked sadly at Corey. "I'm so sorry for what you and—*Charlie*—must have gone through."

Corey didn't know what to say. His hair hid his face, and he shuffled papers to give his hands something to do. His eyes followed the curves of the signatures, one on top of the other. Then they caught his attention for real. They were the same.

"*Exactly* the same!"

He overlapped the two papers—the permission paper and the suicide note—and held them up to the light. Mom was looking at him curiously. One signature covered the other precisely.

"Nobody writes their name the same way twice. Not *exactly.*"

"Unless they...trace?" Mom stared at the paper.

Corey studied the note. The signature had a kind of stiff look. *Doesn't flow.*

"Do you realize—" Corey shouted then lowered his voice. "What this means? Someone else wrote that note. You did *not* kill yourself! Or try to."

All this time, he had been wrong about his mother deserting him! He pulled her up off the floor, threw his arms around her and twirled with her until they knocked against the drawer, which closed with a *wham*. They froze for a second and then laughed and fell against the cabinet.

"I just knew I could never have abandoned you." She gave him a smile Corey hadn't seen in months.

Corey wrapped his arms around his mother, and he noticed something new. The lead weight in his stomach—his constant companion for nearly nine months—was evaporating. Because his mother had *not* deserted him. The anger, confusion, and resentment that caused the weight were based on a lie. Now those feelings were melting away. She was still the Mom Corey remembered, and he felt like he was floating.

For now, Corey could ignore the problems that were about to take the place of the lead weight. He was not ready to voice the questions: Who made Mom disappear? And why? Was there a killer after her—after them *both*?

AUGER MEETS DIRK

Auger thought his dad must have left it—the folder he found on his bed. It contained letters from Dirk Hart, who had launched the family business with booty from Warren's raids on British ships. The letters were addressed to Dirk's grandson, Gregory Hart.

These records had been guarded for nearly a century and a half—but were shared only with those who "possessed the character and cleverness to promote and capitalize on the family name." Auger automatically covered the letter when he thought of Gran and how she felt about "family honor."

Dad had said he wanted to include Auger in his plans from now on, and he mentioned the casino resort on Rocky

Island. And yesterday, Dad had revealed other things, distasteful things Auger did not want to think about.

He looked at the first letter.

Feb. 1855

My Dearest Gregory:

You have now reached the age to receive a most precious inheritance.

I have observed and tested you enough to know you are the one to be entrusted with the family "jewels"—the secrets of the Hart power and wealth. You have learned to lead, and you have the gift of persuasion. You display confidence and choose your words well.

You and I are of one mind. Each of us "gatekeepers" must cultivate like-minded family members, in the generations to come. I know you will guard these jewels of information and pass them on with care.

The folder also contained log entries from earlier times, written by Dirk...*Poole?*

LOG OF A "HART"

August 1812

My arts are wasted on the streets of London, where pockets have already been picked by the wars. My prospects should improve with acceptance into the Royal Navy. I will bide my time until I find an opportunity to better my position.

Other entries made it clear that Dirk had avoided fighting in the British war with Napoleon by talking his way onto a ship bound for North America.

March 1813

After proving myself a trustworthy member of the Royal
Navy, I have gotten myself assigned to escort a supply ship,
bound for Upper Canada, carrying the largest chest of wealth
to ascend the St. Lawrence! Now I must play my cards right.
When the goods are transferred, upriver of Montreal, I will
prepare to "cut the deck."

April 1813

I have managed to separate the "Queen's Bounty" from her
convoy by persuading the crew to take a shortcut among the
islands. I was about to eliminate the crew, sink the chest, and
claim it had been pirated by scoundrels, when a band of
"patriots" appeared. I had to convince their crew that I, like
they, had been impressed by the British from an American
ship and was one of them. Whereupon, Captain Warren Hart
welcomed me into the *Patriot* crew.

We have hidden the chest in the island of the rocks, in a cave
at the northeast end. It should be a simple matter to steal a
boat, retrieve the chest, and make my way back to Montreal.

May 1813

The chest in the cave has been moved. I suspect the first mate,
Worder, persuaded the captain to relocate it. I must set about
gaining Hart's complete trust.

May 1813

I have convinced the captain that this "poor orphan" needs
an anchor, and the guidance of an older man. I have
permission to call him "Father" and no one challenges my
authenticity. I am allowed a bunk in the outbuilding at Hart's

and Worder's property, where I've discovered a young mute woman is a guest in their cabin. She doesn't say a word. Unfortunately, Hart surprised me as I was about to have my way with her. I convinced the fool that she had run to my protective embrace after imagining she saw a bloodthirsty Redcoat.

I have now learned of the existence of many troves of hidden treasure gained from privateering raids. Their locations are well guarded secrets and might best be acquired by "inheritance." I will bide my time. "Father" plans to use his wealth to enhance the war efforts...but if he should fail to survive, no one will question the decisions of his heir.

June 1813

The first mate has grown sluggish; "he" has also grown heavier. The other crew members are blind to the truth that becomes more obvious to me each day.

My opportunity will soon arrive, and I will build me an empire in this new land...

Auger felt sick. Dirk was... *a fraud?* Some London pickpocket just out to steal whatever he could—a *pirate? No way!* Auger stacked the pages neatly and laid them down. He looked away; he tapped his foot. *Patrick* was supposed to be the no-good pirate, not *Dirk.*

Auger's family was looked up to. Not only because of Warren's sacrifice, but because it was thought that his son Dirk had also fought to save the town. Auger had always been proud of his heritage. The family provided employment and shared the pride of Hart's Landing with the descendants of the Patriot crew.

But this document was saying that Dirk had *manufactured* the legend—and wasn't even a *Hart!*

Someone must be playing a joke. Who could have gotten inside the house to plant these papers? Gran was always telling Auger's friends to "go right on up" when they came to visit. Would she even notice who it was? A voice in his head insisted: *That Worder kid is behind this.* Auger really wanted to think so. But he couldn't ignore the other voice: *The dork can barely read. How could he create an elaborate hoax?*

SAM'S CONNECTIONS

Sam woke up feeling nervous—and guilty. *Nervous* because of the quakes and fish poisoning. Could they be related? And because that cop had been asking about Corey and showed the picture of a woman that looked sort of like Corey and sort of like Marie. Plus, Corey hadn't shown up last night after all that whining. And she felt guilty because she hadn't told Corey everything—about a possible connection with Harts, plus the spreadsheet figures. What did it all mean?

The mysterious island flashed in her mind again. It was rumored to belong to the Harts. And Sam wanted to know if there really was a connection to the Harts. She wasn't ready to confront Johnny, but how could she find out more?

UNEXPECTED DATE

Auger was absently pulling another paper, a news clipping, from the folder when his phone rang. He answered while he stared at Grandpa's picture. The article about his grandfather's accident said a woman had died too.

But the female voice on the phone got his attention; it was nothing new to have girls call him, but they would usually give their name. This one was a mystery girl. She had a voice that seemed familiar, but it was low. She intrigued him, and a date could take his mind off...things.

"Let's meet at the Juice Tap at one o'cl—"

"No. Library. And make it eleven this morning."

The girl hung up. Auger stared at the phone, aware that another guy might be put off, but his interest was aroused. His mother had always marveled that Auger could immediately switch focus. But Auger had learned it from his dad: *focus on the business at hand.*

Auger looked at the papers, frowned, and stuffed them back in the folder. He took it to his desk to lock away, out of sight, but the article fell out onto the floor. He kept trying to slide it back in the folder, but it had a mind of its own, and he noticed the name of the passenger, the other accident victim: "Ms. Juanita Santos." Why was she in the car? Had Grandpa left Grandma and Dad for that woman? Was that why they used Gran's birth name, *Hart*, instead of *Downes*? Maybe Fred Hart had been left by both his father and his first wife. Was it a pattern?

Auger hoped his Dad knew what he was doing when he married Rita.

He glimpsed the last line of the article before shoving it into the folder: "Juanita Santos is survived by a daughter, Margarita." Auger grabbed the folder. He'd have to ask Dad about this.

MARGARITA'S REVENGE

Rita Hart wasn't happy about it, but she would have to motor out by the border, supposedly to make a drop. She went to get the tanks from the tunnel—a place where she had been spending altogether too much time, cutting, reaming metal to reduce the weight, measuring, and packing. Soon, she would be able to quit spending her time taking chances on getting caught.

She found the special tanks, but instead of taking two of these, she hid them. Now Jack would think she'd loaded them as planned. His assignment would have put her in a difficult position. *But he's the one who'll get a surprise.*

As Fred Hart's wife, Rita appeared to have everything. But she wanted more. She wanted justice.

Working for the Harts had gotten her mother killed when Rita was a teenager. Sure, Rita had acted out afterwards. It was bad enough losing the only parent she'd ever known. But to be accused of causing the accident! After getting her head straight, it had dawned on Rita that if *she* had been accused of tampering with the car, there must've been evidence that *someone* did. She wanted a clearer picture of the past, even if it meant revealing her own. It was time to take control.

Fred told Rita she would be Queen of Harts Landing on Privateers Day. Was he trying to keep her occupied? Well, she would be Queen. Just not in the parade.

Rita found two clean tanks—*innocent* tanks—and loaded them onto a caddy.

M.A. NOBLE

10 INCOGNITO

Peg felt perfectly natural with Corey snuggled against her shoulder as they sat on the office floor. Yesterday, she'd had no clue she even had a son!

Then he startled her by jerking his head towards the clock. "We have to go home...Howler will be hungry!" He jumped to his feet.

It was risky enough for "Marie" to be seen by the police, but at least cops could be avoided. How could they avoid an enemy they didn't recognize? Yes, there must be an enemy; someone had pushed her into the river—they wrote a fake note to cover it, didn't they? It couldn't be Jack. He wouldn't try to kill her and then *save* her would he?

"We have to leave; people will be coming to work," her son said. "I don't know how we're going to make it home without being seen."

They replaced the papers in the filing cabinet then closed and locked the sliding door. As they went towards the side door downstairs, a display caught Peg's eye.

"Too bad we couldn't disguise ourselves with those." She pointed to the wigs, beards, waistcoats, and trousers adorning a crew of wax Patriots.

A boom rang out over the village.

"It's Privates Day!" Corey dashed to the window. "People will be all over—" He straightened. "What did you say?" He gawked at the old clothes. Peg was sure they were both thinking the same thing.

Fifteen minutes later, the bearded "privateers" left the museum and headed towards Grant Street. Half a dozen Patriots greeted them jovially. Peg walked stiffly beside Corey, hardly daring to turn her head and return the greetings.

Though well disguised, she was petrified of being recognized; every time she caught sight of an officer on duty for the festivities, she wanted to run the other way.

Finally, they darted inside Howler's fence, greeted by licks and wags, and crept though the back door to the kitchen.

"I'm roasting!" Peg knew it wasn't just the outfit making her sweat; it was a weirdly familiar feeling. She threw off the waistcoat as Corey struggled to take off the large trousers he'd pulled over his own pants. Peg followed Corey across the kitchen floor as he went to feed Howler, who was so excited he was knocking his water bowl and splattering the floor.

Corey ducked to grab the dog, and Peg found herself face to face with a photo on the refrigerator. It took her breath away—and triggered a *memory:* standing above a sunlit river under a lilac wreath, saying "I will" to those eyes of aquamarine. She barely heard Corey asking for a towel.

"Mom?" Corey waved his hand in front of her open-mouthed face. All she could do was point at the photo. A giant muskie almost dwarfed the fisherman who appeared to have the head and shoulders of a man and the body of a fish: *the merman she saw in her sleep.* She finally took a breath. She, *Peg Stowe,* had found not only the boy but the man who haunted her dreams. Or at least his picture.

"You recognize Charlie? That's great!" Corey smiled like Christmas had come. For Peg, the photo and her present surroundings triggered other images: eating, laughing with the man, standing at the stove holding a spoon for the boy to lick. Yes, this place felt right.

When she walked into the living room, the image shattered.

"Is this the way you guys keep house?"

Couch cushions were askew, drawers pulled from the writing desk, magazines spilled from their basket. Even curtains had been yanked from the windows.

Corey's hoarse whisper came from behind. "Someone's been here!"

AN INVASION

Corey crept quietly through the house, his mother behind him. He could see that no room had escaped the pillage. *For what?*

"Probably the cops looking for drugs," he said. "Must be professionals if they got by Howler."

"*Or,*" Mom's voice was shaking, "they were looking for *me* here."

Corey put his arm around her shoulder, trying to think of the right thing to say when the clock clanged.

"Oh no!" she cried. "I'm supposed to meet Jack at nine thirty."

"No way! We don't know who we can trust, but we sure can't trust *him.*"

She called Jack's voicemail to say she had developed something contagious and then turned her phone off.

"We forgot the attic," Corey whispered. They climbed slowly. Someone had been here too but had left. Corey noticed a strange look on his mother's face.

"I was here."

Her memory is coming back. "Yeah, you were!" Corey said. "You used to come up here to—"

"No, I mean...a few weeks ago."

"What?" *Impossible.*

She looked out the window and down at the street. She started humming, and then her eyes widened.

"There was an old guy, some weirdo. He kept following me. Then there was an accident and...I came up here."

Corey stared open mouthed. "That day Buddy was—and the car—*you* came in *here?*"

But his mom was concentrating on something else. She closed her eyes and rubbed the fingers of her right hand together then she pinched her thumb and index finger like she was holding something.

"I found papers..." She opened her eyes and pointed below the window. "Right here."

Corey shook his head as if to wake up. "You mean—Sam and I left the journal under the window?" *Pathetic.* He'd had no idea how important the book would become. Then he brightened. "But that's good! If you took the journal, that means Auger didn't get it!"

Corey was grinning as his eyes fell on Howler, panting in the attic heat. "I just realized..." He stroked his dog. "You're the only person Howler would have let in the house that day!"

He turned hopefully to his mother. "So where is the journal?"

Her face fell and she shook her head slowly. "I have no idea."

THE ATTIC WINDOW

"We need a plan." The attic was too stuffy for Corey to think, but if they went downstairs, someone watching the house might see them. Corey went to the attic window to let some air in. It was old and stubborn, and he braced one hand on the raw wood of the sill and pulled at the frame with the other.

"Ouch!" He looked at the sliver in his bleeding finger. He glared at the edge of the broken sill and noticed a gap. *Is everything old and broken around here?* His brows joined as he looked closer into the hollow of the wall, an empty space. No, not quite empty.

Something yellow was visible. He licked a good finger and pried it out. A paper...from the journal. Corey stared. A loose page must have fallen in the crack when he dropped it.

His mother took the paper and read aloud Patrice's words:

> While the crew set up defenses on shore, Warren and I went scouting upriver. I still don't trust Dirk, and I persuaded Warren to stop at the island cave and pick up the treasure chest. I am relieved that we found it a new hiding place.

Mom looked up. "So Pat didn't move the chest by himself."

"*Herself,* remember? Pat was a woman."

"Of course...so *Patrice* and Warren moved the chest." She looked down. "It says here, 'We sailed downriver with the treasure and left it'...*looks like...* 'all on' *something*'Island.'"

She squinted at the page to read the name of the new hiding place. "Is that *Estar* Island?" They had no idea where Estar Island could have been.

"Maybe it has a different name now."

They decided to creep—very carefully—to the office downstairs to search online. Corey turned on Mom's computer, which Charlie had decided to keep once he realized the emails were innocent.

"Here's something about Thousand Islands history." Corey dropped his voice. "We better print it out so we can take it."

He hit "Print." A light flashed: "Paper Load Error."

Duh. He loaded a stack of sheets and pushed "Maintenance" as instructed then realized he had to replace an ink cartridge, too.

Finally, a page printed.

Then another. Then, page after page spewed out. *An earlier job must've been interrupted.* He opened the print queue and saw the file name "Emeline_Redrow.doc"

EVIDENCE?

Corey yanked pages off the printer. They were journal entries. Mom must've entered them before she disappeared and lost her memory!

Corey sat on the floor with his mother as she read about finding the treasure and Dirk and about how Pat didn't trust him. Maybe his Mom couldn't remember reading any of this, but she quickly learned.

"*Patrice* was the mechanical genius. Listen to this."

> Warren says we're a good team: he has battle sense and river knowledge while I can solve problems to make the impossible possible.

> We used my plans to build the hidden hoist with counterweights so we could ascend the Point quickly from water level.

"But why did Patrice pretend to be a man—was it so her father couldn't track her?"

"That's one reason." His mom scanned a page. "She was also hiding her sex so she didn't distract the crew from the mission—they weren't used to fighting alongside a woman. They had to stay focused, and she didn't want to take any chances."

He thought about the legend. "So why did she get overweight and lazy?" Corey was lying on his stomach with knees bent and chin supported by his hands. His mom's gaze held a warm glow. *She remembers how I used to ask questions when she'd read to me.* Even though someone had torn the house apart and was out to get them, Corey felt happy right now, hearing his mother's voice in his own home. He hardly even noticed the new shape of her face—he saw her just as he remembered.

Now she looked thoughtful, scanning a page. "Patrice put on weight because... she was expecting a child!"

"Huh?" Corey sat up.

"Listen to this."

> My time is advancing, and Warren fears for me and our child. He has made me promise to seek safety—even if his life is in danger.

Corey held his breath as he tried to remember something. "*That's* what Warren meant by saying 'Remember your duty' when she left the gunboat He wanted to protect Patrice and the baby—*his* baby—so he was *telling* her to leave!"

"I bet you're right. And listen to this."

> I don't know how much longer I can hide my condition from the crew. I fear Dirk has guessed it, but he says nothing. Perhaps I was wrong about him.

"So what happened to their baby? Dirk would have been, like, an adopted brother to it."

"She must have miscarried...after all, she led a pretty rough life, fighting in battles—just imagine!"

"But if Dirk knew Patrice was a woman," Corey wondered, "why would he claim 'Patrick' fathered *Geraldine's* baby—and try to get rid of it?"

Mom flipped pages. "Here's something about Geraldine from further back."

September 1812

Geraldine Plank is staying in the cabin Warren and I built. She arrived ranting hysterically about the atrocities she has seen in this war.

"A-traw-suh...what?"

"Atrocities. She must have seen horrifying things..."

The only thing that calms her is my lullaby...she even mouths the words along with me. My heart breaks for her! Losing both her child and her husband...no wonder she has turned mute and cannot abide company; we'll not thrust society upon her until she is ready. Meanwhile, she does what we ask, and I will rely on her to attend the birthing of my baby—perhaps the event will bring healing for her.

"Mute? So Geraldine couldn't talk, right? And she was crazy from seeing her family killed, so she must have wandered around...until she got to the Landing."

"Must've ended up here by accident, and Patrice and Warren took her in. And they didn't introduce her to anyone—I bet no one else in town knew about her."

Corey was confused. "But she'd already lost her family. There's nothing in the journal about *Geraldine* having a baby at the Landing. Only that she was going to help Patrice with hers. How could Geraldine be our ancestor?"

So far, the journal was raising more questions than it answered. It didn't agree with anything in the town "history."

"All that literature from the museum came from one source," Mom said. "Geraldine was unknown and mute, and Warren and Patrice both died in the river without telling their secrets."

People only knew what Dirk told them.

Dirk, from a British ship, and who Patrice distrusted. Dirk, who got himself known as Warren Hart's son and inherited Warren's fortune from the spoils of war. *Dirk, who had a lot to lose if there was a true heir.*

Corey and his mother sat in silence broken only by the ticks of the clock.

Then Corey's brows met for a conference. "What if Patrice had *her* baby that same day—after she left the *Patriot* before the battle...before Dirk found her?"

"Maybe she knew she was about to go into labor when she left the ship..."

"And Geraldine helped deliver Patrice's baby during the battle."

"Dirk would have been threatened by a baby—a legitimate Hart heir," Mom said.

"Dirk *did* know that Pat was a woman. That was the secret he figured out!"

"And he probably guessed she was with child."

"But he told lies to keep people thinking Pat was a man."

Mom was staring at another page. "Dirk wasn't even legally adopted."

"Do you realize what this means?" Corey held his breath.

His mother smiled. "It was Patrice's baby that we came from?"

"We did not come from a deserter..."

"Patrice was more courageous than most of the *men*."

"And our *man*-cestor was... *Warren Hart!*" Corey exploded.

Amber eyes locked with blue.

"The Harts are imposters."

Could it be true? Were the Harts identity thieves? Had Auger's family been *taking Hart* instead of using their real name?

"*We* are the Harts." Corey said. "We are the ones who should have inherited the money, owned the town—*I* should've won the trophies!"

HART FAMILY TREE REVISED

Corey glanced at the diagram on Mom's office wall—it was a lie. An *artificial* tree, like those plastic plants. In his mind, Corey replaced the labels with the correct name. Dirk's lie had distressed Corey's family for two centuries, but now their branches could finally be re-leaved.

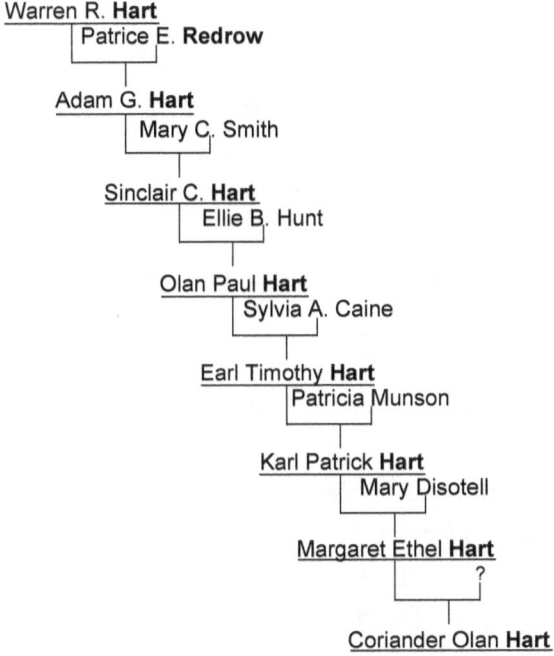

Warren R. **Hart**
Patrice E. **Redrow**

Adam G. **Hart**
Mary C. Smith

Sinclair C. **Hart**
Ellie B. Hunt

Olan Paul **Hart**
Sylvia A. Caine

Earl Timothy **Hart**
Patricia Munson

Karl Patrick **Hart**
Mary Disotell

Margaret Ethel **Hart**
?

Coriander Olan **Hart**

A VISITOR

Corey finally looked back at Mom. "So Dirk wasn't trying to save the baby. He wanted to kill it, and Patrice too." He squeezed his brows. "But if the baby was such a threat, why did he let it live?"

"Maybe Geraldine left with the baby during the scuffle—he probably didn't worry about her telling since she was mute, and it didn't matter if the child lived, as long as no one knew it was Warren's."

Corey considered that idea.

"Remember," Mom said, "Geraldine was devastated by the loss of her own baby—probably a bit insane. She would've *wanted* to think the baby was hers."

He hadn't thought of that.

"Besides," she continued. "Dirk sounds arrogant enough to think Geraldine would be afraid to tell."

"But this printout doesn't *prove* anything. Anybody could make this up and print it out."

"The real journal would be credible evidence." Mom sighed. "But we don't have it."

"Maybe you hid it, safe in your room. Maybe someone's only after the buckle—"

He was interrupted by a growl. Howler had nosed up to the window facing the alley between houses; someone must be out there watching.

Corey and Mom looked at each other and ducked lower to the floor as Howler barked and ran to the front window. *We should have left the house earlier.* They crawled to the kitchen, Corey stuffing the papers in his back pocket. He'd meant to change the pants he still had on from the fishing trip, but there was no time now. They threw their costumes on, sneaked out, and scrambled up the hill.

They finally hid behind the bushes and looked back to watch the house. Someone tall was walking in the opposite direction past the neighboring house; he had had just time enough to get through the shrubs between houses. *That* was the person Howler had been growling at—someone wearing a black cap and a dark blue jacket with maroon trim.

Corey was shaking. He was still dizzy from the shock of finding his mother, and now history itself had changed. But they were in danger. He couldn't be logical. Charlie was unreachable, and the only other person he could trust was Sam—she always knew what to do.

They headed for The Mainsail.

Corey turned his phone off as they crept to the back of the B&B. He didn't know who might be around, and he didn't want his phone to give away their presence.

His mother went to her small room to search for the journal while Corey sneaked through the back hallway. He checked everywhere Sam might be, upstairs and down. When he tiptoed back down the hall to find his mother's room, he heard a voice from the office that sounded like Randy's. But what Corey saw through the door as it closed sent shivers up his spine.

A coat rack still swayed with the weight of a dark blue jacket with maroon trim. Then, *Thwonk!* A black cap hit and caught on the hook right above the coat.

That was *Randy* they'd seen on Corey's street? *Randy* who tore the house apart? The bastard! Corey had had a feeling the guy was up to no good. He tried to hear more as a chair scraped on the floor inside. It was a one-sided conversation.

"Told them, all we knew was the car was gone then reappeared." He paused. "They were dusting for prints, thought it was clean. Then we get a call back, say they found one. *One* print!" He cleared his throat. "You'll never believe whose name turned up."

Oh no! Had Mom left a fingerprint they could identify?

Randy must have turned away from the door, because Corey could hear only bits and pieces.

"...tore the place inside out... found nothing...Worder kid and the woman" and, "...gotta get rid of them."

SILENT SAM

Sam was too shocked to say a word as she sat in the office at The Mainsail and listened to Randy describe what he'd seen and heard. Some very strange things were going on. They compared notes, their voices low. She thought she'd heard someone out in the hallway; probably just one of the new guests finding their way around, but she didn't want to take chances of anyone hearing their discussion, and she signaled Randy to lower his voice.

Afterwards, she went to the kitchen to grab lunch; she called Corey. No answer. She laid the phone down on the table to eat her sandwich. Her mind had been spinning, trying to add everything up about Johnny, about Marie. About that island. *I'd like to see it closer.* She glanced at the clock again: one minute to eleven.

"Oh no, I'm gonna be late!" She picked up a folder and stuffed it in her bag as Randy came down the hall. He yelled as she ran out, "Check in with me by..." The clang of the clock muffled the last word, but she was sure she heard "*two.*"

BETRAYED BY A GLOVE

Corey got himself back to Mom's room, quiet as possible, and told her what he had heard about the fingerprint.

"A hole in my glove—how could I be so stupid!" She shook her head at the brown cotton glove she pulled out of a drawer and onto her right hand.

"I bet I touched the mirror with it when I looked back..." She covered her eyes. "I still can't believe I ran over a man." She buried her face in her hands, one bare, one gloved.

"The fingerprint isn't the worst thing," Corey said. They'd thought someone else was out to get them; now he was sure that Randy was involved. He wondered how much Sam and Johnny really knew about Randy.

He turned on his phone to call Sam and saw that she'd called him but left no message; he called back and left her a message.

"I...don't know where to go now." He avoided Mom's eyes. How much longer could he keep her safe? They sat on the bed staring at the door.

Then his mom hit her head with her palm and grabbed his hand. "It's Friday—my appointment!" She pulled him to the door. "We'll go see the one person I can trust."

DR. POOLE'S INTRUDER

The downtown office building appeared deserted. The open stairs at either end were hidden from the street, and visitors could go upstairs unseen. Halfway down the hall, a strong hand twisted a key, and a door swung open. It swung back.

The room was set up like an office...for therapy? The archives were in a cabinet to the rear. Session recordings were labeled with dates. The intruder selected a recent session and inserted it into a player. *Click.* A female voice began.

"...you are feeling more and more relaxed....' *Fast-forward.* Another female: "...I am in a dusty attic, holding a bundle of ancient papers..."

The woman with two faces was back in operation.

Several more session recordings were popped in and out. The dead woman had returned, but without her memory, and the therapist seemed to be helping her extract recollections. *This has to stop.*

"...important to your psyche that you find the buckle, it seems to hold a key to your identity—its loss would be devastating...you must speak of it only in the safety of our sessions."

In a more recent recording, the 'client' was saying, "I am standing in an office; I hear rustling, I switch buckles and give back the false one." *Forward* and then, "...the real buckle falls to the bushes."

In a few moments, the recordings were replaced and the cabinet locked.

So there is a journal...one that could ruin the Harts.

Now the therapist knew everything the woman knew. The therapist would have to be dealt with.

One hand grabbed the doorknob from inside before its owner hesitated. Sharp eyes swept the room. Everything appeared to be in order. The intruder stealthily pulled the knob, slipped out, and closed the door.

A TRAITOR

Corey and his mother had arrived at Dr. Poole's office in time to hear a familiar voice coming from inside. It was...Mom's?

How can that be? Corey turned to look at his mom, just to be sure she was really standing out here beside him.

"It's a recording," she whispered, eyes wide.

Duh. Someone inside was playing back Mom's appointments. Corey and his mother listened, close to the door, as someone brought up one session after another.

In a few moments, they'd heard enough to realize two things. Mom had left the journal with Dr. Poole for safekeeping. *Great news.* And someone did try to kill her, for the buckle. *Bad news.* They still didn't know where it was, or why it was important—only that it had dropped into the bushes, which they'd already searched.

Mom jerked at Corey's arm and put her finger to her lips. The door knob was turning!

They barely made it into the door well of the next office when they heard the door open. Then they heard fading footsteps. They peeked around the wall to see who was interested in what Mom knew. Judging from the looks of the intruder sneaking down the stairs at the other end of the hall, it was a red-bearded Patriot.

"Quick," Corey whispered. "We have to follow him."

When they reached the street, they saw a red-bearded Patriot by the Juice Tap...one walking towards them...and several more in a crowd of battle re-enactors headed for the wharf. They all had on the same type of jacket.

Corey and his mother gave up and ducked behind the library; they sat on a stone bench by the statue of Warren Hart. A nearby plaque stated that the Harts had established the library in eighteen-something.

"I completely forgot my appointment for this week had been cancelled," Mom said. "At least we know the journal is safe."

"Unless the intruder found it in there and took it."

Her face fell. "Oh."

"If they did, at least they won't kill us for it—"

"No, it would be the buckle they'd kill us for. Wish we knew what it was about."

Corey pulled the journal printout from his pocket and gave it to his mother. She scanned it for answers.

"Patrice says she gave Warren the special buckle to keep 'close to his heart,' and they agreed to keep it secret until after the war."

"Doesn't help much."

"Maybe it has a map of the islands."

Corey turned on his phone. "I'll give Sam another try." He hit the speed dial and was about to leave another message, but then he heard Sam herself. "Hey, you're there!" he said. No answer. "Uh...Hello?"

Then he heard her voice again. It was coming from the other side of the statue. He closed the phone as he stretched his neck to see Sam sitting at a concrete table behind an oak tree. He grinned with relief. He'd found his ally. He opened his mouth, about to call her, when someone else leaned into the picture, over a pile of old papers, as if to give her a kiss. The guy's head was close to hers as she put her hands on his chest. The head was blond, the eyes cold steel. Corey squeezed his eyes shut as his head started to pound. Icy prickles crept over his skin, but his chest was a brick of heat.

A jumble of images danced through his mind: Sam as Warren Hart, humiliating Corey at the hockey game; Sam as a vision of beauty, reading his family secrets; Sam as a friendly sleuth pretending to help him find the journal. Was she telling Auger about it now? Did she find it and give it to him?

Next came an image of Sam as a back-stabbing pirate wielding a cutlass, and Corey could feel its sharp blade between his shoulders.

DRYING TEARS

Peg could see devastation in her son's eyes as he hyperventilated. She walked him back among the trees bordering the library property, where he sank onto a suspended fallen tree and gripped its branches. Only his chest moved, rising and falling rapidly. Peg sat beside him, examining his face; she barely saw his lips move as the word "traitor" came out. The amber in his eyes had turned to mud.

"That was Sam, your friend...?"

"No." He'd found a voice, a cold one. "A deserter."

Peg felt bad. Things had already been hard for Corey. She herself had left him alone for months, and even though she'd come back, how was he better off? Someone was out to get them, and they had no friends. She put her arm around him and told him he had *her* now, but she knew it couldn't erase the pain of losing a friend. Peg could handle being wanted by the police, even being stalked by a killer. But watching her son suffer was heart-breaking. She covered her face.

****

The one person Corey had thought was his friend was—a traitor. He'd once thought his mother had deserted him, but she would never have abandoned him. How did things get so twisted? Would Corey ever be able to trust his own judgment again?

He knew one thing. He had his Mom; she was the one anchor in his life, and he had to protect her. He looked at her. She was trying to hide it, but he could feel the tree under them vibrating with her sobs.

He hated making her cry. They were facing real danger—she must be terrified. But he had to keep himself together for her. He managed a smile. "At least I'm sure of you." He draped his arm around her shoulder.

She dabbed her eyes with her rough jacket.

"Here, I've got something softer." Corey reached into his pocket. His fingers poked into a hole before closing on a wadded mess, tangled with something hard. He pulled off the tissues and handed them to his mother as he gazed at the dark thing in his other hand. "I forgot I had this...it was Buddy's."

His mother quickly blew her nose and reached out. "Let me see that." She squinted at the object. "Looks like the thing he kept fondling when he followed me."

"It came off in my hand when I loosened his belt."

She rubbed on a spot until a small *W* then an *H* appeared, and she took the brass object, enclosing it in her own hand. She took a sharp breath and dropped it; the blood drained from her face.

"That," she said, pointing at the object on the ground, "is why I was pushed into the river!"

Corey stared downward as the truth dawned on him. Warren Hart's brass buckle had been in his pants for two days.

11 DOWN TO THE BUCKLE

"We had a hot lead to the buckle...*and you lost it?*" The boss gripped the phone tightly. Jack was on the other end, coming up with excuses, but the bottom line was, both he and Marie had failed.

Buddy was clearly the key to the buckle. He spent his time at the *Point*, where he hid in the trees and kept watch for an invasion that would never come. So that rustling in the bushes last September—the distraction that allowed Peg Stowe to switch buckles—had been *Buddy*. The Stowe woman must have let go of the real buckle before grabbing the rail, and the object had landed near Buddy.

Buddy had another habit that suggested he possessed the object: his compulsion to save anything he found and return it to the owner.

These facts might never have been connected to the buckle if it weren't for the final piece to the puzzle: the gossip about some pervert stalking females. But Buddy never intended to take off his trousers; it was something else he meant to remove—to return to its owner. And only one female caused him to reach for his belt: *Peg Stowe*.

The cleverest mind in town had deduced the truth and made plans to locate and protect the buckle's secret. The boss allowed a brief smile of self-congratulation before scowling. Lesser minds had thwarted the object's discovery.

"Marie not only failed to find the thing; she put Buddy in the hospital. Now you've let it slip through *your* fingers too?" Pause. "So the belt turned up at the hospital...but no fastener."

Four fingers drummed on mahogany.

"Who was the last person to see Buddy fully dressed?" Another pause. "I see. Well." The drumming stopped. "

"You know what to do, even if you have to comb each of the Thousand *Die* Lands." A chuckle escaped tight lips and faded quickly.

AUGER'S PRIVATES

"Auger, what's wrong?" He'd seemed okay when they met, even flirted. Then he started acting funny. Sam had to put her hands out to keep him from pitching onto the cement table. Now he wobbled on the bench and stared into the woods behind the library.

"Did you hear me? About Johnny being related?"

He looked dumbfounded. "Sorry." He scrambled out of the curved stone bench, jarring his folder, which splayed several yellowed edges. He happened to rip one off as he grabbed the edge of the table, and he just jammed it in his pocket as he darted to the men's room.

Sam had shared her theories with him; she only needed some missing pieces, but Auger couldn't or wouldn't give them. She put out her hand to neaten the papers that stuck out from his folder but stopped when she noticed the old handwriting. She couldn't help taking a look; it was from Auger's ancestors. This page was from Dirk Hart.

June 1813

It is done! My tip-off has had the desired effect: the British have vanquished the Patriots (assisted by my aim with the cannon). I am now a "hero" to the townspeople, of whom there were no witnesses. I had commanded them to retreat to the safety of their homes, escorted by Jackson, the only other crew member ashore. I refused to "expose the women, children, and disabled to the British wrath." Jackson has been very useful in confirming "Patrick's desertion." He believed he saw it with his own eyes. By ensuring all townspeople were concealed, he has unknowingly made possible the sinking of both the *Patriot* and the *Spitflame*.

I later tried to force the location of the treasure out of "Patrick," but she would not reveal it; I believe she would have given in at the threat to her baby, but the damned mute woman stepped in. She was surprisingly strong! After Geraldine ran with the child, I was able to force Patrice off the edge.

Surely, I thought, I would find a map or note about the treasure among the woman's belongings. But my search revealed nothing, save for a chest of clothing, and the cutlass that had already been altered by its owner so as not to cause suspicion. I was examining the item when crew mate Jackson showed up, the man to whom the mute woman had fled. I explained the situation and reassured him that Patrick was "no longer a danger." I did not have the opportunity to get rid of the woman, but I am confident there will be no challenge to my story. She seems content to have her "own" child.

Sam was dumbfounded. In the folder, she found other entries and read one from twelve years later.

September 1825

The "Harts" are revered by the citizens of Harts Landing despite our charade. "Father's" buckle, which would speak with a well-placed touch, remains mute; and the truth in "Patrick's" cutlass is camouflaged by an ingenious stroke! The truth is hidden in plain sight, and I am confident that the citizens, blinded by their veneration, will never doubt the "Harts."

And she read one of the letters from many years later...

May 1855

My Dear Grandson:

I am founding a little monarchy; with the help of my "subjects," I have grown our secret landing into a town that attracts visitors who stay, drink, and eat at our "Hart" taverns and inn. I have no doubt my offspring will show their true blood in furthering the goals of their forefather and will continue to increase the family power and influence.

Warren Hart was a fool. Far better to acquire wealth for yourself and your family than to lose your life for "country and honor."

My one regret is that I never did find the vast treasure removed by Patrice. But I have full confidence that you will succeed in the pursuit of further riches, with or without the missing chest.

Was this for real? No wonder Auger was sick. How would he react if he found Sam reading it? *Better get his private papers back in the folder.* She knew Auger was proud of his Hart heritage, and he would not want to be seen as a fraud.

AUGER REGROUPS

Auger mopped his face with a wet paper towel. He had put on a good show before Sam had asked that question. He had no idea how he was related to Johnny, but he couldn't admit that to her. How could she know more about him than he did? After Dirk's notes, it was the final straw. He'd headed for the men's room to heave.

Gotta keep it together. Somehow this stuff would blow over, and he'd be his old self. Maybe even take Sam on a real date.

Before Auger left the restroom, he heard something through the window that opened onto the woods. There were two figures murmuring by the trees. On was that Worder kid. Auger knew one thing: he didn't want that dork—or anyone—finding out about Dirk Hart. Those old papers would never see the light of day again.

He went back out to tell Sam he'd had some kind of virus but he was over it.

TO KILL FOR

Corey's eyes bugged out. He bent over and gently brushed off a worm as he picked up the buckle for a closer look. "This is the thing I punched Auger Hart for?" He turned it over. Though tarnished and dirty, it was the right size. And it had a dent on the face. "It's been in my pocket all this time." Corey shook his head.

His mother squinted at the object. "It's got a hidden spring—" She raised her head and asked the sky, "How did I know *that?*" before resuming her inspection. "You just pinch it there. No, *there.*" She used the corner of her fingernail to press as she squeezed.

The back separated from what appeared to be a sealed edge. She took out a folded piece of paper and carefully opened it.

Something wispy fell out, and Corey caught it. "Yuk, cobwebs!"

"No, it's hair," his mother decided as Corey stared at the braided fuzz. Then Corey noticed something inscribed on the inner brass plate. He squinted. *Captain of My Heart.* "Hey this must've been a present from Patrice."

His mother nodded and started reading the yellowed paper out loud.

"Province of Upper Canada...*twenty-fifth* day of *August*...the Year of our Lord, One Thousand Eight Hundred and...*Twelve.*" Her eyes shifted lower. "...being joined in the Holy Bands of Matrimony..."

Corey looked over her shoulder. "Warren Rubin Hart and Emeline Patrice Redrow."

It was a marriage certificate.

Corey held up the hair. "And this would be..."

"Two locks of hair woven together, from Warren and Patrice."

Corey and his mom looked at each other and at the buckle with its secret contents.

"This is the thing..." she began.

"...that *someone* would kill for." Corey snapped the paper and the hair back into the buckle.

He felt the hole in his pants pocket. Without the wad of tissue, the buckle could fall out. He slipped it into his shirt pocket.

GETAWAY CHALLENGE

Corey could taste danger. They needed to get somewhere safe to figure things out. They couldn't take a car; the cops would get them. But it would be perfect out on the river. Who would notice them among the boatloads of people in disguise? They could go upriver to Mom's cabin on Wellesley Island.

Corey walked down Main Street, his eyes shifting back and forth. His mother was on the opposite sidewalk—better not be seen together. He recognized a few storekeepers because they stood by their shops, but most people were impossible to identify.

Singing and laughter spilled from the Priva-Cheers Saloon. Corey tensed and looked straight ahead as he walked through the chattering crowds. He caught a few words that made his brows spring to his hairline.

"Five-year-old found it...packet of cocaine...Pine Street."

Pine Street. That was where Corey had swerved into the ditch before the cops stopped him. Someone had planted cocaine under his seat—*that's what dropped off the bike!*

No one could possibly know that Corey was the one who dropped the packet; still, he half expected to be accused. He walked faster. *Only a block to the wharf.*

Then something poked him in the back. He glanced down at the walk; an extra shadow moved along with his.

"Where d'ya think *yer* goin'?" It was a low, rough voice.

He pictured a gun digging into his back. *Now what?*

The voice said, "Hart friend or foe?"

Huh? "F-friend..."

The object was removed.

"Well, all *righty* then!" The voice was now jolly. "Have a drink, Patriot!"

Corey jerked his head to the side to see a reveler holding a plastic flintlock pistol and a tankard of Patriot's "ale."

"No thanks." Corey kept walking. He tried to ignore the man, who kept harassing Corey until distracted by a chesty Patri-*ette.*

It was another block before Corey could take a full breath. His reaction to the tourist had been lame. *How can I ever face a real killer?*

His breathing started to even out as he approached the pier, but it was nearly battle time and it was crowded with tourists. Corey tried to act casual as he checked out the boats tied at the pier, pretending to be one of the history buffs and privateer wannabees who gawked at the weapons and war gadgets. Then he glanced out at the dock space he'd been headed for. The *Stowe Aweigh* was missing.

He forgot it had been impounded. What to do now? He was sweating; he loosened his coat. People were jostling him and rocking the dock, and he stumbled. He stiffened as something was slipped around his neck. Was he being strangled right out in the open? He looked down and grabbed at the "noose."

It was only a pieces-of-eight medallion. Corey really had to get a grip. He grunted, "Not interested." The vendor yanked and pulled it over Corey's beard and hat before running off to rope in a real customer.

Corey had forgotten about all the wild characters that would be loose. He felt like a rowboat in a squall; he wanted to ground himself on a bench, but they were all full.

"Need some help?"

Corey backed up and hit a post.

It was Johnny. Corey's relieved grin turned into a scowl when he saw Sam's phone in his hand.

"She left her cell behind, but she was expecting an important call, and I couldn't find her." Johnny lowered his voice. "I heard your message—what you were wearing...and that you needed help. What can I do?"

Johnny was the one who had stood up for Corey and saved his butt more than once. He should be told the truth about Randy and Sam...but it would have to wait.

"I need to get out on the river."

"My boat is over there." Johnny pointed. "Key's in it, all gassed up." He whistled as he walked away.

Corey should have known he could count on Johnny, even if Randy was a monster and Sam was a backstabbing deserter.

FREE!

Someone bailed me out? Charlie was flabbergasted to get out of jail, but he wasn't about to question why. He looked forward to being home, but when he got there, the house was a wreck. What had happened? And where was Corey?

Charlie remembered that he had his phone back, and he checked messages. The first one was from Corey, who said he couldn't come to visit but had a "gigantic surprise." *Now what?*

Second message was from the police. *They just let me out, now they want me to call back?* He dialed the number and listened to the detective. Charlie stood with his hand to his ear even after the phone slid to the floor, where it kept repeating "Mr. Stowe? Are you there, Mr. Stowe?"

Charlie went to the fridge. He took out a can of Genny Light. He sat down in the living room with it as he scowled at the picture on the wall.

Why would the police be asking about his deceased wife?

He picked up his phone and heard the final message as he turned the beer can around and around in his hand. It was a request from someone he couldn't refuse. He put the unopened beer away and headed downtown.

JACK REPORTS

Contagious? Marie was about to catch more than the flu. Because of her lame excuse, Jack had to do the special "planting" on the other side of Rocky Island, the one she should've done. He'd made sure to leave those border Patrol fellows a refreshing bottle of "coke"—on the rocks. Just in case Rita didn't take the loaded tanks later, like she was supposed to. She had been getting rebellious.

And he'd gotten back in time to recognize and follow Marie and the Worder kid to the library, where they found the missing object. He could have grabbed it and eliminated them both, right there, but the boss's idea was better: "Just flush the fish right into the bowl." Where they would be taken care of in *private.*

"I'm heading out again," Jack told the boss, "for Rocky Island." He was pleased to see the two heads in the boat at the pier. "Don't worry, I'll stay behind, just far enough."

GETAWAY BOAT

Corey heard shots; he noticed the crowds getting thicker. Redcoats were threatening a band of Patriots on the street. Shouts and skirmishes drew tourist eyes in the other direction as Corey pulled the boat away from the pier.

"Can't you go any faster?" The voice came from behind.

Corey smiled. His mother had stopped at the food stand, with her hat pulled low. But after Corey untied lines and dropped to the helm, she'd slipped into the back seat.

They scanned the bay full of watercraft. Locals, tourists, and nearby island residents had come to see the Privateer Day battle, and chaos ruled the waters. Corey struggled to pick his way among fishing boats, ski boats, and jet skis mixing it up with gunboats, flat-bottomed Durhams, and even what looked like an old bathtub, all racing for the best viewing positions. But so far, the only ones losing the battle were the officers trying to keep order.

They had finally exited the bay when Corey heard his phone play three notes, and he pulled it out to see a text message from a strange number. It was Sam—*the traitor*—she must not have gotten her phone back from Johnny. She wanted to know where Corey was, wanted to talk about something important. *Wants my location so she can rat on us. Not gonna fall for that.* He stuffed the phone in his pants.

Mom sat next to him and handed him a sandwich.

"I was just curious how you knew it was *this* boat?"

He looked at her blankly. "What do you mean?"

"My work boat, you know, for the dive site. I didn't realize the keys were in it."

He stared at her as his brows crushed together. He opened his mouth to speak...

Boom! The canons roared. "Go!" Mom screamed.

The battle had commenced. A British ship approached from one side and a Patriot gunboat sailed from the other while muskets and flintlock pistols rang out; Corey opened the throttle to get out from between the warring vessels. He had the odd sensation that the river was heaving and the islands trembling. *It's just all the noise and confusion.* A blue motorboat several hundred feet behind them had to get out of the way too. Looked like it was turning upriver.

When Corey and his mom reached the other side of the battle zone, their breathing returned to normal. They ate their sandwiches as they turned upstream.

"What did you mean?" Corey asked through a mouthful of tuna on rye. "About the boat..."

"It's the one I use to go to the dive site."

"But it belongs to..."

"Jack."

"Johnny."

12 A CHANGE OF HART

Fred Hart had come back to the stairwell of his downtown office building and removed his red beard. He stuffed it under the steps. He put on a new hat and beard and adjusted them; he slipped his spyglass into his waistcoat. Rita was supposed to ride in the Harts parade; she certainly wouldn't want to miss being the center of attention as Queen. As if she needed to remind anyone of her position. Fred shook his head with a smile.

The reenactment had gone well. Now tourists and locals alike were partying, drinking tankards of "ale" in the streets and singing pirating songs. *Privateers* were honored at the Landing, not *pirates*, but tourists were infatuated with pirate lore and always would be.

Where was Rita?

It was time for Fred to climb to the raised podium in front of his office building.

"Fellow citizens, we will turn back the enemy to keep our Landing safe for another year. I must exhort you to be strong, loyal, and courageous, just as our founders..." As Fred articulated the speech, he was thinking ahead. He'd finish his address then duck behind the library and meet with someone who owed him a favor. Someone with his own build. Fred knew that paying the hospital bill and posting bail would come in handy. *Stowe is in my debt.*

And no one would know that Fred had left the village.

Fred entered the library yard and met his son coming out with that girl from the inn; she hung back while Fred pulled Auger behind the wall for a conference. As his son left, Fred said, "Find Rita and call me, and keep tabs on Grandma—her aide was bringing her to the parade." Fred wanted to know where everyone was.

Then he found his stand-in and transferred his captain's costume.

AN OLD BOAT

Corey was glad to pull over to the north side of Rocky Island, where they'd be out of sight of the revelers. Mom was describing Jack, her so-called brother, and he sounded just like Johnny. But Jack was a cocaine smuggler, and he'd been lying to Mom—how could he be the guy that Corey admired?

Then he remembered. *I'm a horrible judge of people.* Corey was the one who always whined about people judging *him.* But he had trusted and mistrusted the wrong people.

His thoughts were interrupted by the sputter of the engine, and soon the boat was dead in the water. Johnny had said the tank was full, so Corey hadn't bothered to check.

He searched for a gas can. No luck. Mom found a couple of wetsuits and threw one at Corey.

"Better suit up." She was right. If someone was looking for them, they sure didn't want to be sitting ducks. Corey dropped anchor and tore off his coat, hat, and beard. He pulled off his jeans and yanked the large suit over his underwear and shirt. Mom struggled into a suit and got a tank and some head gear from the back. She dumped the tank overboard and threw the other gear in the water just as a shot rang out.

Corey thought it was from the staged battle...until he saw Mom's face and let his gaze follow her pointing finger to the helm. It had a bullet hole.

They both plunged into the water.

Corey arranged the second stage regulator and felt Mom fix the tank onto his back. He submerged and tried to steady his nerves—he had always heard that "if you panic, you're dead." Mom sucked a few breaths from the alternate regulator and signaled him to the north.

He peeked up and around the corner of the boat to see where the shooter was. The other boat was closing in! He and Mom should go deeper. He looked around. But where had she gone? He swam where he'd seen her heading. *She hasn't got a tank.*

Something blocked his path, the wreck of an old bateau, a flat-bottomed boat, stuck sideways into the rocks. He started to swim around it—he had to get the tank to Mom. They would be spotted if she had to surface!

Then he saw someone swimming towards him from the north. Someone wearing a tank. Corey ducked behind the old boat, but not before he'd been seen...by a diver with sapphire eyes.

Oh. It was Mom.

They were right near the boundary between the U.S. and Canada, where Corey had seen his mom when he untangled Sage's fishing line. Now she had picked up a tank from the same place. This time, she was using it for the air.

They hid behind the bateau, under the projecting side so it trapped their bubbles as they watched the surface. Corey couldn't make out details, but he could tell the boat driver was pulling off a large hat and beard—and had red hair.

Corey felt sick. Johnny had been like an uncle. Shouldn't Corey be going to Johnny for *help*?

No. He'd better get over it. Johnny was probably searching their boat...er, *his own boat*. He must've brought a gas can on board to fill it, because now he was starting the engine.

Corey stayed hidden and followed his mom back towards the northeast end of the island. They swam in a trench deep enough to hide them for a couple hundred feet. It had an overhang that collected their bubbles...he hoped. They could see a lot of rocky pillars sticking up between stretches of deep bottom, carved by glaciers ages ago. Those unseen obstacles were the reason for a lot of sunken ships under the St. Lawrence. They drew divers like a candy shop drew kids, but the place could be hell in strong current if you didn't know what you were doing. Corey had heard of more than one diver who didn't come back alive.

Corey took a chance and looked out from behind a pillar; Johnny was trolling in his own boat, his eyes probing the water all around. The trench wouldn't hide Corey and Mom for long.

Near the northeast shore of Rocky Island was a pile of rock slabs—granite that had fallen to form an enclosure. There was an opening at the corner big enough to slip inside. He didn't like the idea of being in a small enclosed space underwater, but they didn't have a better choice. Mom turned on the flashlight she'd grabbed from the boat. Inside the enclosure was space enough for them to glide either way around an old row boat. It must've settled there before the rocks fell around it.

After examining the stern and midsection of the boat, Corey gestured to his mother to go towards the other end of the enclosure, but she pointed to the entrance. Corey remembered that she didn't have much air.

Maybe she thinks Johnny's gone by now.... Or maybe Mom had a sixth sense about her battery because before they got back to the opening, her light failed. They hurried towards the hole they had entered, but just before they reached it, a slab slid down over it like an angled garage door, closing their daylight hole.

FLATTENED

Darkness closed around Corey; it was like being in a solid cage with the walls squeezing in on him. He started breathing faster. He detected a slight buzzing. *Calm down.* He got a grip on his panic just as he felt something crawling on his face.

It was his mother's hand reaching up, feeling for his head. *If she's trying to console me, it's not working.* No, she was searching for something. Then light was flooding her face. He shook his head, which made the shadows around her nose grow and shrink. *Oh.* He had forgotten she'd fastened a headlamp on him earlier.

Together, Corey and his mother pushed against the new barrier, but it wouldn't budge. As Corey drew air in and out, the noise reminded him of a *Star Wars* character. He kept repeating to himself *keep calm, keep calm.* He and his mother would *not* die under the river!

Corey made several gestures to his mother; they would have to search the other end of the enclosure. She gestured back and glided around the starboard side of the row boat. Corey rushed along the port side to see if there were any openings, and he periodically jerked his hands up against the rock ceiling to locate any segments that might give way. Near the bow, he edged over the side of the boat and stretched out on the raised seat to get leverage. But the planks collapsed, and he dropped into the boat's bottom.

Corey tried to climb out, but his tank caught; he couldn't move to the right or left. His breathing got faster as he started to panic. Then, just as he thought he would lose it, he seemed to move outside himself; he was looking down on his body, right through the rock cage. He saw himself jerk his head up to shine the light forward, but the headlamp knocked against the rock and slid backward so his body was in darkness.

Had the lack of oxygen caused him to hallucinate? He didn't think more about it because a sudden vibration shook him right back into his body.

DEJA VU

Peg Stowe moved along the starboard side of the rowboat by grabbing the edges and following the murky gray outline illuminated by Corey's lamp. She saw the light shine above the bow of the boat, on stacked rock slabs, and could see no way out. She looked lower. There! Rock slabs separated to form an opening. She squeezed herself under the bow of the boat and worked her way down the hole. *There had to be an exit.* Their lives depended on it. She was heading towards a soft light coming from farther down the channel. She took a deep breath—or most of one.

There was no more air in her tank. Would she find air if she went forward? Could she get to Corey in time if she turned back? Her indecision wasted vital seconds, until the island trembled and made the decision for her. Or was it the pounding of her heart that pulsed her back towards Corey?

Her head spun; her chest prickled and ached for air. Then the pangs triggered a recollection: *I've done this before.* She'd been sure her life was over then, last September, but— almost impossibly—she had found air underwater.

Wait. Was that a real memory? Yes, and it triggered others. She *knew* she had no brother. Jack was just a smuggler who had fished her out of the river and used her.

Much of Peg's mind had been asleep, but it was waking up, and she was sure she would recapture all of her memory.

The realization seemed to release oxygen locked inside her. With a burst of energy, she followed the light to where Corey struggled in the boat. She squeezed over the side and grabbed Corey's regulator. Finally! She sucked air a few times and shoved it back to Corey's mouth. Then she freed him from the boards wedged between him and his tank.

Sharing both the lamp and the tank, Peg led her son through the tunnel. After several turns, they came to a widened area that forked. They were exchanging frenzied gestures when Peg noticed, once again, how labored her breathing had become.

The remaining tank had run out of air.

AUGER'S DISTRACTION

Auger was glad to forget about Dirk for a while. He maneuvered the shuttle boat from the pier near the resort.

"This is great!" Sam sounded excited. "We get to avoid all that chaos in the village."

"I wouldn't want to put you through that." Auger flashed a smile. "Besides, we'd just be in the way there." *And there's no way I'd go through all that riffraff.*

After they'd left the library, he had barely recognized Rita at the pier, definitely not dressed for the parade. He'd offered her a ride. That's when the ground had started shaking again and the big sign came down.

Then he'd also found Gran. He and Sam had hiked up to the cliff to see if they could spot her car somewhere in the village—but they were surprised to find Gran's car right up there in the museum lot.

Inside the museum, a new display had caught Auger's eye. *That fake buckle from the resort.* Apparently, his dad had moved it there. Auger had picked the thing up and felt the bashed-in center next to the *W.* The thing looked pretty authentic, even had some kind of finish to make it look old. Then when Gran showed up with her surprise, he'd stuck the brass thing in his pocket.

Gran had a new gift for him: the captain's outfit! It was a little early for it, but everyone knew Auger would become King of Harts Landing next year—and he'd look awesome as Warren Hart.

His grandmother didn't feel like watching the parade at the village. *Good.* Sam wanted to see if that Worder kid was out on the river, and Auger wanted to distract himself from that nonsense about Dirk. Gran said she'd have her driver drop them at the private pier near the Hart estate.

Now Sam sat next to him as they sped upstream.

The musical tones of a cell phone came from a back seat.

FISH TRAP

"Got the fish right in the tank, Boss." Jack said to his phone as he sat on the rocks at the edge of the island. "Believe me, they won't be going anywhere—I closed the lid myself!"

Those idiots thought they could hide from him. They'd left a trail of bubbles...just a few, but enough for a sharp eye like his. At the rock enclosure, he'd found that huge, unstable slab, and with a little help it fell solidly over the opening.

In fact, everything had been falling into place. This morning he'd found Sam's phone on the table after he'd returned to the B&B from dropping the "loaded" tank at the border. Then he'd heard the Worder kid's voice message to Sam, telling what Corey and his mother were wearing. Jack had spotted the two leaving the office building and watched them behind the library. When he'd heard their plans to head up the river, Jack had just enough time to get to the pier and drain the gas.

Now the boss gave him further instructions to "check on the island operation." As Jack stuffed his phone in his pocket, he noticed a motorboat rounding the island, heading for the drop zone by the border. *Rita's heading into the trap.*

He edged along the rocks, past a concealed inlet, back to his own boat. He had left Sam's phone on Randy's boat—he'd been distracted after firing his revolver. He hadn't meant to pull the trigger—he was just practicing his aim and got carried away. But he knew the boss would *not* have been pleased.

Jack started the motor and eased his boat towards the island's hidden cove, but before rounding the rocks, he noticed the Border Patrol had reached Rita. He smiled.

He tied up inside the cove, and as he scrambled up the incline, he patted the weapon at his side. He hoped to use his skills for real very soon.

PAYBACK

Rita had seen Jack on the rock, phone to his ear. Did he even have a clue who his boss really was? That identity would soon be revealed. For now, she had to deal with the authorities. The Patrol had showed up by the border, as expected.

"Ma'am, we're going to have to inspect those tanks," an officer had said.

"No problem." Rita had smiled and showed the tanks. She'd inspected the boat itself this morning before heading out—Jack put on a good act, but he couldn't fool her. Just as she'd suspected, Jack had planted several incriminating packets, but before pulling away, she'd found a good place to "replant" them.

Rita relaxed as the men searched the boat, and she thought about her recent discoveries. She had been only a child when she'd sneaked into that room Mama was cleaning. Even then her artist's mind had captured and filed the image she'd found, the photograph of a man. The image had remained with her all these years, and recently her inner shutter had clicked on a match. The old guy, Buddy—if you looked past the wrinkles, balding patches, and extra padding— was *Bartholomew*, supposedly missing in action. She'd found the picture again, just to make sure—still hidden at the estate. And the young Bartholomew had an undeniable resemblance to Jack.

But she'd found more than pictures this time, and she knew the Harts weren't all they appeared to be. *I thought I was the fraud.* By now, Rita had learned a thing or two about people—and she was about to reverse psychology.

She heard a splash. One of the patrol guys had dived into the water.

Her jaw dropped. She hadn't worried about what might be underwater—after all, there was no scheduled contact today, and there should be no tank dropped there, but she should've realized Jack would cover all his bases. She dug her fingernails into her palms as she waited. Her mind spun. What if, despite all her precautions, she took the heat for this whole operation? She gnawed her manicured nails.

Finally, the diver broke the surface and whispered to his partner, who came towards her.

"Sorry, Ma'am..."

Rita held her breath.

"...to have bothered you," he continued. "Have a nice day."

She stared as they returned to the official vessel. Then she collapsed to the driver's seat.

Rita recovered quickly. She had learned a thing or two in the last few weeks, and it was time to make her move. She would visit the island, where she had more influence than Jack imagined. Carlos, the "construction" manager was an acquaintance. And she was carrying a persuasive device, which still had several shots.

FRED'S ALLY

After Charlie left as "King of Harts Landing," Fred remained behind the statue in the courtyard. He had just slipped a simple rubber mask over his face when someone yelled, "Sam!"

Randy, that fellow from the inn, was knocking on the door to the women's restroom. "Are you in there, Sam?"

Wasn't this guy the partner of that dive shop manager? *He would be very interested to see the pictures in my briefcase!* Not that Fred would show them. Fred had been suspicious about Rita for some time, and he hadn't been surprised when the private detective came back with pictures. Pictures of her and that Johnny. What *had* surprised Fred were the pictures of Rita hiding something on Charlie Stowe's boat. She'd gotten Charlie Stowe arrested.

"Sam!" Randy called again. "Where are you?"

Fred squared his mask and stepped out from behind the statue to make a new acquaintance just as the earth shuddered.

Twenty minutes later, Fred was motoring out of the bay towards Rocky Island.

THE CAVE

Corey's lungs strained for air. Terror pricked his body as he squirmed in the narrow channel. *Calm down if you want to stay alive.* He had more than himself to think about. Only a few days ago Corey's name meant "loser," and he'd thought his mother had abandoned him. Since then he'd gotten his mother back and found out his ancestor was a hero.

He fought the fear; he closed his eyes and calmed his mind. A split second expanded to a timeless world: Corey was a ship gliding to port, a gentle breeze filling his sails. He dug deep to find the pilot within, the true navigator inside him.

Corey's eyes flew open; he knew what to do. He dropped the tank, motioned to his mother, and swam hard to the right. He figured he was going southwest, parallel to the shore. The channel turned a sharp left—into a solid rock wall.

He didn't think, didn't even hesitate. He ducked and swam under the wall through the opening where the water flowed. The channel headed in towards the center of the island; the upper boundaries of the channel widened and stretched as Corey burst into the open air, wheezing and sucking hungrily. As he tilted his head back, his gaze met granite walls and ceiling. *The cave of Rocky Island.*

"Shhhh..." Mom was behind him. "I hear a voice." It came from the other side of the rock wall to his right that stretched upwards towards the dome and projected several feet into the large cave, keeping Corey hidden. The stream was now contained in a narrow cutout in the cave floor, but it disappeared under a bridge-like expanse of rock then appeared again on the south side. Corey stared, unmoving, as the cave walls reflected the glow of lights and echoed the mechanical whirr of fans.

He pulled himself onto the ledge under the wall. He flattened himself against the wall and inched along it, his cheek brushing the rough, damp granite. He peeked around the wall, and when he saw what was on the other side he almost fell back into the water.

Sam was against the opposite wall, hands behind her. A rectangle of duct tape covered her mouth. Someone was standing over her with...a *gun*? Someone with cold gray eyes, and a face that still bore the mark of Corey's fist.

Auger Hart.

I should have called Sam back. Had she really betrayed Corey? That's not how it looked. Auger was no ally. Now Corey had to protect his mother *and* his friend.

"Stay hidden," Corey hissed to his mother, who now stepped among loose stones on the ledge. Corey took silent steps; he would surprise Auger while he was looking the other way.

But the surprise was Corey's when falling rocks splashed from the ledge behind him.

Auger's head snapped towards the sound, and his steel gray eyes bored into Corey.

FRIEND OR FOE

Auger's stare triggered an explosion of memories for Corey: insults thrown at Mom, howls rolling over the river, Corey's bloodied fingers on the cliff.

Rage awakened his inner beast, and Corey flew at Auger.

"Awrrrrgh!" He slammed Auger to the ground, and the boy's head met the rock where the fallen gun had clattered. He lay still.

Why didn't Auger fight back?!

Please be alive! Auger's eyes were closed, and he looked so innocent Corey felt guilty. Corey propped Auger's head with a rock and held his fingers to Auger's throat. He breathed with relief as Auger gave a moan.

Sam was writhing and twisting, her eyes darting back and forth.

"Don't worry, he—can't hurt you now." Corey was still a little unsure what had happened. As he turned to untie her, he noticed a crevice in the rock wall, maybe an opening that led out to the castle.

On the other side, the wall was lined with tables, sinks, shelves of flasks and, near Sam, a tall, open cabinet. He sniffed. There was that rotten egg smell he remembered from the fishing trip—must've been from the chemicals.

As he turned back to untie Sam, a movement caught his eye, from the shadow by the cabinet door. He could just make out the human form in an 1800s navy coat, and on it fell the hair of a dark wig and a beard. Mr. Hart's privateer suit. His hands were behind his back. Had Auger done this to his own father?

Sam grunted and waved her head, her eyes wild.

"Take it easy, Sam. I'll get that off you then free Mr. Hart too." Her head was still turning and twisting.

He had grabbed the tape when he heard a low whisper, "Stay there" and the sound of metal scraping rock. Corey turned and stared into the weapon—held by the hands he'd thought were tied.

Fred Hart was behind this? But Mr. Hart had been good to them! He'd paid Charlie's bill and brought Howler back. Corey opened his mouth, but nothing came out.

"I dried doo dell yoo!" Sam stretched her lips to unstick the rest of the tape from her mouth. "Auger was helping me!"

Corey tore his eyes from the gun to look at Auger, still laid out on the rock. Had he screwed everything up? Corey slowly turned back to his challenger, who had returned to the shadow after grabbing the gun.

"I—I thought you were a *friend.*" Corey's eyes fixed on the gun aimed at his chest. "You really had me fooled, *Mr. Hart.*"

The laugh that rolled out from under the beard made Corey stumble backwards. This was not Mr. Hart.

SUSPICIONS

Fred Hart's suspicions had grown stronger ever since he'd conferred with Auger at the library. Now, he powered away from Harts Landing as his passenger spoke over the noise of the motor.

"Never would have believed it." Randy punched a fist into his palm, and his grimace joined the creases of previous scowls. "Like I told Sam, Johnny was looking for something at Charlie Stowe's place. I saw it after he'd torn it apart—" Randy drew a big breath. "I knew something weird was going on, Johnny being gone so much, Sam finding those computer files—then I overhear Johnny saying the boy and his mother are *disposable*?!" Randy's brown eyes blazed over dark shadows as he checked his watch for the fourth time. "Sam was supposed to call me by noon—it's not like her to forget."

"I was going out to Rocky Island anyway." Fred had a feeling something might happen there during the battle. "It looks like the signal is coming from there."

"Thank god for the phone tracker." Randy tapped his fingers on the hull. "I almost forgot I had it."

"All those cancelled reservations and data loss...my tech guy finally traced the problem." Fred lowered his voice to a mutter. "Someone's been creating distractions."

Randy started to ask about it, but Fred had to focus on navigating. Demonstrators and revelers filled the waterways, some heading out, some in, for the post-parade festivities, and many had taken numerous drafts of Patriot's brew. Fred wove his way through the chaotic throng and approached a houseboat filled with college kids as they cheered on a young woman casting her costume off, piece by piece, to the music. Fred held the boat astern of the house boat.

"I dug up some old family letters." He waited for a jet ski to clear the area. "Seems my Uncle Bartholomew—the one missing in Nam? He left a pregnant girlfriend." He glanced at Randy, who was still drumming his fingers, and added softly, "That would be Johnny's mother."

The fingers stopped. "Wait. Your uncle was *Johnny's father?*" Randy let it sink in. He pounded his forehead with his palm. "Oh my god. His mother must have told him last summer—that's why he wanted to come to the area." His voice became harsh. "And I thought we came because we both loved the Islands."

Randy sat back in his seat, his eyes smoldering as he looked at Fred. "Guess there's a lot Johnny never told me. But Johnny's father—your uncle—he died in Vietnam, right?"

"That's what I thought." But Fred had been shocked to learn otherwise. "You know that man that ended up in the hospital—Buddy?" I did some research. Turns out he's Bartholomew Hart." Fred scowled at the rotund pirate in a passing ski boat, threatening them with a toy sword.

"That old guy that hangs out by the bar, that's Johnny's father?" Randy was quiet for a minute. "But there's other stuff...that doesn't add up."

"Like how that rental car ended up in the hands of a dead woman?" Fred swerved around a canoe. "She was my assistant, Peg Stowe. One day I saw someone going into my rental building, to the office that's supposed to be empty. This morning I found recordings of a *Marie*...it's the Stowe woman." Fred was pretty sure he knew who the therapist was, too.

"Wait, you mean the Marie that stays at my B&B—?"

"Says she has a brother, 'Jack,' who gives her a place to stay."

"*What?* Johnny used to go by 'Jack'—but he doesn't have any sister I know of." Randy looked lost.

"Well, it sounds like someone is lying and using her."

Randy looked gray. "I don't know Johnny at all." He threw his hands in the air and slumped in his seat. "I just need to find Sam."

Fred glanced at the tracker and checked the location of Sam's phone. He headed for the north side of Rocky Island.

Fred did not mention the things he discussed with Auger this morning. He swung the boat around the end of the island. Was it possible that he himself was not a Hart? And that the buckle had evidence?

EYES OF COMPASSION

Peg had not planned to reveal herself yet. But something drew her out, like a magnet, from behind the rock wall.

It was the voice.

"*I* know who you are..." Peg's lips twitched into a hopeful smile as she walked forward, her eyes riveted on the other woman.

The voice had unleashed a series of impressions: a stuffed oak chair, a darkened room, a skilled and compassionate listener. This woman had been helping Peg remember.

"*Dr. Poole.*" Peg had never seen her face clearly, but Dr. Poole had been the one she had entrusted with her secrets. Maybe everything was all right now. Her doctor was here to...

What *was* her therapist doing here? Peg stopped moving. And what was that thing she was pointing at Corey?

Peg looked again at the face of the woman who had just stepped out of the shadows. She did recognize those eyes—but now they had a sinister quality.

The woman was punching buttons on her phone; a familiar pattern played, and Peg began to relax, letting awareness subside. She took a deep breath, let her mind... *No!* Something in her fought back. Something began to awaken. Fresh images flashed in her mind, and Peg saw that Dr. Poole, the woman who had helped her remember, had also made her forget. In fact, Dr. Poole had been mining Peg for information!

"You..." Peg gasped. "You've been *using* me." The therapist's cold eyes gleamed back, over a slow serpent smile. It was the same smile Peg had seen on a brisk September night, before she fell into the river.

"You! You tried to *kill* me!"

Other voices barely penetrated Peg's buzzing mind. Corey: "Mom's doctor?" Sam: "What are you talking about—

that's Mrs. Hart. Corey: "Mrs. Hart...you mean Fred Hart's wife?"

The snake eyes grew narrower and the mouth hissed. "Enough riddles." The woman took a step towards Peg and pulled off her beard.

Peg's mind spun with images of three women: the attempted murderess at the Point, the therapist with soothing voice, and this threatening gunwoman. Now all three lined up, overlapped, and merged into one. And her name...

A voice interrupted Peg's thoughts.

"What are you doing?!" Auger shouted as he sat up, pocketing his phone. "Put that gun down, Grandma!"

Now Peg remembered. It was Fred's mother, Mackenzie Hart.

M.A. NOBLE

13 FRED'S DISTRACTIONS

Fred noticed the Border Patrol heading upriver as he rounded the west end of Rocky Island. He headed for the source of Sam's phone signal: a blue ski boat.

"That's *my* boat!" Randy shouted. Fred pulled alongside so Randy could jump over, and soon he was waving Sam's metallic pink cell phone. At the same time, Fred's phone chirped with a text message from Auger.

Fred snapped his phone back into its holster. "We need to get to the cave at the northeast end."

But Randy, still standing in his own boat, was listening to Sam's messages. "Corey's suspicious—of me?" He held the phone out and stared at it. "Corey says he and his mom had to get away, wearing *disguises.*"

"We'll find out more soon." Fred helped Randy back into his boat. He didn't tell him the details of Auger's message. He was preoccupied as he pulled the boat away. He'd worked his butt off for the business, fighting obstacles, and now he understood who was behind them. *Mother,* the Hart company's Chief Financial Officer. She gave the impression of innocence, even softness, but she had been tying up funds and hiding assets, making sure Fred didn't look too closely. She had assured Fred that she had put together a capable team for the castle project, and Fred had been glad to leave it in her hands. Now he stared at the Round Tower as they passed by, marveling at his talented mother. She had kept track of business even while working as a therapist at the psychiatric care center from which she had just retired.

"Hey, watch it!" Randy's shout jarred Fred back to the present.

They were headed straight for the rocks.

WHO'S WHO

Corey gawked at the gray hair and wrinkles that had been hiding under the beard. He must be in a weird dream, with Sam tied up in a meth-lab cave, Auger's grandmother dressed like a privateer.... Now the woman winked at her grandson, saying, "Good job playing possum, Augie."

Corey shot Sam a look that asked *Is this for real?* She hissed, "That crazy woman kept obsessing about the buckle. She made Auger come here, like she knew you'd show up. Thought I was helping them—even thanked me for informing Jack." Sam looked confused and embarrassed. "I—I went along at first then I blew it, and...she *taped* me for talking too much. She gave Auger the gun while she tied me—she's *freaky* strong!"

Corey had seen the woman in a wheelchair last winter. For fifty or sixty, the woman had healed well.

Now Mom was trying to reason with her. "They'll be looking for Corey, they saw him leave—"

"I know more than you think." Mrs. Hart seemed to be gloating. "You were both *hiding* from everyone. They'll assume the boy has followed his mother..." Her voice turned sappy. "To the depths of despair, at the bottom of the river."

"But my—my stepdad knows we're here!" Corey blurted.

"That's a lie. I have my *Jack of Harts* to keep me informed." A horrible chuckle escaped her lips.

"Jack of...?"

"My nephew." Her grin dissolved. "He did try to blackmail me when he learned we were related, but he's been useful." She looked directly at Corey. "And since he buddied up to your stepfather, he's kept me up to date."

"Jack..,*Johnny.*" Corey turned to Sam and grunted, "Did you know about your father?"

"My fa–Johnny? *He's* not my father! Randy and I figured *him* out. That's why I was trying to reach you on the phone."

Corey's brows reached his hairline. "So Randy is..."

"My father!"

Corey dropped to the rock. Nothing had been what it seemed. He looked up at Mrs. Hart. "What about Sam? She's no threat."

"There's much to be gained for her and her father. *If* they cooperate."

Sam glared at the woman. "Randy would *never–*"

"But if they can't keep their mouths shut, we'll have to dispose of them, too." Mrs. Hart turned to Auger. "Tape her mouth again." Auger took his time sticking the tape to Sam's lips. "And tie the boy's hands." Auger pulled Corey to his feet and caught a length of rope from his grandmother. He made Corey turn so the woman could see his hands tied. Corey was losing the feeling in his hands, like the rest of his body.

"You can't fire...it'll be heard!"

Mrs. Hart smiled sweetly. "Do you really think *today* anyone would notice?"

Fireworks, muskets, and cannon. A wave of cold passed through Corey's numbness.

The woman's smile disappeared. "But I won't need to use *that* form of persuasion if you and your mother do as you're told."

What did that mean? Was she going to torture them? Was she going to let them go if they promised to keep quiet? Sam was squirming against the rock wall. Was it possible...had Auger loosened Sam's hands when he'd stuck the tape on her mouth?

Auger was slightly behind his grandmother, but wasn't he slowly moving forward? *Sneak up and take the gun.* The gravel crunched under Auger, and his grandmother swung her head towards him.

Auger halted. "Gran, you don't have to bother with these people!"

His grandmother backed up to give him her attention while keeping the others in view. "And why is that, Auger?" Her eyes had softened.

Auger's hand jerked to his pocket. He pulled out something whose rubbed surface glinted in a shaft of light. "I've got the buckle."

Now he had everyone's attention.

"I ripped it off the dork—" Auger threw Corey a superior look. "Earlier, on shore." He opened his hand to reveal a buckle and a piece of yellowed paper.

Suddenly, Corey recalled the pirate selling necklaces on the pier. His face burned with anger, and he strained hard against the ropes binding his hands.

****

"You clever boy!" Mackenzie's heart pounded with joy. Her Augie had gotten the buckle that eluded everyone else. She'd known he was smart, potentially ruthless. And this girlfriend had surely been his confidante. Too bad she got cold feet and couldn't keep her mouth shut.

"So, I guess there's no need to bother with anyone here," Auger was saying, "Dad could make sure—"

"*Frederick?*" Her voice sounded sharp, even to her. "The fool was going to water down the Hart legend...*and* make that—that Sanchez woman the queen. Really, the women Fred gets involved with." She put some sugar back in her voice as her eyes swept over to Auger. "I know it was hard, Dear, but you were better off after your mother was persuaded to leave."

"Wh-*what?* Mom left because of you?"

"Auger, you'll come to see...greatness means sacrifice."

"What are you saying?" His voice trembled.

"The plan, in the papers I left you. You, dear boy, are the most important part." She clamped her teeth in a wide smile. "*You* will finish what our ancestor started."

"But...Warren Hart wasn't our ancestor."

"Of course he wasn't." Mackenzie laughed. "Dirk Poole was."

FRED'S REVELATION

Huge slabs of granite loomed as Fred yanked back the throttle and jerked the wheel, but with the assistance of several four-letter words, he avoided smashing into the rocks.

"Hey! Over behind those bushes—" Randy had been swinging his head every which way to check for clearance. "Looks like a boat. Must be a channel here somewhere."

Fred eased the boat towards a hidden waterway, and Randy swept at a branch that swung aside as if hinged.

"That's Johnny's boat." Randy pointed to the small cove ahead, and Fred maneuvered alongside the other boat. He was about to suggest they head up the shore path when he noticed Randy's shocked look. Fred followed his open-mouthed gaze to the console of Johnny's boat. It was adorned with a bullet hole.

Fred couldn't hide information any longer. He told Randy about the text from Auger. When Randy heard that Sam was in a cave with Johnny and a madwoman, his face went white. It was all Fred could do to keep him from tearing off through the island. He made Randy follow him along the island's edge as they looked for an entrance to the cave.

"I should have seen the signs." Fred's voice was low as he rounded a large rock and grabbed at sparse bushes to keep balance. "I knew my mother had 'two faces.' I just didn't connect things until I heard those recordings." He was too anxious now to keep secrets. "I'm sure she hid Peg Stowe, pumped her for information, and planted suggestions because she wanted that *buckle*." Then Fred stopped so quickly that Randy plowed into him. "That's what her so-called bridge games were all about—she was having sessions with 'Marie'!" He frowned and crept forward as Randy urged him from behind.

"She had Dad change his name, made him CEO so she could focus on her therapy practice—but *she* always kept control." Fred panted as he scaled a boulder. "She was a Yale grad—brilliant." He was out of shape; he needed to get to the gym more.

The two men climbed several more rocks and around clumps of bushes.

Randy's breathing had also quickened. "I always thought... your mother was...a *fragile* lady."

"Hah!" Fred grabbed a birch tree to steady himself. He lowered his voice. "She said she broke her legs falling on the ice here last winter." He held a branch so it wouldn't snap into Randy's face. "I suspect something more dangerous. She pretends she's recuperating—but I saw her pumping iron. She's got back her bull strength."

"*Sammy...*" Randy urged Fred forward.

The guy must be worried sick. Fred felt drops of sweat on his own face. There! He saw a pathway. He skidded down a rock and landed on a carpet of pine needles. It reminded him of the mess he'd tracked home as a boy. The maid, Juanita, had cleaned it up without complaint. She had died in the accident when Dad gave her a ride home. Mother had hated the maid; she must've thought Dad and the maid... But is father was just being kind. After the accident, the cops had come around. Fred's eyes widened. The brake line had been cut.

Mother?!

The thought made Fred forget where he was; he tripped on a tree root, and Randy pulled him up. Sweat trickled down Fred's neck, and he remembered waving that last time, as Dad left to take Juanita home. *Mother got rid of them both?* Then he remembered the old news clipping Auger had showed him: the woman's daughter was a Margarita.

PLAY THE ACE

Mackenzie Hart noticed her grandson's eyes fixed on her weapon; Auger was obviously as enthralled as she was with power. He was playing the devil's advocate, weighing all the options—or was he testing her? *Good boy either way.*

"Those old letters...they're just wild talk. Dad doesn't think—"

"Right!" She tapped her head with a free finger. "Your father doesn't think." She had insisted on giving Fred the *Hart* name, but it wasn't enough to change his nature. "Frederick is soft. Manipulated."

"You think Dad is controlled by *Rita?*"

"A gold digger, like her mother..." Mackenzie felt her eyes misting as she looked into the distance. "If your grandfather, Gerold, had only kept his focus." She shook herself. "But they had become obstacles."

"Grandpa and Rita's mother—you *killed* them?!"

235

Mackenzie gazed at Auger. He was still young, and he needed to learn the facts of life. "We sacrifice those who obstruct the mission. I had to take the reins."

"Let these people go, Grandma," the boy sputtered. "They won't stop your resort plans." Mackenzie hid a smile. Auger was putting on quite a show, playing good cop/bad cop!

"Auger, we can't leave loose ends, and they are bound to talk. We alone must possess the Hart name." Her lips quivered. "We'll make it synonymous with patriotism—" She caught her breath. "Imagine the battles, music, light shows—all highlighting the Hart heritage."

Her eyes refocused. "Then we'll parlay our good name into the power of politics." She beamed at her grandson. "That's when we play our ace. That's *you*, Augie."

Auger's mouth hung open.

"After finishing law school, you'll easily conquer the region, the *Empire* State, and finally..." Her voice lowered. "Go national."

Auger stumbled backward.

"Yes, the Oval Office!" She gave a regal smile, "You will make *Hart* the most powerful name in the world...Dirk himself foresaw it."

Auger spoke as if dazed. "I *was* planning on law school, but—Dirk couldn't have known. What are you *talking* about, Gran?"

"It's right there in his letters." She quoted: "'I will build me an empire...'" She beamed with pride at her grandson. "'And it will be fulfilled in August.'"

THWARTED

Samantha was stunned. To think that Dirk was planning more than a few months ahead—the woman was nuts! Now she was going on about how the "mission" would require major capital.

"The casino and lab will start us off," she told Auger, "but we need deeper pockets. Don't worry, I found our *treasure* right here."

"The Patriots' chest?"

"No, but excavations revealed more than this cave..." The woman's eyes shifted back and forth. "I found a source of power right under our feet! We'll ship it down the river and on to enrichment facilities."

Sam realized that Johnny was really Jack, Mrs. Hart's nephew, and that the "scuba sales" she'd found on the computer were drug money. Now other connections were emerging: fish poisoning, earthquakes, and mining...

"Uranium!" she blurted. "You're shooting chemicals into the earth—"

"Poisoning the fish!" Corey added.

Mrs. Hart ignored them. "We kill two birds with one stone: our castle will hide equipment and lab waste and it will serve as the crown jewel of island resorts." She paused. "But all our plans depend on use of the Hart name." Her voice was cold. "These people stand in our way."

This was a disaster. The woman planned to eliminate Corey and his mom. Sam should have prevented this—if only she'd figured out Johnny sooner. She had to do something. Maybe she had a chance...Auger had loosened her knot. She eyed a fist-sized rock next to her as she pulled at the rope.

"You're a *genius*, Grandma..." Auger was saying. His grandmother was eating it up. "I—I'm seeing your vision." He edged closer to her. "And I'm ready for my initiation. Let *me*..." He held out his hand.

The woman smiled, but her voice was firm. "Not yet, Auger, these things can be tricky. Give me that syringe." She gestured towards a table. "No one will question it if a Worder overdoses."

"I'll be reasonable," Mrs. Hart told Corey's mom, who looked with horror at the object that appeared in her own hand. "You can send the boy off yourself. I'll give you a count of five before I do it myself." She aimed the gun at Corey.

Mrs. Stowe's hand shook, and her eyes flashed in terror.

"One...two..."

Mrs. Stowe gasped as she gripped Corey's hand.

"Three, four..."

She threw the needle down and shielded Corey, who struggled to do the same for his mom.

"Five!"

The woman's face had tightened in concentration when her arm jerked to the side from the force of a well-aimed rock. She lost her balance, releasing her grip, and stumbled as the gun fell to the stream. Everyone stared, speechless, as the woman crashed, headlong into slab of granite.

She was confused and dizzy, probably suffered a concussion. Auger helped his grandmother out towards the boat. Before disappearing, he turned to the rest. "Do you think I would have *let* her—" He nodded at the syringe. "Just distilled water...and I unloaded the handgun earlier."

No one moved. Then Corey and his mom both grinned at Sam.

"You can pitch!"

"Even without bullets, that woman—"

All three talked at once about the bizarre events. Had Sam really prevented a disaster? Would they make it out alive? She had finally started to relax. She headed towards

Corey to untie him when she noticed a movement by the bridge. A figure had appeared, haloed by the daylight.

"Looks like I'm in time to finish the job."

Sam gawked. Here was the man she had lived with, even called "father, the man she thought had cared for her and Randy. Now the sight of him made her want to vomit. She had worked so hard to save them all that her wrists were bleeding. Now her so-called dad was going to ruin everything? The rage that welled up inside her erupted in an ear-splitting shriek.

"You monster!"

DELAYED

Fred knew his mother was eccentric. But he hadn't realized until today that she was capable of anything sinister. Now he understood: even if she found that old buckle, she would see Peg and Corey as a threat because they knew the truth. What would she and Johnny do to them?

Fred was sweating; he had to get to the cave. He could see a path that might lead to the entrance, below and to the right. They just had to scramble down these rocks and—

A scream resonated from the cave.

"That's Sammy!" Randy made a panicked dash from behind. He slipped on a rock and grabbed Fred; they both lost their balance and fell to the water below.

M.A. NOBLE

14 COREY'S COURAGE

"How could you—" Corey sputtered. He had thought they were finally safe; now this snake shows up. He yanked at the rope around his wrists. He wanted to choke Johnny with his bare hands.

"You're *not* my brother," Mom shouted.

"Right, Marie. But I'll spare you from watching the kid go." Johnny aimed his weapon at her. "Auntie will be very impressed."

Corey's heart was in his throat and he struggled until his wrists burned. He couldn't just stand by! He had a purpose—one that had nothing to do with history. He had heart, which was more important. He cared about his mom and his friend, and even if he was a Hart he would always be just a deserter if he didn't act.

Corey charged. But he only had time to block his mother as Sam shouted, "*Corey, no!*" and a shot rang out. He fell backwards, and everything went black.

A HOLE IN THE HART

"*No!*" Peg screamed. It was bad enough to face death again herself after finding out who she was—but for her *son* to be shot? She couldn't believe he was lying lifeless in her arms.

"He, he got in the way." Jack looked from Corey to his gun. Then his voice gained confidence. "Don't worry, you'll join him soon."

Peg glanced up through teary eyes as she rocked Corey's body, and a hazy vision, a haloed being, met her gaze, approaching from behind Jack. Maybe it was an angel who would take Corey and her to a better place.

But the angel proved solid with a powerful kick; Jack staggered forward, and the revolver clattered and slid down a crevice as the red-haired woman bellowed, "You set me up!" She held out her camera. "And you can tell the Boss I have the shots to prove everything."

Peg was disappointed to find that she was still alive and sitting in a cave holding her son, who had given his life for her. She laid her hand tenderly on his chest. Was that a slight rising and falling? Her senses were playing tricks. She moved her hand over a rib. She looked higher. The vein in Corey's neck pulsed. And amber eyes were opening. She barely heard his whisper.

"Auger was bluffing...about having the buckle."

REUNITED

Corey phased in and out of consciousness but heard the shouts: "You're alive!" and "What's that thing stamped onto his chest?"

He heard his mom's laughter mixed with sobs and felt her kisses on his face; he saw Sam's lips quivering into a wide smile; he noticed two men had arrived dripping wet. One folded Sam in long arms as the other looked for something— or someone.

Corey must have passed out again, but now he groaned as he was lifted to a stretcher, and he heard the man—it was Fred Hart—talking to his wife.

"So you got yourself involved in drug dealing."

"But I never wanted—"

"The worst thing was being blind..." Fred stared at Rita.

On Rita Hart's face, Corey recognized the look he'd worn so many times himself: shame. A tear streaked past her trembling lips.

But Fred had more to say. "*I* was the blind one, too busy to see you needed me."

Corey was glad to see his wife's eyes shine with hope over a relieved smile.

With his rib stabilized and a blanket tucked around him, Corey was more comfortable. By taking shallow breaths, he could even visit with Mom and Sam as the boat glided towards the Landing, where he would be transferred to a land ambulance.

Something had been bothering him. "Why did Auger have that fake buckle—and that ancient piece of paper?"

"He picked the buckle up at the museum when we found his grandmother. Oh—" From her pocket, Sam pulled out and waved the yellowed scrap Auger had dropped in the cave. "It's something he accidentally tore off at the library."

Corey stared at the objects. So Auger really had been on their side, using decoys to fake his own grandmother out.

"The real buckle shielded Warren Hart..." Sam stared into the distance. "And now you." She touched his arm. "And you shielded your mom." She whispered, "You're a hero, like your ancestor."

Corey couldn't afford to feel proud; he barely even felt safe. He'd kept expecting someone else to show up with a gun, even after the authorities arrived—which Auger had sent.

But as they approached the Landing, he was starting to believe that he and his mom had their whole future ahead of them. And that Mom would have her past, too. He smiled at the sapphire eyes that gleamed at him.

As they headed through the bay, Corey noticed something was missing. The Hart sign no longer hung over the entry, and part of the opposite pier was smashed where it had fallen. The quake must have done it.

Now the parade king was walking down the pier towards them. *How did Fred Hart get here ahead of us?* But that man wasn't Fred Hart; someone else wore the captain's costume, and his hand trembled as he reached for Mom.

"Peg? Is that really you?"

"*Charlie?*" Mom touched the man's face. Then they just held each other without words.

A furry mass wagged its body near Corey while strong arms held him back.

"Howler!" Corey ignored the ache in his chest as he stroked his best friend. "How did you get down here?"

"Got loose earlier," Charlie said without taking his eyes off his wife. "Almost got crushed by that sign." Corey was sliding into the ambulance when he heard Charlie add, "He'd be a goner if the Hart kid hadn't grabbed him."

15 SAIL ON

Corey's sail filled, and he raced the windsurfer over the bay. He was healing quickly, getting stronger every day. He gazed out over the rolling river and pictured a treasure chest. The gold was out there somewhere. He and his mom still hadn't discovered where Estar Island was. At least now their history was public, thanks to the journal—which had been found in Mrs. Hart's suite. There was even a loose page, stuffed in the back, that described how the cutlass had been engraved with the words *First and Last Mate.*

Johnny and Mackenzie Hart were both in jail. Rita's trial was coming up, but Fred had gotten her the best attorney they could afford. Mom would get off since she wasn't under her own control. Mom and Fred Hart were partners now. Maybe after they straightened out Mrs. Hart's mess they could make some money. Charlie had quit drinking and was building his guide business.

A wave was coming. Corey pushed his back side out then jumped. *That should impress Sam.* She was sitting on the beach pretending to read a book, but he knew she was watching. Corey had added a few pounds and was working out. With Sam's help, he had even expanded his vocabulary.

Now he watched his own muscles flex as he maneuvered the board. He swung the boom to let the breeze push past the sail's backside in a tack to bring him to shore; then he would jump lightly off the board in front of Sam.

A large vessel came into view from downriver, and Corey gawked at the billowing white sails. He'd heard about programs where kids could learn to navigate on those "tall ships." As he thought how great that would be, he forgot to pay attention to his own sailing.

Splaunsch. Corey found himself completely immersed. Then the mast and sail came down on his head. He clawed his way out and sputtered as he heard Sam's giggle...along with a male snort. Auger Hart.

Corey dragged the rig onto the beach.

"You looked good out there." Sam tried to hide her grin as she watched him roll up the sail.

"Thanks," Corey grunted.

"Still dorky, but improving." Auger winked at Sam as he leaned on Randy's van, parked behind her. Sam beamed back at him.

Did she really go for that trophy kind of guy? *So superficial.* Corey furrowed his brows as he wiped the board down. Why should he care? He didn't have that kind of relationship with Sam. She was a friend. So why did his stomach knot up when she smiled at Auger?

Auger still had that confidence of a hockey god. He was supposed to be the loser! He acted like his ancestry didn't matter.

But wasn't that what Corey believed? He was confused. Was Corey a loser or a winner? A Worder or a Hart?

"You decide who you are." That's what Mom had said—but she didn't have to worry about *her* name, now that she remembered it. Charlie had offered to give Corey his name, too, to adopt him, but *Corey Stowe* just didn't seem right.

He finished dragging the surf gear to the rental stand as he heard the van start. Corey didn't look; he didn't want to see Sam drive away with Auger sitting next to her. He started walking home as he heard Auger's yell: "Catch you later—*Back*Worder!"

Funny, it didn't make his gut clench any more. In fact, Corey really was a back *Worder* if you thought about it—a

Redrow. But he was a unique mix of his ancestors. He felt the hard edge of the brass buckle in his pocket. The bullet dent had been pounded out to extract the certificate inside. Too bad the old paper was pretty much destroyed.

Corey hadn't walked half a block when the van pulled up.

"Hop in!" Brown eyes flecked with gold targeted him through the open window.

"I—I thought you were taking Hart with you." He stared at the empty passenger seat.

"I thought you could use a ride." Sam leaned over and pulled the door handle. "And in case you forgot—I *am* taking Hart."

M.A. NOBLE

16 FACILITY FOR CORRECTIONS

It would take months for a trial and a decision on final placement; meanwhile, Mackenzie Hart would make the best of things at the county jail. After all, she really was a *Poole* and, like her ancestor, she could bide her time. She would use the tools at hand to accomplish her mission.

It was unfortunate that an operation with such potential had been shut down. But there were other treasures to exploit. And no matter how tight the security in here, her tools could never be confiscated.

The corrections officer appeared with the item she had requested.

"Thank you, Oscar. You have done as I asked." Her voice was lulling as usual. But this time, she added, "I see you are feeling good about pleasing me. And you are becoming more relaxed..."

As she had always told her clients, "We make progress one small step at a time."

****

M.A. NOBLE

Thank you...

for reading *Taking Hart*. If you enjoyed it, please let others know! Also, you can email me: MANoble@rocketmail.com

Next, in *Taking the Gold* :

Corey sets sail on a tall ship to win Samantha, face his treacherous father, and beat the villain to the British gold hidden in the 1000 Islands.

TAKING the GOLD Excerpts

I must have been imagining things. Corey had just turned southwest when he thought he saw it again. He jerked his head back towards Singer Castle. There. Flashes. Three short, three long, three short. An SOS! It had to be Sam.

* * * *

"What have you got there?"

Corey's palms were damp. He should have left the cup below!

"I'm from Kentucky, and if that's bourbon, I'll know it."

A drop of sweat streaked down Corey's cheek.

The captain lifted the cup to her nose. "Just as I thought. Some people can't handle their soda pop."

* * *

The motor hiccupped. Corey adjusted the choke, but it kept sputtering, and before he left the channel behind, it died entirely. Corey glanced again at the upbound ship, now larger on the horizon, remembering something Charlie had said.

He stared into the lights of the freighter that bore down on him.

CHARACTERS
Names and Descriptions

NOTE: Some characters are listed under multiple names; some have another identity revealed in the story.

2012 CHARACTERS

<u>Corey Worder</u>: 16-year-old descendent of the War of 1812 Patriot known as Patrick Worder

<u>Peg</u> (Margaret Worder) Stowe: Corey's mother, who disappeared into the river; only a suicide note was found

<u>Charlie Stowe</u>: Corey's stepfather and Peg's husband; a fishing guide

<u>Samantha</u> (Sam): girl who befriends Corey and lives at The Mainsail Bed & Breakfast (B&B)

<u>Randy</u>: tall, dark, scowly owner of The Mainsail, one of Sam's two dads

<u>Johnny</u>: friendly, red-haired owner of The Mainsail and part-time manager of the dive shop; one of Sam's two dads

<u>Auger Hart</u>: 17-year-old hockey player known as a descendent of town hero Warren Hart

<u>Fred Hart</u>: Auger's father, CEO of the Hart Corporation

<u>Rita Hart</u>: Fred's wife and Auger's stepmother; owner/artist at the Glass & Brass art gallery

<u>Mackenzie Hart</u> (Gran): Auger's doting grandmother, in a wheelchair after taking a fall; known as charitable and proud of the Hart legacy

<u>The Boss</u>: Power-seeking head of hidden operations that threaten the St. Lawrence River

Jack: Dive shop manager and cocaine dealer who has formed an alliance with the Boss.

Marie: Jack's partner, who keeps a low profile to evade capture and imprisonment; she believes Jack is her brother but has trouble remembering the past

Dr. Poole: The therapist who uses hypnosis to treat Marie

Buddy: Roly-poly man who lives behind the bar, panhandles at the Point, and sings an old river song

The St. Lawrence River: To its many residents and returning visitors, the St. Lawrence is a character that draws many lovers. Carrying the waters of the Great Lakes to the Atlantic Ocean, it helps form the US-Canadian border along northern New York State. Throughout history, its Thousand Islands (actually, closer to 2000!) has enabled privateering, piracy, smuggling, and romance.

1812-13 CHARACTERS

Warren Hart: Sailor, formerly "impressed" into the Royal Navy and taken to Kingston, where he escaped to captain the *Patriot's* privateering crew, which ambushed British supply boats in the 1000 Islands; known as the hero of Harts Landing for saving the town from British wrath

Patrick Worder: Offspring of a British Naval officer, Worder left Kingston with Warren Hart to be his first mate; later known as a deserter and pirate who stole the Patriots' treasure and tried to kill his own child

Dirk Hart: Sailor celebrated as the son of Warren Hart and co-hero of the Battle of Harts Landing

Geraldine Plank: Mute woman who had lost her husband and child tragically and who wandered, deranged, to the Landing, where Warren Hart took her in; known as the mother of Patrick Worder's baby, Adam

FACTS BEHIND THE FICTION:
The War of 1812 in the 1000 Islands

Pirates and privateers in the St. Lawrence River? Yes, the Thousand Islands—with its varying depths and river currents, hidden shoals, and hundreds of small islands and coves—has provided a backdrop for mystery, trickery, and treachery throughout American history. Real life pirates, spies, and privateers have used the maze of river channels and islands to accomplish missions both selfish and patriotic.

During the War of 1812, British ships carried supplies and military pay across the Atlantic and then upriver on the St. Lawrence to Montreal. (Yes, on the St. Lawrence, upriver is *southwest*.) Then the cargo was carried in flat-bottomed boats farther upriver, past the rapids (and possibly offloaded again west of Prescott to a lake-sailing ship) to Kingston in Upper Canada. On its way, the cargo would pass through the Thousand Islands before entering Lake Ontario; British gunboats protected these vessels from ambush among the maze of islands and coves where an enemy could hide.

What was the War of 1812 about?

By 1812, the citizens of the new American nation were angry at Britain. The British supported native raids on American settlements in the Ohio River Valley. They also embargoed European trade, which hurt American commerce. But one of the major offenses of the British was to force sailors off American ships and make them serve in the Royal Navy. (The British considered Americans born in Britain as royal subjects, and they needed many sailors in their fight against Napoleon; they took both British and Americans off ships.) This British act of forcing American sailors was known as "impressment," and to Americans it was injury and insult. The British actions showed a lack of respect for the newly formed United States.

The American nation declared war and invaded Britain's nearest possession: Upper Canada. Soon, both the British and the Americans raced to build fighting ships. Their main naval bases were on opposite shores of Lake Ontario near the head of the St. Lawrence River. The British operated from Kingston, in Upper Canada, while the Americans built and launched vessels at Sackets Harbor, New York. East of these towns, the Great Lakes drain into the St. Lawrence River, which flows northeast past Montreal and out to the sea.

To supplement their limited navy, the American government encouraged citizens to attack British vessels. These private citizens and their boats were called *privateers* and were allowed to take possession of goods they found on enemy ships. They were not to be confused with *pirates*, who lawlessly plundered ships of any nation. Privateers were authorized by their government to attack the ships of its enemy. In the War of 1812, a "Letter of Marque" signed by President Madison was permission from the U. S. government to attack and seize British ships.

Not all Americans agreed with the war. In fact, many Americans dwelling along the northern border continued, secretly and illegally, to trade goods with their Canadian neighbors, and they used the islands to hide their smuggling activities.

CREDITS

*Many worthy individuals have given help and advice,
but any faults that remain in the book are my own doing.*

–*M.A. Noble*

Thanks to the following for their contributions:

SPECIALISTS

Historian Bob Garcia, with the Ontario Service Centre of Parks Canada

Educators

Victoria Levitt (SUNY Potsdam)
Pedro Ponce (St. Lawrence University)
Christopher Sweeney (SUNY Canton)
Robert Badger (SUNY Potsdam)
Jeffrey Chiarenzelli (St. Lawrence University)
David Valentino (SUNY Oswego)

1000 Islands/St. Lawrence Business Owners

John Ashley (Blufin Dive Shop)
Allen Benas (1000 Islands Fishing Charters)
Capt. Rich Clarke (Sign Man Charters)
Khris and Donald "Moe" Hunt (Hunt's Dive Shop)

REVIEWERS

Linda Barbour
Sage Brown
Herb Bullock
Troy Creurer
Bonnie Danis
Barbara, Jamie, Mark, Chris,
    and Darian Fenton
Rosemary, Karl, David, Kim,
    Charlie, Karlie, Becky, and
    Edward French

Bob Hockett
Meagan Macauley
Lois McAllester
Roger, Alexander, and Ginny
    Noble
Erin O'Conell
Corine Stoll
Ginger and Isobel Sweeney

ABOUT THE AUTHOR

M. A. Noble lives in St. Lawrence County between the Adirondack Mountains and New York's Canadian border. She enjoys music, outdoor activities, and writing to entertain.